MW01131768

MESSENGER

Book Two

By

A.L. Crouch

Dedicated to the two men who lost their lives doing what they loved, running the Rock and Roll Raleigh marathon on April 13, 2014.

Run on forever, friends.

Therefore, since we are surrounded by such a great cloud of witnesses, let us throw off everything that hinders and the sin that so easily entangles. And let us run with perseverance the race marked out for us.

Hebrews 12:1 (NIV)

One

I deserve this, I told myself as his steel toe slammed into my ribs with a grotesque crunch. The air rushed from my lungs like a punctured balloon, the last of it escaping with a stifled wheeze. His fist connected with my jaw, throwing my head back into the tiled floor.

I did nothing. The taste of blood pooled inside my mouth, but I said nothing. He wanted to kill me. I was grateful to him for it.

"That letter you wrote for Boss to recite at his parole hearing didn't fly. Boss got another ten year flop in here cause of you," he seethed, hammering his foot into my outer thigh.

I bit the inside of my lip to keep from crying out, adding to the metallic taste on my tongue.

"You ain't nothing round here now," he continued. "Boss was protecting you cuz he thought you was educated, that you could help him out. But you ain't nothing but a goof."

Another kick to the ribs and I felt the slosh of swelling beneath the bones. The throbbing edged me closer to puking with each caustic pulse, but I stayed silent. I warred with the logging for death and the inherent will to survive. My vision flashed with white heat and then blurred with every gasp of air.

As the room began to spin, I spotted my cell mate rounding the corner. He came to a halt, his eyes widening and flashing to mine. He readied himself to charge, the anger on his face palpable. Glaring at him, I held up my hand as a signal to not interfere.

"So, you can expect some heat now." The assault continued. "Yeah, you're a marked man. You got one in the hat, baby. We're coming for you."

My attacker crouched down beside me. His breath smelled of stale cigarettes and rancid meat. For the first time since he jumped me from behind, I got a good look at him. It was Smiley, one of Boss' goons, so named because of the matching rows of gold-plated teeth he flashed at me now. Through my blurring vision I could see they were browning around their edges.

"Badge coming! Wrap it up, man," someone ahead of us shouted, a lookout no doubt.

Smiley took a quick look behind him and then flashed me a golden grin before ramming another foot into my thigh.

"You best watch your six. You ain't gonna know when we're coming, but your days are numbered. You best believe that. Boss ain't gonna let this slide."

Smiley ran off in the direction of the warning, leaving bloody footprints which faded with each step. The cold linoleum punctuated each merciless throb as I struggled to find the desire to pick myself up. Blood continued to ooze from my brow.

"*Guero!* You found some big trouble this time, man. What the hell happened?" Miguel, my cell mate, was at my side. He lifted my head and I struggled to sit up. Without a doubt, some ribs were broken.

"We gotta get you out of here before a badge sees you. He'll sign you out to the SHU for sure. Let's go, man. It's almost time for lockdown."

With Miguel's help I got to my feet. I took a second to assess the damage. The blood on the floor was unsettling, but I reached up and found that the cut on my brow was minor. Miguel, twenty years my senior and as many years into his life sentence, looked around. Then he hastily removed his shoes and mopped up my DNA trail with his socked feet. When all traces of blood were gone, he replaced his shoes and ushered me forward.

He would not help me walk. I wouldn't have let him if he tried. In prison a man must walk tall no matter the circumstances, a fact old-timers like Miguel knew well. We almost made it back to our cell.

"Foster!" The deep, booming voice called to me. I turned, the blood still running from my forehead. "We got a problem that needs dealing with?"

At six feet four with the build of a pro wrestler, Officer Edmonds was more intimidating than half the inmates in North Carolina's Central Prison. He was also the most respected. Fair but firm, Edmonds had a short fuse for nonsense.

"No problem." I said, not daring to look him in the eye. "I fell."

"By the looks of it, you must have fallen from the roof. Inmates are restricted from the roof. Do I need to lock you up in Solitary to make sure you stay in bounds, Foster?"

I could feel the eyes of my fellow inmates as they gathered to watch, waiting for my response. Edmonds was giving me an out, a way to get myself locked in a private sell in the Security Housing Unit for my own protection, but I knew the SHU would offer me no refuge even if I wanted it. Solitary confinement had its own consequences. Sure, I would be momentarily safe from Boss' death threats, but the SHU was temporary. To get time in the SHU for protection was a punk move that would only garner me further problems when I returned. It wasn't an answer.

Besides, in solitary confinement there were worse advisories to deal with. Better to take my chances with the violence-fueled society in the close security block than to face the demons in my own head.

"No, sir," I said coolly. "I'm just clumsy. I'll make sure to watch where I'm going from now on."

Edmonds stared me down, no doubt ascertaining the severity of my injuries. I still did not meet his eyes. There was nothing he could do for me. With a grunt, he finally turned his attention down the block.

"Make sure that you do," he said over his shoulder. "You might not survive the next . . . fall."

"Let's go, *Guero*." Miguel patted my shoulder. "I don't like the attention we're getting out here."

We walked on. I kept my body rigid even though the pain in my side was excruciating. There was no hiding the swelling of my brow or the blood that continued to seep from it, but to show weakness of any kind in here was to invite a world of trouble. As welcomed as death would be, I learned a long time ago that there are worse things a man can face than death. In lock-up, where hope is a joke and he who inflicts the most pain is king, inmates perfect the art of harassment and torture. It's all some of them have left to live for.

"Here you go, *Guero*. You gotta clean yourself up, man," Miguel said when we finally made it to our cell.

I looked at the rusted clock above the sink. Almost time for lockdown. If any more trouble was coming tonight, it only had ten more minutes to arrive.

"When that blood dries on that khaki uniform it's gonna turn purple. Not a good look for a manly man like you *Guero*, unless you trying to match that eye."

Miguel held out a clean, white undershirt, and although his jokes were not well received at the moment, I was grateful he was there. I inched the stained shirt up over my head as he removed his shoes and ditched his socks in the laundry bag. As suspected, my undershirt was also stained crimson. Pulling it off too, I used it to mop up my face as I inspected my side. A sickly, yellowish purple was forming along my rib cage. A break or two for sure, but there was nothing to be done. Even if I could check myself into the infirmary without having to rat on Smiley, there was nothing they could do but help to manage the pain. I would have to manage that myself.

"He came out of nowhere. Hit me from behind, the coward," I said, taking the clean shirt from Miguel and pulling it over my pounding head. Then I took my bloodied undershirt and ran it under the cool water from the stainless steel sink in the corner of our cell. The cold, moist cloth felt good against the broken skin above my eye. I held it there until the bleeding stopped.

Miguel leaned against the side of the bunk, his arms folded across his chest. "That's cuz you a big guy, and everyone knows what you did to your last bunkie. Smiley knew he had to get the jump on you, man."

"I guess," I said, wiping the inside of my mouth with a clean corner of the now useless rag.

"What you mean, you guess? What the hell were you doin' in the blind, man? I thought I taught you to stay in view of the cameras or a CO at all times, *Guero*. The way you been actin' around here lately makes me think you have a death wish."

Shrugging him off, I did my best to rinse the blood from the damp shirt. When the water ran clear, I pitched it into my laundry bag and lowered myself onto my bunk. Miguel watched me, his eyebrows raised. He wasn't going to let this go.

"What that *vato* want with you anyway? What'd you do to him? You disrespect his *clica* or something? Boss' crew ain't nobody to be messing with, *Guero*."

"You think I don't know that? He asked me to write his letter for the parole board. I guess it didn't go very well." I sighed. "And stop calling me *Guero*. We talked about this. My name is Logan. Eleven years in this cell with you and I still don't know if you're calling me an idiot or something."

Miguel stooped over to look me in the eyes. "Stop trying to change the subject. Why are you doing favors for that *loco hijo de put. . .?*"

"English, Miguel!" I snapped, rolling onto my injured side. The pressure squelched the throbbing and made it easier to breathe. *Thank God.*

"Why you agree to write the letter? No parole board in the world would put that drug lord back on the street early."

"He asked. Just like they all ask when they need their GED papers looked over, or want to write a love note to their girlfriends. They need my education to make them look smart. It's the only thing I've got in here, you know that. Besides, Boss asked me personally. It's not like I could I say no."

Before he Miguel could argue, footsteps clomped on the dingy tile outside the cell.

"*Aguias*," Miguel whispered and stood up straight. "Look alive *Guero*."

I used the rim of the top bunk to pull myself to my feet with a grunt. The throbbing returned with a vengeance and threatened to floor me, but I straightened out as Officer Edmonds came by with his hand-held tally counter. He gave me another look-over.

"You recovering from that fall, Foster?"

I nodded to him and did my best to grin. "Nothing but a scratch."

With a click of the counter he was on to the next cell. A few minutes later a shout of "all clear" signaled the guard at the controls to lower the cell doors. A shrill, metallic clang and we were shut in for the night. Relieved, I lowered myself back onto my bunk. Miguel grabbed a book from his cubby and climbed up into his bunk.

Lights-out wasn't for a couple of hours, but there was no chance I was going to be able to escape into a Tom Clancy created world with this headache. I lived for these hours of peace each night when both Miguel and I read ourselves out of this place. Out of the paint peeled bars and the smells of urine and sweat. Out of the castle-like monster that was our mandatory home.

Tonight there would be no escape though, only the dull ache and incessant pounding that was a couple of broken ribs, a severely bruised thigh, and a split gum and brow.

I tuned over onto my injured side again and again the throbbing ebbed. Closing my eyes, I imagined a life outside this current reality, but it was no use.

"Big white boy with blonde hair." Miguel said out of nowhere.

"What?"

"That's what *Guero* means," he said. "Suits you."

I chuckled despite the pain the movement caused. "Thank you, I think."

Miguel lowered his voice to a whisper. "Boss set you up. There's no way he thought anything you wrote was going to get him paroled out of here. Not a *loco* monster like him. Besides, he's got enough of the language skills to write his own letter."

I rolled onto my back again and tried to take a deep breath but it was too painful. "But why set me up? What does he want from me? He's never had any beef with me before, why now?"

"Cuz man, you're thirteen months to the gate. Some heavies can't stand to see a dude get outta here when they can't. It's a power trip, man," he explained. "Plus, like I said *Guero*, everybody knows what you did to your last bunkie. They know that when someone brings you heat, you'll explode like you did on that poor *bastardo*. Taking you out when no one else has had the *cajones* to . . . it's like a badge of honor."

"So, you're saying if I had a life sentence he wouldn't mess with me? Makes no sense, Miguel," I scoffed.

Miguel shuffled in his bunk, the movement caused my body to wobble. "Man, you been in here almost twelve years and you still thinkin' like you out the gate. It's different in here. We don't all have your smarts, man, and Boss didn't get to be the shot caller round here by making moves that make sense to folks like you. It's simple, *Guero*. Take the man out that everybody else is afraid to touch a year before he walks. He takes more than your life then, he takes your freedom too. Boss feeds off that kind of power, man."

When Miguel explained it, it made sense. I wanted to be angry. I *should* have been afraid, but all I could feel was relief, relief that maybe I wouldn't have to face freedom next year. My freedom was what I feared more than anything. Not because I didn't want it, yearn for it even, but because I understood more than anyone that I didn't deserve to ever leave this place.

"Maybe I'm not meant to get out of here Miguel. Maybe the big man upstairs has a different plan for me," I said, rolling back over onto my side, eager to end the conversation.

I heard a wisp of fabric as Miguel hopped off the top bunk. He rolled me to meet his angered glare. Miguel was a slight man, his dark skin weathered and cracked from too many days working on the road crew. His jet black hair was peppered with white, but he had the grace and agility of a young, broken mare. When Miguel was angry however, he was scarier than hell. He never told me how he landed in Central, or why he carried a life sentence. I never asked, sure that someone somewhere had made him very angry.

"You listen to me, *Guero*. We been together in this hellhole a long time, and for eleven years I have watched you beat yourself up over them girls. Now you getting close to having served your penance and you want to punish yourself longer? When you gonna forgive yourself, man?"

"I don't want to talk about this, Miguel."

"Man, you don't never wanna talk about it. It's eatin' you up, man. You made a mistake more than a decade ago. You were a kid, *Guero*. Let it go. You ain't honoring those girls' memories at all by ruining your life too, you remember that," he said, then backed down with a sigh. "We'll take care of Boss. I've had your back all these years. You better not let that go to waste and get yourself killed now. Ain't nothing going to keep you from getting out of here and moving on with your life. You best come to terms with that, Logan."

Miguel hopped back up into his bunk with a huff. He'd used my real name. There was no arguing with him when he did that. He used it as if he were giving a final argument. *The end, no further comments*. I heard him flip the page of his book and then all was quiet, save for the usual coughs and murmurs of the block.

Rolling back over, I tried to disappear, to go dead inside, and wander into nothingness, but I couldn't. Miguel's words swirled in my head and I couldn't flush them down. He was right. I couldn't forgive myself. I didn't know how. In the past eleven years, not a day went by that I didn't think about what I'd done.

I was just a stupid kid then, untouchable. Fresh out of college and on top of the world.

On my way. That's what the text had said. That's what had been so damned important. So important that I don't even remember where I was on my way to. Only half a mile from home,

I didn't think twice about taking my eyes off the road to send that text to my frat buddies.

I should have known she'd be out running on the side of the road that evening. How many times had I passed her on my way to my last class or going for drinks downtown? She ran every evening just before sundown, when the humid Carolina air thinned out and the cool spring breeze scented it with honeysuckle and pine. Her long, red hair swayed with every step as she smiled from underneath her visor when I passed.

I should have known.

When I finally closed my eyes to sleep I saw her, as I did every night. I saw her sprawled face-down in the street, her legs bent in awkward angles. Her red hair was splayed across the pavement in a pool of blood, just like it was that evening. I'd swerved at the last second, but it was too late. My car slammed into the ditch and I was rendered unconscious for a few minutes, maybe longer.

When I came to, I peeled myself out of the car and went to her as the first sirens sounded in the fading evening light. She was so still . . . lifeless. Not breathing. I found out during my trial that her neck snapped with the impact.

I was taken by paramedics into the nearest ambulance as rescue workers flooded the scene. It wasn't until we were pulling away that I noticed her jogging stroller. Mangled, it laid upside down in the ditch beside my car.

Two

Every day is the same in prison. It starts with the six am formal count. I'm usually up hours before we are called to stand outside our cells, but when I woke this morning my body was a vessel of pain. The throbbing at my side was replaced during the night with debilitating stiffness. It was hard to breathe. I lingered in my bunk until Miguel hopped down and sat at my feet.

"No pushups for you today, *Guero*?" he snickered.

I shrugged. "What can I say? I must have done too many yesterday."

Miguel grabbed my hands and helped me to my feet. The pain was excruciating at first, but once I was upright it eased a bit. Breath came with more ease.

"You gonna make it today, man?" Miguel asked. "You look even whiter than usual."

I knew I must look like pure hell. Gently running a finger over my brow, I found that the gash had scabbed over some. When I lifted my shirt though, I was alarmed at the shade of purple that had spread across my chest. There were no protrusions to suggest a punctured lung or internal bleeding though. I found comfort in the fact I was able to breathe normally now that I was moving around some.

"Just sore. I can handle it," I said, grabbing a clean uniform shirt from my cubby.

"You going to breakfast?" he asked, sitting on my bunk to tie on his boots.

"Not hungry."

"Not hungry, or you think one of Boss' guys is gonna jump you at chow?" he asked, standing up to look me in the eye.

I grabbed my work boots. "I'm not scared, Miguel."

I sat on my bunk to tie them on, but when I reached for the laces I cried out with the sudden explosion in my side. Miguel shook his head and bent down and laced them for me.

"That's what I'm afraid of."

He pulled me back to my feet. I laid a hand on his shoulder and gave it a squeeze to let him know I appreciated him.

"You need to eat, *Guero*," he said. "You need to keep your strength up. I'm not going to let one of them *vatos* get the jump on you."

"You've managed to stay out of trouble for the last twenty years, Miguel. You going to start some now?"

"Whoever told you I've stayed out of trouble?" He winked, then went to the sink to brush his teeth.

When they raised the bars I was dressed, brushed, and feeling less stiff after making my bed. I stood on the opposite side of the cell door from Miguel as Officer Duke approached, counter in hand. He looked up at me and was taken aback.

"What the hell happened to you, Foster? You finally decide to go 'gay for the stay' with the wrong gump?" he chided. "Next time sweet talk him first, you might have better luck."

Tall and as slender as a stripper pole, Officer Duke derived pleasure from tormenting the convicts under his supervision. A typical schoolyard bully, he used his power to humiliate whenever possible. Like all other inmates, I despised him.

"I'll keep that in mind," I said through gritted teeth.

"Or maybe you just like it rough," he snickered, then clicked the counter in my face and walked on.

"Stupid hack," Miguel whispered under his breath as we waited for the all clear.

When our block was released, we made our way to the chow hall. I took my tray of slop to the table in the far corner where we always sat. Miguel took his seat across from me. No one ever sat with us and I was fine with eating my meal in peace. This morning was different though. Every eye was on me. Curious glances and lifted eyebrows watched my every move.

The news of Boss' threats must have spread throughout the block during the night. Not surprising. A man couldn't take a dump without everyone on the block knowing what color it was. They thought they were staring at a dead man. What they didn't realize was that they'd been looking at one for the last twelve years.

"It's fine, *Guero*," Miguel whispered.

We never spoke much outside of our cell, there was no need. We'd lived in such close quarters with one another for so long that we could tell what the other was thinking. Staying to ourselves was the best way to stay out of trouble.

I forced the runny grits into my stomach and washed it down with the hot, metallic-tasting coffee.

"I'll see you after work," I said, standing with my tray.

"Watch your back today," Miguel nodded.

There was a benefit to leaving breakfast early. Being the only inmate in the east tunnel meant I could walk to work comfortably. Once I was through it, trouble could only come from behind. I moved quickly, not eager to get to work, but not wanting to give anyone the chance to box me in either.

In the mornings, the east tunnel was guarded by Officer Brady, dubbed Squeaker for his high pitched voice and scrawny physique. Were it not for the 9mm pistol strapped to his side, Squeaker would be the least intimidating correctional officer in the long history of the prison. The way his eyes darted, catlike and ready to pounce as his agitated hand hovered over his sidearm, communicated to us that he would not hesitate to shoot for any reason. So he was left alone.

Nodding to Squeaker, I made my way from the tunnel to the seedy, three-story prison industries building. I knew to go around to the back door of the plant and knock. It was too early still for the front door to be unlocked for inmate workers. After a few seconds the door opened with a metallic groan and Mr. Jones popped his bald head out.

"Logan, you're early. Anything wrong?" he asked, his moustache turned down in a concerned frown.

I shuffled my feet in the gravel. "No sir, just up early and ready to get a jump on my count."

He looked unconvinced, but sighed and opened the door anyway. The familiar smell of aluminum and paint filled my nostrils as I stepped into the license tag plant. Mr. Jones shut the door behind me and locked it.

As much as I wanted to pretend this was a normal factory, like the one I had in my father's plant in high school, being locked in the building while my boss wielded the key was a sharp reminder of where I really was. A guard would escort us to lunch and at the end of the day I would most likely be frisked or scanned with a metal detector before being allowed to return to my block.

"You can help me bring up the machines and get them ready to go." Mr. Jones walked over to the large aluminum spool and adjusted the feed of the thin, reflective metal.

I made my way to the tool and die machine, affectionately called Papa Smurf by the men who operated it, and switched out the dies before turning it on. The blue machine hummed to life as Mr. Jones came to stand beside me.

"You gonna tell me why you're really here this early? That gash on your forehead is mighty telling." he said.

Sighing, I lowered my head. I wasn't ready to confide in him. Mr. Jones was a fair boss. He treated us not like prisoners, but as valued employees. I trusted him, and after working for him for a decade, I knew that he trusted me too. Up to this point in my sentence, with the exception of my first month here, I'd stayed out of trouble. Mr. Jones was the only free man on campus who called me by my first name. He looked at me as a person, not just another inmate. Telling him I was jumped by some drug lord's goon might change his opinion of me.

"I ran into a little trouble. I'm handling it though," was all I said.

He looked at me and rubbed the stubble on his chin. Without any further questions he nodded and pat me on the back.

"I was just about to grab a cup of coffee. You look like you could use some. We have a few minutes before the rest of the crew gets, here."

"Sir?"

"Oh, come on Logan. When was the last time you had a real cup of coffee?" he asked. "I've got the good stuff brewing in my office. Come on, it's fine."

"Thank you, Sir," I said, but paused, reluctant, before following him into the hallway normally restricted to inmates.

Mr. Jones' office was the first one on the left. He could keep watch over the entire plant form its sizeable bay window. When he opened the door, the smell of expensive Columbian wafted towards us like sea spray. I'd never smelled anything as good in my life.

"Have a seat, Logan," he said as he poured out a mug of the heavenly brew and handed it to me.

I sat in the empty chair in front of his desk and closing my eyes, breathed in the steam from the hot mug. Mr. Jones poured himself one and sat behind his desk and put his feet up on its mahogany surface.

"There is nothing better than a great cup of coffee in the morning. The wife gets pissy when I buy these beans at the specialty shop, but I say it's worth every penny. What do you think?"

"I think it's worth every bit of my paycheck, and I will gladly give it to you," I said, taking my first luscious sip.

Mr. Jones laughed. "You enjoy it, Son. You've been a great employee. Gonna miss you when they spring you next year. I was thinking you should start training a replacement soon."

"Thank you, Sir, but isn't is a little early for that? I still have thirteen months," I said, dismissing the thought.

"I know that, but it will be here before you know it. It takes a while to learn the machines like you know them. Got some newbies coming in next week. We'll talk then," he said, taking another sip.

There was a commotion outside as the inmate employees shuffled in and took their places at their assigned stations.

"I'd better get out there." I finished my coffee with one hot gulp, savoring every last second of it as it burned down my gullet.

"Take it easy today, Logan. I see you favoring that right side. Don't need my best employee holed up in the infirmary."

I nodded, setting my mug by the coffee pot. "I will. Thank you again for the coffee."

On the production floor, I took my place behind Papa Smurf. Luckily it was my turn to stack plates, an easy job with minimal movement. Santiago and Bishop, who ran the machine with me, were already stamping plates when I got there. They stopped what they were doing when I walked up.

"Damn! Smiley did a number on you alright." Bishop gaped.

"It's not as bad as it looks," I assured.

Bishop was dark-skinned, bad tempered and serving an eight year sentence for breaking and entering, a crime for which Bishop claimed he was wrongly accused. According to him, the front door of the house in which he took thousands of dollars-worth of stuff was unlocked. So he reasoned that it couldn't be breaking and entering. It was simply luck.

"Yeah, well you look like hell," he countered.

"Thanks," I said, stacking the plates he had already stamped.

"Yo, what you gonna do about Boss? Word on the block is he wants your head, man," Santiago said with a trill of impending tragedy.

"Yeah, so I've heard," was my answer.

Santiago, a small but ruthless runner for the Mexican Mafia, was transferred less than a month ago from San Antonio. Constantly disgruntled at the lack of his gang's presence here at Central, he fed off of drama. He would not have the satisfaction of reveling in mine.

"But what you gonna DO?" he persisted as he changed out the die.

"You gotta do something, man," Bishop warned. "This ain't just gonna go away on its own."

"I don't know." I sighed. "Right now I just want to work."

Bishop lowered the stamp onto the next plate and then passed it to me.

"I know a guy," he said. "He could take care of this for you. Make it go away."

"Sure, and then I'll owe him a favor or commissary for the rest of my stay." I chuckled. "No thanks. I have to deal with this myself."

"You see? That's why a man needs brothers, *Ese'*," Santiago mused. "If a bulldog steps up to me, I have my brothers to back me up. They take care of it. Take a bone crusher to the *Puta*. My *Clica*'s got my back."

I took my stack of plates to the belt and started a new pile.

"Are you inviting me to join your gang, Santiago? I'm flattered," I said with a wry grin.

Santiago let out a loud howl of laughter. "Yo man, I like you and all, but you're a little pasty to be part of my crew, if you know what I mean."

"You don't need a gang, man." Bishop snickered. "They kill each other off as much as they be killing other folks."

Santiago shrugged, "Can't deny. Gotta keep order one way or another."

"What I'm saying, man, is you already got a rep as a heater. After what you did to your bunkie way back, people are waiting for you to bring the heat to Boss. You don't and you'll live out the rest of your jolt a marked man."

"What happened back then was different. I'm not the same man I was then," I said, turning my back to them to focus on my stacking. I sent another pile down the line.

"I suggest you bring that man back," Bishop said before he and Santiago busied themselves with other gossip.

When we were released for lunch, I kept with the work crew as we made our way through the tunnel. To my relief, chow was uneventful. Santiago and Bishop sat with their respective racial groups, separate from one another. It didn't matter if you were good friends while on the job, when you were out of the shop you stuck with your own kind. Miguel and I decided long ago to go against the norm. We refused to belong to any kind. I sat blissfully alone in my usual spot undisturbed while I ate my stale bologna on white.

The workday dragged like any other, with the exception of the throbbing at my side. The stiffness there had me moving slower than I would have liked. Bishop and Santiago watched me from the corners of their eyes, but did not complain.

At three o'clock on the dot, I helped shut down the machines and clear the conveyors. I was about to check out for the day when Santiago grabbed my shoulder and pressed something into my hand between our two bodies. The shard of metal was cool against my palm.

"I like you, Foster," he said into my ear, under breath. "You ain't never done me wrong. You're gonna need this. It's time to bring the heat, man."

He started to walk away. I pulled him back.

"Where did you get this?" I whispered behind gritted teeth. "I can't take it. What if they do a frisk and search outside the block?"

Santiago took a quick look around and then turned back to me. He held my hand closed around the shard.

"I broke it off the end of the aluminum spool before they changed it out, man. Don't nobody know about it. It's strong. All you gotta do is scrape it against the brick or the pavement, man, and it'll be sharp as hell too. Hide it in your sock. Ain't like they gonna suspect you anyway, man. You ain't never caused no problems at work," he whispered.

"I can't . . ."

"You gonna need it, *ese*'. Take it." Santiago squeezed my hand and thrust my closed fist into my chest and then followed the rest of the work crew out of the plant.

Heart racing, I looked around and tried to think. If I walked out with this thing in my hand I would be taken down by a CO for sure. I had to get it into my shoe, but the cameras were on me in the middle of the production floor and they'd already seen Santiago's questionable closeness.

I darted into the bathroom and threw my boot off in the stall. Putting he shard under the insole, I thrust my foot back in. If there were metal detectors, as there often were coming back into the block, they would pick up the metal toe. Hopefully that would clear the whole shoe.

Flushing the toilet, I walked quickly but nonchalantly behind the last of the work crew. As much as I didn't want my new contraband, I did feel more confident going into the east tunnel. I knew I could take Smiley if he came at me again. This time I was ready for him. But if a gang of Boss' men came for me, at least now I had a fighting chance. If I wanted it.

As I feared, there was a checkpoint set up at the end of the tunnel. I looked behind me, thought about going back, but it was futile. The plant would be locked up for the night and the tower guard would catch me if he saw me going beyond the shop toward the mental wing without an escort. If I tried to ditch the scrap in the tunnel, the tunnel guard would see.

So I filed in line behind Santiago and told myself not to hold my breath. Act natural. That's how you were supposed to act when you were hiding something. Prison lesson number one.

Santiago shot me a knowing glance as Officer Edmonds and another officer, metal detector wands waving, searched everyone coming back into the blocks. There was nothing I could do but keep my eyes forward and await my turn. Edmonds ran the wand up and down Santiago's body and made him spread his legs, then cleared him to go. Before he walked on, he gave me a slight nod of encouragement as I stepped up to the wands.

"Spread 'em," Edmonds commanded in his deep voice and I obeyed.

He ran the wand over my torso. When he reached my right calf, the detector whined. He moved it away and brought it back to the same spot. When it whined again, he lowered it until he reached my shoe. The whining grew into a scream.

"Remove your shoe, Foster," he commanded.

"It's the steel toe, I'm sure," I shrugged.

"I said remove it."

I took the boot off and stepped back from it, wondering how long I would be locked in the SHU for possessing a concealed weapon. Edmonds scanned my boot as I wiped the damning sweat from my injured brow with the back of my hand. Luckily, the toe made the wand screech more than the metal hidden beneath the insole. Edmonds picked up the boot and after looking inside, turned it upside down and shook it. When nothing fell out he tossed it to me.

"Had to check," he said. "You're clear."

Stepping into my boot, I began to walk away.

"You going to have any more falls this evening, Foster?" Edmonds asked, making me pause.

"I don't plan on it," I answered, walking away as casually as my stiff side would allow.

On visitation days, while most inmates were with their families, I usually took advantage of the abandoned track and ran a few miles before evening chow. There was no way I was going for a jog in my condition, but I considered walking a few laps to ease the rigidity in my aching muscles.

I would have no visitors today. It had been eleven years since I'd allowed one. My family tried a couple of times in the beginning, but I refused to see them. The Logan they knew and loved was dead. Better they never get to know the monster locked up in here. It was better if they just move on.

The letters still came, but they remained unopened in the bottom of my cubby. My mom and dad lived only an hour and a half away in Greensboro. These years must have been hell for them. For that I hated myself all the more.

I'd allowed only one non-legal visit since my detainment began. Grace Kennedy came to see me my first month in Central. Still in shock and mad at the world, mad at myself more than anything, I'd made my way to the visitation room expecting to see my lawyer. Who I saw instead was the mother of the woman I'd killed, the grandmother of the child whose life I ended before it ever had a chance to begin.

I knew who she was because she'd given a statement at my trial. With tears in her eyes, she'd pleaded with the judge to give me the minimum sentence my conviction would allow. I never understood why until she came to see me that day.

Sitting across the small table from her, I forced myself to look her in the face, but I couldn't meet her eyes. Grace's expression was stern, but she exuded a peace that I hadn't felt since this nightmare began.

"What are you doing here?" I asked her.

She shifted in her seat and adjusted the collar of her rain coat. "I had to see you. There's a message I have for you that you need to hear. I read it this morning and I knew I had to come."

Her cracked leather purse lay perched on the floor beside to her chair. She pulled from it a small, white Bible which was worn and dingy around its beveled edges. At once my body tensed and panic pulsed through me at the sight of it. Hell was already a tangible reality I faced down every day. The last thing I could bear to hear was how much worse it would be for me on the other side of this life. I'd already resigned myself to the fire.

She read Hebrews 12:1, her voice shaking. "Therefore, since we are surrounded by such a great cloud of witnesses, let us throw off everything that hinders and the sin that so easily entangles. And let us run with perseverance the race marked out for us."

She closed the Bible and placed it back in her purse. When she looked up into my face, a single tear slipped onto her cheek.

"Not a day goes by that I don't think about my girls. My daughter, Simone, was so full of life. She had to overcome so much. She was a single mother, you know." Grace's wrinkled lips curved into a joyless smile. "Faith was just a baby, barely six years old. I want you to know that I will miss them dearly. I want you to know that your mistake took two of the dearest things in my life away from me."

It was the first time I'd heard the name of the child I'd slain. Faith. I had killed Faith. *How poetic*, I thought as my face heated.

My palms began to sweat. Not wanting to hear any more, I struggled to contain the anger bubbling inside. I longed to explode, to burst into flaming bits of rubble, but I knew I owed Grace this moment. I deserved to hear every word she said. When she reached her feeble hand across the table and rested it atop of mine, I met her eyes at last.

"I read that verse to you because it speaks of letting go. I want you to know that I've let go of my anger towards you. I've forgiven you, Logan. Since that very evening, I have forgiven you. I'm here because I want you to let go of your mistake, to forgive yourself. You made a stupid choice when you picked up that phone while you were driving, but two lives have already ended because of that choice. It would be the worst kind of tragedy for you to lose yours too. There's too much good left for you to do in this life."

I couldn't stop the tears from falling onto our joined hands, but I yanked mine loose and wiped at my eyes anyway.

"You forgive me? How can you do that?" I growled. "I killed them."

Grace nodded her head. She had a look of concern for me on her face that I could not fathom. Was she playing with me? Tormenting me? How could anyone forgive what I'd done, especially this woman whose world I'd just destroyed?

"Yes, you killed them, but I believe God has forgiven you, Logan, and so have I. You need to find a way to forgive yourself. Hope is still alive, still with me. Hope survived, and so must you."

I don't remember much of what happened then. The confusion was dizzying. It's the anger I recall above all else. Throwing my seat back, I stood and glared down at her.

"Who the hell do you think you are?" I remembered yelling. "You can't forgive me. God hasn't forgiven me. He sent me here, to this hell on earth, to rot. I deserve it, every torturous, disgusting minute of it. You understand me? I don't want your forgiveness."

I remember storming out of the visitation room then, and seeing Grace bow her head as the door swung shut. I remember stalking back to my cell where my bunkie was waiting for me, like he always waited for me. The next thing I remember was standing over his unconscious body, his face an unrecognizable puddle, my hands covered in blood.

Grace was the last visitor I ever allowed. Since that day, only an occasional visit from my lawyer had me sitting at those tables. Though I thought about that day often, I didn't regret the things I said to her. She needed to see the monster I really was. There were days though, the darkest of days, when I clung to Grace's words.

Three

Miguel wasn't back from road crew yet. I grabbed another pair of shoes from my cubby and kicked off my boots. Luckily, I could slip my running shoes on without having to undo the laces, which would have been impossible without Miguel's help. I considered what to do about the scrap of metal hidden at the bottom of my boot. Looking around first, I plucked the aluminum from the insole of my boot and slid it beneath the insole of my running shoes. Then I slipped them onto my feet and left the cell.

As usual for this time of day, the track was empty. I longed to jog away the stress of the past twenty-four hours, but I couldn't risk it with my injured ribs. Instead I walked the gravel as fast as my bruised lung would let me. At first my head and side throbbed with the movement, but once my heart started pumping, the pain faded and blissful warmth came to the areas of my body that hurt the most. I looked out into the empty field on the other side of the razor-wired fence and contemplated my impending freedom. I thought about Boss' desire to kill me before I made it to the other side of the gate, and didn't know what I feared more.

My thoughts were interrupted when the intercom blasted my name. I had a visitor. Knowing it wasn't a social visit, I prepared myself for a long talk with my lawyer about my upcoming release. By the time I made it up the hill to the visitation room I'd broken a sweat. My breathing came in labored wheezes. I welcomed the chance to rest in the cool, manila-colored room.

When I remembered the search awaiting me before I was allowed to enter the room, I thought about going back to my cell to change out shoes, but decided not to. It was a pat-down at best, at worst I would have to disrobe, but there would be no metal detectors and the aluminum scrap was secure inside my insole. Nothing to worry about.

As luck would have it, I was given a lazy pat-down and allowed to go on my way. I opened the revolving door and scanned the tables for my lawyer. At first all I saw were fellow inmates chatting away with relatives and friends, their smiles forced or over-exaggerated. The air smelled of perfume and fabric softener, a rare bouquet when your pallet was accustomed to the musk of the block. I closed my eyes for just a second and breathed it in. When I opened them again, I suddenly felt out of place.

My lawyer was nowhere to be found. I did see that at a table in the far corner, a middle-aged man in a suit and tie waited patiently for someone. I didn't recognize him. He stood as I approached.

"Mr. Foster?" he asked.

"I'm Logan Foster," I answered, tentatively.

"Mr. Foster, my name is Harold Dillinger. I represent Mrs. Grace Kennedy's estate," he said, motioning to the chair in front of him. "Won't you have a seat?"

I hesitated with the mention of Grace's name. The sharp edge of dread poked at my gut. Had she finally decided to sue for damages? To press charges of her own? That could mean additional jail time if she pulled it off. After all of these years, had she finally accepted that I deserved to be locked up for good? I sat reluctantly, keeping my eye on Dillinger, trying to gauge his next move. Then his words dawned on me.

"You said you represent her estate?" I asked, having a seat.

Mr. Dillinger sat and crossed his hands atop the table. His clean-shaven face was unreadable.

"Yes, I do. Mr. Foster . . ."

"Please, call me Logan," I insisted.

"Logan, when was the last time you had contact with Mrs. Kennedy?" he asked.

"I've only ever met her once, eleven years ago. What is this about?"

Mr. Dillinger looked down at his hands and then back to me. "Mr. Foster . . . Logan, I regret to inform you that Mrs. Kennedy passed away this last Sunday. I am here on official business per her request in her final will and testament."

I held up my hand. "Wait, what? She died? May I ask how?"

Dillinger nodded patiently. "She succumbed to lung cancer."

"Lung cancer," I repeated, considering his words. "And you say you're here because she requested that you visit me? Why? To let me know that she died?"

My mind raced, considering the possibilities. *Did she want me to know that she'd suffered these last eleven years? Did she want her death on my head too?*

"I'm here because she left something for you in her will," he answered. Leaning over, he picked up his briefcase and laid it on the table. "I was to bring it here and deliver it to you personally."

The clasps on the briefcase released with a double click and he raised the lid. I watched with curious dread as he shuffled around. When he withdrew the small, white Bible my heart stopped. He shut the case and handed it to me. I didn't move.

"She wanted you to have this. She was very adamant that it be given directly to you, Logan," he said, the Bible still in his hand.

"Is this some sort of a joke?" I asked, looking around the room.

"No sir, it's not a joke." Dillinger sighed and lowered the Bible. "Look Logan, I don't know what the deal is with this Bible or what it means to you or doesn't mean to you, but it was her last wish that you take it. Please sir . . ."

Taking the Bible from him, I stared at it, small and worn in my hand. I had no words.

"I am sure she would be very pleased that it is in your possession. Now, if you will excuse me, I have another appointment . . ." he said, rising from his chair.

"Tell me one thing," I interrupted.

"Yes?"

"Did she die well? I mean . . . was she happy? In life?" It came out a whisper.

Dillinger nodded, understanding. "She was a very happy woman. She will be greatly missed by many. Good luck to you, Logan."

With that he turned from the table and exited the visitation room. Sitting there, I stared down at the delicate Bible in my hands. There was something sticking out from between its pages. I flipped to where the bookmark, a golden angel wing, held the page. Hebrews 12:1 was highlighted in yellow ink.

Slamming the book shut, I rose from my chair, the metal legs scraping against the polished tile. I was frisked more thoroughly on the way out of visitation. No longer caring about the metal contraband in my shoe, I stared blankly into nothingness as the officer ran his hands up and down my legs. He looked through the Bible before handing it back to me and sending me on my way.

I ambled back down the hill towards my block, ignoring the stares and whispers of my fellow inmates as they made their way to chow. By now every inmate in the prison knew I was a marked man. None of that mattered to me. In that moment nothing mattered. I entered the cell block and passed the hallway trash can. Without a second look, I tossed the Bible in.

Four

When Miguel strolled into the cell just before 4pm count, I was laying in my bunk. His tanned face was flushed and sweat trickled down his temples. With a sigh he walked to the sink where he washed his hands and splashed cool water on his head.

"You know, before I got put away I used to look forward to springtime. Now every year I hate it more and more. It's hotter than my Aunt Maria's tamales out there on the roads, man. This summer is going to be brutal."

When I didn't respond he turned to me.

"How you feeling, *Guero*? You run into any trouble today?"

I sat up and found that the stiffness in my side had returned, but to a lesser degree.

"No, no trouble. I expect it will come soon enough," I said. "Let it come."

"You going to chow? I'm starving," Miguel asked.

"No, I'm not hungry tonight. You go ahead."

Miguel sat beside me on my bunk and cocked his head to the side. "What's this mood, *Guero*? You worried about Boss?"

"Not in the way you think."

Removing my shoe, I lifted the insole and motioned for him to look inside. He leaned over. When he saw the aluminum scrap his eyes widened. He looked around and then scowled at me.

"*Qué demonios estás pensando? Estás loco, Guero*?"

"English, Miguel!"

He shook his head, starting over. "Are you crazy? I want you to stay safe and all, but there are better ways, *Guero*. You'll kill someone with that, and then where will you be?"

Sighing, I took the metal from my shoe. I looked at it a moment and then thrust it at him.

"Santiago gave it to me. I need you to take it from me, Miguel. The way I'm feeling right now . . . I don't trust myself with it. Take it, please. Get rid of it."

He looked down at the scrap in my hand and then back up at me. When he met the desperation in my eyes, he grabbed the shard and stuffed it into the back of his pants just as Officer Edmonds' boots sounded in the hall.

"I'll get rid of it," he said as we took our places outside our cell for count.

Afterwards, I went back to my bunk. Miguel hesitated and shot me a concerned look before walking off towards the chow hall.

Laying back down in my bunk, I thought about Grace. I tried to imagine what her life was like in her final years. Mr. Dillinger said she'd been happy. Had she gotten over the deaths of her daughter and granddaughter? Was she able to move on? How often had she thought about me? Clearly, she still believed there was a part of me worth saving. The Bible she left to me told me that. But why? Why couldn't she just accept that I'm not the person she hoped I was? That it was too late for me?

I wrestled with the anger that thoughts of Grace brought to the surface. She'd offered hope, a cruel thing to dangle in front of a condemned man. There was no hope. There was nothing, no one, that could save me now. How dare she try to make me think otherwise?

Rising carefully, I went to the sink and filled a paper cup with water. I drank it down and was filling it back up when I heard footsteps clomp up to the cell.

"Looks to me like you're hiding from someone," a familiar voice chuckled behind me.

"You found me easily enough, Boss,' I said, tuning slowly to meet his grinning face.

A slender yet muscular man, Boss leaned against the cell entrance. His smooth, black skin glistened beneath the florescent lighting, highlighting the two tears that were tattooed beneath his obsidian eye. Smiley stood beside him, his arms crossed at his chest.

"To what do I owe this pleasure?" I asked, the anger raw and volatile within me.

Boss chuckled and scanned the cell. "I think you know damned well what I want, Logan. By the looks of you, Smiley here made it pretty clear."

"You want me dead. Why, because I couldn't get the parole board to let you go? You ran a drug ring that supplied heroin to the entire east side of Chicago. There was nothing I could have written to that parole board that would convince them to let you go. You knew that before you even asked me to do it."

"See, that's where you're wrong." Boss stepped inside the cell, his lips tightening over his bone straight teeth. "I ran the east AND the west."

Smiley laughed, following Boss into my cell. He stood in a fighting stance, ready to take action at the slightest indication from Boss.

"You were right about one thing though, I do want you dead," Boss continued.

"Why?" I asked.

"I have my reasons."

This time I laughed, fixing my eyes on Boss. "It seems we both want the same thing."

"Well then, this should be easy," he snickered. Smiley took a step towards me.

I shook my head, feeling the veins in my neck bulge.

"Unfortunately for you though, I've decided not to give you the satisfaction. See, I understand guys like you." I took a step toward Boss as he clenched his jaw. "You're scared. You know that by the time you see the outside of this prison again, you will have lost your power on the streets. And that terrifies you. That's why you have to set your sights on someone like me, who is getting out soon. You have no control over your own life, so you want to take control of someone else's. You need that power, don't you?"

Boss glared at me. I stepped even closer, the anger inside impossible to contain. "The funny thing is, Boss? You don't even realize that you're the lucky one."

"I'm not scared of a damned thing," Boss breathed, leaning in until I could feel the warmth of his breath graze my cheek.

I motioned to Smiley, "Then why do you need him?"

Smiley took a step closer, but Boss held up a hand and he froze.

"Why don't you wait for me in the yard," Boss said to Smiley, but did not take his eyes off of mine. "I want to take care of this myself."

"Boss?" Smiley questioned, stepping closer.

"I said go!" Boss hissed.

Smiley hesitated, his fists clenched. Then he slowly turned and left the cell, kicking the rail in the hallway as he stormed off.

"You see? Now it's just you and me, Logan. You're the one that should be scared."

"I'm dead already, there's nothing you can do to hurt me, Boss." I said, remaining rigid as I glared at him.

"Oh yeah?" he asked, reaching into his waistline. He retrieved a blade, shrewdly wrapped with fabric scraps. "How about we test that theory?"

My mind raced to the scrap of aluminum Miguel had no doubt discarded by now. Then I thought of Grace and the Bible laying in the bottom of the trash can. Red hair and an overturned stroller flashed before my eyes as Boss lunged at me, throwing me to the floor. He jabbed at me with the blade, but I caught his arm and struggled to keep it from my chest.

With a forward thrust, I swung my free fist and connected with his jaw. Saliva sprinkled my face as Boss reeled backwards. I rolled over and tried to get my legs under me. Before I could stand, he was on me again. I grabbed onto his wrist, battling to keep the blade away from my face.

"I'm going to send you straight to hell, Logan, where you belong." Boss sneered down at me, blood dribbling from his lower lip.

He focused all of his strength into his arm and thrust it forward, forcing it free of my grip. I jerked my head to the side just before the blade hit the floor beside my ear with a metallic screech. I didn't give him time to draw it back up before I rolled over onto his hand where it clutched the blade.

"I'm already there," I breathed, twisting his arm at the wrist.

Boss let out a howl and dropped the blade. I let go of him and reached for it, but he rammed his knee into my injured side. The breath rushed from my body in a mangled scream. My vision blurred with white heat as I collapsed, gasping for air.

Boss scrambled to his feet and glared down at me, a satisfied smile curling his lips. He stalked over to where his blade lay beside my bunk. Still gasping, I reached for it, trying to get to it before he did. With a laugh, Boss rammed his steel toe boot into my injured ribs with a crunch. The shock of the blow sent me reeling, the pain vibrating throughout my body. I couldn't breathe, couldn't cry out. Clutching at my side, the world around me spun and faded.

Unable to inhale a breath, I waited for unconsciousness to come, and with it death. Boss would no doubt finish me off once I passed out. Making peace with it, I welcomed an end to this pain . . . to my miserable existence. I was ready to face whatever awaited me on the other side of the darkness.

"You're not as tough as they say," Boss snickered, wiping the blood from his lip.

He picked up the blade. I heard the thud of his boots on either side of me. Bending over, he lifted my shoulders from the floor by my shirt collar. He put the blade to my throat. I was able to suck in some air with my head now elevated, but the pain was only beginning to wane enough to move. I struggled, but it was no match for the weight of his body on mine.

"I'm really am going to enjoy this," he said. I felt the blade press into the flesh of my neck. I closed my eyes, ready for the end, and awaited the first slice.

Instead I felt Boss' body lift from mine with brute force. His head flew into the metal bunk, sending him sprawling beside me. I looked up into Miguel's raging face.

"You okay, *Guero*?" he asked, helping me to my feet.

Still gasping, I was finally able to inhale. I felt weak on my legs. Miguel started to put his arm around me, but I shrugged him off.

"You should leave," I said between heaving breaths. Boss, holding his head, was struggling to get up off the floor. The blade was still in his hand.

"No," Miguel argued. "I won't leave you like this."

I took another gulp of air and staggered towards Boss. "Go, Miguel!"

Miguel looked from me to Boss and shook his head. "Don't do this. You're not like him, *Guero*. You made me hide that shiv so you wouldn't hurt nobody. You're not a monster like he is. Walk away, man. Let's go get a CO to deal with him."

I turned to Miguel, anger and hopelessness taking possession of my body. "You think because I've been locked up with you in here for so long that you know me? You don't know me, Miguel. I am a monster!"

Miguel stepped closer to me and held out his hand. "Logan, I do know you, *mi amigo*. You don't want this. What you did to those girls was an accident. You been seeing yourself as someone who'd do that to them on purpose. You're killing yourself over them. That's what makes you different from him. He don't care about nobody. Come with me."

Hesitating, I looked at Miguel's outstretched hand. The anger faded as I considered his words. Though I could never see myself as anything but a condemned soul, I knew I could never be like Boss. My thoughts turned again to Grace. I imagined her looking down on me and was shocked to discover that I cared about what she would think. Confused and disarmed, I stepped toward Miguel.

"Watch out, *Guero*!" Miguel screamed out suddenly.

I whirled around in time to see Boss lunge for me with the blade. Jumping out of the way, I waited until the blade was clear of my body. Then I hurled my clenched fist into Boss' face. Renewed anger fired up like flames from a dying ember from within me as Boss fell to the ground, his jaw hanging at an awkward angle. Again my thoughts flashed to Grace, to her feeble hands holding the small Bible as she read from Hebrews 12:1.

". . . let us run with perseverance the race marked out for us."

This is my race, my destiny, I thought as I slammed my fist into Boss' face again.

"That's enough, *Guero*," Miguel pleaded, but I continued to beat into Boss' face.

Miguel ran from the room as I pulled back my bloodied fist. Before I could use it again, officers flooded the cell. Edmonds clasped his muscular arms around my torso. I screamed out in pain and collapsed against his firm grip. My side reeling, I gasped anew for breath. He dragged me away as other officers bent down to tend to Boss, their boots slipping on the puddle of crimson seeping from his nose. The last thing I saw before my breath left me and I lost consciousness was Miguel, a mask of sadness on his face as he mouthed, *I'm sorry*.

Five

When I raised my weary eyelids, I saw I was alone in a small room. It didn't take long to recognize the peeling white paint and rusted toilet. The single window in the dented steel door refracted light into the room at strange angles. I'd been placed in solitary confinement, the SHU.

Looking down, I saw that I was cleaned up and dressed in a fresh orange uniform. My boots were replaced with soft soled slippers. I gritted my teeth against the dull ache in my side as I sat up to lift up my shirt. The bandages wrapped around my torso limited my movement. I didn't dare peed beneath the wrapping.

My head was foggy. It took more than one try to get to my feet. I walked to the door with the intention of looking out, but caught my reflection in the window. The cut on my brow was bandaged up as well. My brown eyes looked dark and heavy, my face sunken as if I hadn't slept in years. I wondered how long I'd been out. Outside, a guard sat in an armchair reading a magazine. Knocking on the window until I got his attention, I motioned the guard over. He looked surprised to see me and sat his magazine down as he stood.

"They said you'd be out at least until morning," the guard said as he stuck his chubby face in the window.

"How long have I been unconscious?" I asked.

"About six hours. It's almost lights out. They said you have a few broken ribs and need to take it easy for a while," he answered. "That was some fight you had in there. I hear the clean-up was hell, man."

When I remembered the fight I started to shake. *What had I done?* I looked down at my bruised knuckles, now cleansed of all that blood.

"Boss . . . is he?"

"He'll be out of the count for a while. You gave him a pretty bad concussion. Needed some stiches too. His nose is busted to hell, man," the guard chuckled. "You even broke his jaw."

I leaned against my arm on the door with a sigh, relieved that I hadn't killed him. "How long am I in here for?"

The officer shook his head. "I'm not sure. Not long. They saw the blade that Boss came after you with. Heard they had to pry it out of his hands."

Again relief. Being locked up in this small room with only my own thoughts to keep me company terrified me more than anything Boss might have done to me. Though my head was fuzzy, my mind in a fog.

"Why do I feel so weird?" I asked, rubbing my temple.

The guard laughed on the other side of the door, a loud, guttural sound. "Man, that's the painkillers. Guess they're doing a number on you, huh? They said it would knock you out for the rest of the night, but I don't think they gave you enough. You're a pretty big guy."

"I haven't taken any medications since I've been here. I forgot what it's like."

With another laugh, the guard walked away. "Enjoy it, man. You should sleep soundly tonight. They said you could have some more in the morning. Lights out in five."

I stumbled to the sink and brought water to my mouth with my cupped hands. The cold liquid soothed my scratchy throat. It took me a while to lower myself onto the single bunk and I was thankful for the bandage that kept the pain to a minimum as I moved. Laying on my back, I stared at the ceiling and replayed the events of the evening in my mind. I thought about the scrap of aluminum that Santiago had given me. If Miguel hadn't taken it away when I asked, I knew without a doubt that Boss would be dead.

The lights in my cell went out. In the hall they dimmed to a low glow. My mind was heavy and focusing became difficult. I closed my eyes and let my mind wander into the fog that surrounded it. Blissful nothingness engulfed me as I sank back into sleep.

When I opened my eyes again, it was still dark. Feeble light seeped into the small window, casting eerie shadows within my cell. The corner of my eye caught movement. Turning my head, I stared in confusion as something blocked out the light from the window as it passed. It passed again, a flash of red.

Tracking the movement, I forced my weary eyes to focus. I was about to dismiss it as a guard patrolling in the hall, but then it passed again. This time I watched as white fabric skimmed the wall below the window. Whatever it was, it was inside the cell with me.

I struggled to sit up. The pain, worse than before, made it difficult to move. When I was upright, I rubbed my eyes and stared again.

That's when I saw her.

Her red hair swayed against her white dress as she paced the floor in front of the cell door.

My heart raced. Panic filled me with pulsating dread. *I'm not seeing this. This isn't happening*, I told myself. It was a bad dream. I needed to wake up.

When she saw that I was awake, she stopped pacing. She turned to me and I gaped, horrified, at her familiar face.

Though she was fuzzy, like looking at a reflection through frosted glass, she was just as I remembered. Beautiful and luminescent, with the exception of a jagged white scar that ran from her forehead to her chin on the right side of her face, the woman I killed stood before me.

"Simone?" I breathed. It was the first time I'd ever said her name aloud.

I backed as far into my bunk as I could. She stepped closer and put a finger to her lips. I stared, unblinking as she approached, willing myself to wake from this nightmare.

"Logan," came a velvet whisper which made the hairs on the back of my neck stand on end. She stood before my bunk while I trembled.

"You have to go," she whispered again. "Save them."

"You're dead. I . . . I killed you!" I choked out.

"You have to go," she repeated.

"What do you want from me?" I asked, my voice raising to a shrill cry.

I tried to look away, but the desperation in her green eyes held me captive. They pleaded to me. I couldn't move. Glued to my bunk, the terror threatened to swallow me whole. *It was the pain meds*, I told myself. *They were making me see things that weren't there. My guilt brought her to me. She wasn't real, she couldn't be real.*

"Save them," she said, stepping even closer.

"You're not real," I shrieked, holding up my hands in a vain attempt to shield myself from the intensity of her stare. "I am so sorry for what I did to you. So, so sorry . . ."

My voice came as a hoarse cry, tears wetting my eyes as I tried to look away. She reached for me. I ducked away with a shriek just as the lights in my cell turned on. Like the shadows, she was gone.

"You okay in there inmate?" the guard yelled from the window.

I looked up to see his chubby face framed by the glass. Letting out a shaky breath, I looked about my room, my eyes wide. Panting, I ran a hand across my damp forehead and tried to collect myself.

"You had a nightmare, man. No worries. No one is getting at you while you're locked up in here, I promise," he tried to reassure me. "Go back to sleep, there's still a couple of hours before wake-up."

"Please," I hollered after him as he started to walk away. He turned back to the window. "Did you see a woman?"

"Those meds have you all jacked up," he chuckled, then walked away.

The lights went out again. I sat in the shadows and tried to process what just happened. I wanted to believe that the pain medication was messing with my mind, but the dull ache in my side had turned into a sharp, stabbing pain during the night. The drugs had long worn off.

Slowly laying myself down on my side, I folded me knees into my chest and trembled until morning.

Six

I stared at my breakfast tray knowing I needed something in my stomach, but unable find my appetite. Deciding that the banana was the most doable, I forced it down my throat then stuck the tray back into the slot in the door. The pain in my ribs too great to lie down so I leaned against the wall and thought again about what transpired just a few hours ago. *Had I really seen her?* It wasn't possible, yet I couldn't think of any way past what I'd seen. She'd been with me in my cell. Simone. The woman I killed alongside her child.

"I must be going crazy," I whispered.

Which a loud click, the cell door opened. Officer Edmonds stood in the doorway. He looked me over, his face solemn. I stood, both embarrassed and relieved to see him.

"So, I didn't fall," I said with a shrug.

He nodded. "I gathered that. How're the ribs?"

"I've felt better," I said with a forced grin.

Edmonds shifted his feet, "I didn't know about your injuries when I grabbed you."

"Yeah, I know," I said. "You did what you had to do."

"Yeah well, they've got medication waiting for you in the pill line," he said, meeting my eyes.

"I can go?" I brightened, desperate not to spend another night in the SHU . . . with her.

"You going to tell me about it?" He raised an eyebrow.

I looked away from him. "There's nothing to tell. It's been dealt with."

Sighing, he came into my cell and crossed his arms over his chest.

"You know we took a six inch blade off of Boss? Make no mistake, he was there to kill you, Foster. Now, you busted him up pretty bad. He'll be in the infirmary for a while, but a beating like that gives a man something to prove. You understand? Sure you don't want to file a report? It could get him transferred to max security. At the very least it would make him think twice before coming for you again. Do you understand what I'm saying? "

"I'll take it into consideration," I lied.

Edmonds stared me down, no doubt trying to get a read on me. Then shaking his head in defeat, he turned for the door. "I'll have them bring in a fresh uniform, then we'll walk you back to your cell. The doc wrote you a lay-in form. No work for you today."

Edmonds locked the door behind him. Relief washed over me. I would not be trapped here for another night. Better to face the sea of stares and snickers on the block than come face to face with my demons again. I was lucky to be in good standing with Officer Edmonds. For a fight, an inmate faced more than a week in the SHU, no matter what the reason.

Going to the sink, I scooped up another drink of water and then splashed my face, hoping against all hope that the image of Simone, the way she looked at me with those desperate green eyes, would fade. It couldn't have been real. She was only a figment of my imagination brought on by a mix of stress, isolation, and pain medication. That was all.

By the time I was escorted to my cell, dressed again in close security khaki, Miguel had already left for chow. I was given a strong warning not to cause any more trouble, then left alone to rest in my bunk. They'd given me ibuprofen and Percocet in the pill line. I declined the Percocet, but decided the ibuprofen was harmless enough. Laying on my bunk, I waited for the chemical relief.

I tried to clear my mind, to think of anything else besides Simone. Closing my eyes, I imagined running the track, which had always brought me a fragment of peace. I wished more than anything that I could get in a few laps. Instead, I imagined that I was out there, the blackbirds in the neighboring field my only company. Feeling the cool spring air graze my face, I listened to them squawk.

Then a voice was lifted above the breeze and bird song.

"You have to go. Save them." Her voice was urgent, pleading to me from my subconscious.

I shot up in my bunk, regretting the movement immediately. Clutching my side, I forced her voice from my mind. *She wasn't real*, I told myself, but I couldn't shake the feeling that she was with me, somehow. Even now.

"Hey, what time is it?" I yelled to a guard as he passed my cell.

He looked to his watch. "Quarter to seven."

"Thank you," I said as he continued his patrol.

Carefully rising from my bunk, I decided that I had just enough time to make it to work. There was no way I would get any rest sitting in my bunk all day with my mind in a jumble. I needed to go to work, if for no other reason than to feel normal. *It was just a normal day*.

It took me longer to get to work than I anticipated. Winded easily, I took it slow, ignoring the stares and whispers as I made my way through the east tunnel. Squeaky stared at me in surprise when I nodded to him. I wondered if he was one of the CO's called to respond to my cell the night before. The sight must have been gruesome, there was fear in his eyes as he watched me pass. At the very least he'd heard about it in detail.

By the time I entered the shop, my coworkers had already taken their places behind the machines. They looked up at me and gawked.

"Logan!" Mr. Jones hollered as he came to me from his office. "What are you doing here?"

"I needed to work today, sir," I explained.

He looked me up and down, "You look like hell, Logan. You're supposed to be on lay-in for today, maybe even tomorrow."

"I know, sir, but I want to work."

I felt the tension build in my shoulders. Mr. Jones knew everything. He would see me differently now, I was sure. Though when I looked up and met his eyes, there was no fear there like I saw in Squeaky's. If anything, there was concern for me in their slate depths.

"Why don't you come outside? We'll discuss it," he said, motioning me towards the back door.

When I turned to follow, I saw Santiago and Bishop gesture to me from Papa Smurf. Santiago pumped his fist, a proud smile on his face as Bishop clapped his hands silently as he nodded in approval. Funny how beating a man within inches of his life made you a hero in prison. To the other inmates, I'd accomplished something great by taking down Boss. What it proved to me was that I was every bit the man I feared that I was. I would not be celebrating.

Mr. Jones dug his keys out from his pocket and unlocked the deadbolt from the back door. I followed him outside and let the door close behind me with a metallic groan.

"First thing's first, are you okay?" Mr. Jones asked.

I was taken aback. Surely this man had heard what I'd done and was putting himself at risk by being alone with me. Yet he was asking ME how I felt?

"Sir?"

He sighed and cleared his throat. "Look, I heard about the whole thing. What the CO's didn't tell me I heard from all the chatter in here this morning." He motioned to the inmates on the production floor on the other side of the door. "Sounds like you were in quite the situation. Glad you came out on top, Logan. You should be resting though."

"I almost killed a man last night and you're worried that I need rest?" I whispered, unable to keep the shame from my voice.

"A man does what he has to do in a situation like that," he said, running a hand over his bald head. "You know, when I was stationed in Afghanistan back in the day, they used to have these dog fights with the strays just outside of camp. Despicable as they were, I learned something from watching during patrol once. You see, they would find a pup that was no more than a few months old. They would train it to fight, get it to where it was mean as hell and ready to shed blood. I watched them throw it in the ring with the kindest, most gentle dog they could find, just to see the dog get ripped apart."

Mr. Jones looked up at me from under his wire-rimmed glasses and I met his eyes reluctantly.

"Funny thing happens when a good dog gets thrown into the mix with a trained killer. He discovers a side of himself that he didn't know was there, and he does what it takes to survive. Sometimes the good dogs win, Logan. Now go back to your bunk and lick your wounds, you've earned it."

"Sir," I fumbled for the right words. "I need to be here. It feels . . . normal here. I'd rather be productive."

Jones studied my face and warred with the decision, his brows furrowing as he thought. Finally, he nodded and blew out a loud breath.

"Okay," he said, "I get it. I understand. You can stamp plates today. Just know those guys in there are all worked up. Can't promise they'll stay off your back. Seems you're the new shop hero."

He unlocked the door and held it open for me.

"I'm no one's hero," I said, walking through to take my place next to Bishop behind Papa Smurf.

When Mr. Jones was well into his office the chatter started. Ignoring the whispers and profane congratulations as best as I could, I got to work stamping plates. I passed them to Santiago who I could tell was biding his time before saying anything. Bishop just grinned like a proud parent beside me as he changed out dies. I looked at them both.

"I don't want to talk about it," I announced.

Bishop raised his hands in a gesture of innocence, but smiled wickedly down at me, the whites of his teeth contrasting his ebony skin. Santiago shook his head and chuckled, then leaned in close despite my declaration.

"Man, all I wanna know is . . ." He looked around and then leaned in closer. "Why didn't you shiv the guy, man? You know, with what I gave you? Shut that *puta* up forever, know what I mean?"

I sighed and lowered the stamp onto the next plate. "I said I don't want to talk about it."

Santiago laughed and backed off. "Alright, man. Gotta give you mad props though. You bout took him out with your bare hands. You're alright, Logan."

As I handed Santiago the next plate, Bishop leaned down into my ear.

"It's always the quiet ones," he said, slapping my back with a laugh.

At lunch I faced with the same chatter and snide, congratulatory praises. I ignored them all and focused on getting my sandwich down. When I stood with my empty tray, I locked eyes with Smiley. He stood with his arms crossed at the end of the food line, the threat clear on his face. Turning from him, I threw my trash away and walked back towards the east tunnel. It wasn't over between Smiley and I. I knew he would come for me eventually, as soon as he got the okay from Boss. Nothing was over, it was just a matter of time. In prison, a man has nothing but time.

The remainder of the workday passed far too quickly. Helping to clear the machines, I dreaded leaving work. I needed to stay busy, to keep my mind on constructive things. Even as I powered down Papa Smurf, my mind wandered to Simone and the way her red hair had flowed behind her as she paced my cell. Shaking the thought from my mind, I followed the rest of the inmates out of the plant.

I stopped by the pill line and again declined the Percocet, but downed the ibuprofen. When I got to my cell, I slipped into my running shoes and made my way to the track. By the time I got there, the pills were starting to numb the edge off. The stabbing pain at my side and temples dulled to a slow throb again. I was thankful that only a few inmates were in the yard and that the track was unoccupied. Walking was the best I could do, but it was better than nothing.

I watched the birds fly overhead and tried to clear my mind of this place. Of Boss, the fight . . . of Simone. Despite my efforts, Mr. Jones' words came to me. "*Sometimes the good dogs win,*" he had said. He thought I was a good dog, unlike the mad dogs around me waiting for the chance to shed blood. He looked at me and saw someone different. I struggled to understand why. Surely he had read my file. He knew what I was.

As I rounded the corner, I looked up to the empty field behind the razor-wired fence. Long grasses and weeds, yellowing beneath the unseasonably hot sun, swayed in the light breeze.

I thought of life before the accident. A sparkling new engineering degree, vacationing with friends, and moving onto the next phase of life was all that mattered to me then. The world was a blank canvas, waiting for me to make my mark. How different life would be, I thought as I turned another corner, if I had never gotten into my car that day.

My thoughts shifted to Simone. What would she be doing right now if I never existed? Would she be out on the roads running as she had done so many evenings before? Maybe she would have run a marathon or gotten remarried. And Faith, her little girl. She would be nineteen, almost as old as I was when I ended her life. She could have grown up to become someone great. I stole that chance from her. What a mark I had made.

I rounded another corner and looked back over to the field to watch the blackbirds peck at the parched ground. Movement among the tall, swaying grasses caught my eye. Gossamer white fabric surrounded the red hair that blew along with the breeze.

I froze, my eyes fixed on the woman who stood there, translucent. Her green eyes pleaded to me from the other side of the fence. My heart pounded in my chest, making the throbbing in my side worse. I was glued to the gravel where I stood, willing Simone's image out of existence. Instead she took a step forward. I heard her velvet voice in my ear as if she were right beside me.

"Logan," she whispered.

Horror shook me to my core, but I was compelled to step closer. *She wasn't real, she couldn't be real.* I had to know for sure.

"You aren't real," I called to her.

She glared at me as I stepped closer. I could see the scar that marred her pale, cloudy face.

"Save them," she pleaded.

"What do you want from me?" I called, "Save who?"

I walked to the fence, keeping my eyes locked on hers. Convinced that she was a figment of my own twisted imagination, I reached for her. *She isn't real*, I told myself even as my hand trembled against the chain link. She took a step towards me and reached out her hand.

"You are the only one who can stop it," she said. As she approached, I noticed the tears in her glassy eyes.

"I am so sorry," I whispered, the water standing in my own eyes as her hand sought mine. I felt the electric warmth of her touch.

"Back away from the fence inmate!" A gruff voice screamed at me from above.

I looked up to the guard tower above. A CO stared down the barrel of his shotgun as he aimed it at me.

When I looked back to Simone, she was gone, the warmth on my hand the only evidence that she was ever there. Backing away from the fence, I raised my hands into the air.

"I'm sorry," I shouted, "I . . . I thought I saw someone."

I turned back quickly, my heart racing. By the time I made it to my bunk, I was panting. The trembling in my arms and legs made it hard to catch my breath. I walked to the sink and ran cold water over my face, trying to jar myself from whatever strange place my mind was trapped in. I turned to see Miguel returning to the cell from work. He stopped short when he saw me, a smile spreading across his face.

"*Guero*! They let you out," he said, slapping my shoulder. "Thank God. Man, I'm sorry I had to rat you out to the badges, but you was really going to town on Boss. I tried to tell them that he was the one . . . Wait, what's the matter with you? You look like you seen a ghost or something."

I wiped my face with a towel and sat on my bunk. "I think I'm going crazy."

Miguel waved me off and went to the sink to wash his hands. "Man, you're just shook up from your time in the SHU. Few days and you'll be straight."

"I keep seeing her, Miguel. It's like she's here with me. She keeps saying things . . ."

Miguel turned from the sink, skepticism plain on his weathered face. "Man, you think you're the only one who sees skirts around here? Men weren't made to be around only other men for years at a time, man. Does something to their head. So, is she hot?"

Miguel wiggled his eyebrows.

"Damn it, I'm not joking," I huffed, lowering myself onto my bunk. "It's her, Miguel. The woman I killed. Simone."

Miguel's smile faded. His head hung as he sat beside me. "Oh, I see. So, you seeing what? Like her ghost?"

I hesitated, knowing it would sound crazy, trying to figure out how best to explain. "I don't know. Last night I woke up in the SHU and she was in the cell with me. She spoke to me. I thought it was the pain medication they gave me, but Miguel . . . I just saw her again, out in the field by the track."

Miguel nodded as he considered my words. "*Eso es algo de mierda loco.*"

"English, Miguel!" I yelled.

He blinked and looked up at me. "That's crazy, *Guero.*"

"I know," I sighed, standing with a wince to pace the cell as Miguel sat contemplating.

"You said she spoke to you? What did she say?"

Stopping, I looked back at Miguel. His expression was hard to read. "She told me I was the only one who could save them."

"Save who?"

"I don't know," I said, resuming my pace. "It doesn't make any sense. Do you think I'm crazy?"

Miguel stood, "Yes."

I threw up my hands. "Great!"

"Listen, *Guero*," Miguel stood in front of me, forcing me to stop pacing. "We all a little crazy up in here. A man can't be locked up in this place without going a little *loco*. Sounds to me like you've got some unsettled business. That mess with Boss brought up some stuff that you've got to deal with, man. You need closure."

"How am I supposed to get closure, Miguel? I killed her . . . a long time ago. I've been locked up here for almost twelve years. That's my closure."

"No," Miguel shook his head. "That was justice for what you did. What you need is to make peace with yourself over it."

I sighed and sat back on my bunk. "Not this again."

"Yes, this again," Miguel propped a foot next to me and leaned in. "You've been tearing yourself up for over twelve years. Maybe you are seeing her because it's time to close this chapter, *Guero*."

I thought about what he said for a minute. It made sense, though I didn't want it to. More importantly though, it was something. It was a reason for why Simone was visiting me, whether she was all in my mind or some kind of ghost.

"So, what do I do?" I whispered.

"Find out what she wants." He shrugged. "And give it to her."

"But who does she want me to save?"

"That, *mi amigo*, is what you have to figure out," Miguel held out a hand and helped me back to my feet. "Now, let's go get some chow. It's taco night."

Again, I was the center of attention as I chomped silently in my corner next to Miguel, who seemed amused by the constant nods and gestures of approval. A quick glance around the chow hall assured me that Smiley was nowhere near, for now. All I could hope was for my injuries to heal before he came at me again. Let that be a problem for another day.

For now, my mind reeled with the concept that Simone was all in my head. My subconscious was playing a terrifying game and I had to figure out to solve the riddle.

"Let's get out of here, *Guero*. I swear, these tacos taste less like Mexico and more like ground Mexican every week. I think I found part of a poncho in that last one," Miguel said and emptying our trays, we walked back to our cell.

As much as I couldn't stand to lay still in my bunk earlier, I was actually looking forward to the quiet time. There was so much to consider, and I doubted Simone would visit me in the cell surrounded by other inmates on the block. So far she'd appeared to me when I was alone, only to vanish when anyone else came around.

Stepping out of my shoes, I grabbed the nearest Tom Clancy novel from my cubby and sat down to read. I knew it would be hard to focus, to forget about Simone for even a couple of hours, but I had to try.

Miguel kicked off his shoes and climbed into his bunk. I felt him move around, then finally settle as I opened to the first page of *Patriot Games*.

"You never answered me earlier," Miguel said before I could read the first sentence.

"What are you talking about?"

"The woman you've been seeing. Is she hot?" Miguel chuckled.

"Are you making fun of me now?"

"No, not at all, *Guero*." He sounded apologetic. "I honestly just wanna know. I mean, I see lots of women drive by while we're out on the roads cleaning up, but I'm not so lucky to see one in my room at night. Tell me . . ."

I sighed and lowered the book. "She's dead, Miguel."

"I could be into it."

"You're disgusting."

Miguel laughed, I felt him shift in his bunk. "No, seriously. What does she look like?"

With a sigh, I conjured Simone's face. "She is very beautiful. Long red hair, green eyes. Her face isn't that clear when I look at her, she's fuzzy. Like looking at someone through a haze of heat on the highway. She has a scar. It runs along the right side of her face. I think I put that scar there."

"Damn, that's deep," Miguel whispered. "I hope you figure out what she wants, *Guero*."

"Me too," I whispered, then raised the book again.

It didn't take long to doze off. For a while my mind drifted in perfect emptiness and rested there. Soon though, I was bombarded with images of bloodied pavement and spinning stroller wheels.

When I opened my eyes, the nightmare hung like a thick fog above my head. The cell block was dark. The occasional cough or snore provided the only lullaby. My book laid face down on my chest. I stood to place it back inside my cubby.

She stood on the other side of the bars, in the middle of the hallway, when I noticed her. Falling onto the floor, my heart raced at the sight of her. I scanned the hall for any other movement, for anyone else who might see her and let me know once and for all if I was losing my mind.

"Miguel," I whispered, but heard only an unconscious snort in response.

Simone stepped closer, her white dress glowing in the darkness. I raised my eyes to meet the sadness in hers and slowly got to my feet.

"What do you want from me?" I choked out a whisper. "What do you want me to do?"

"You have to save them," she answered. "Before it's too late."

I looked around again, to see if anyone woke at the sound of her voice. No one stirred.

"Who? Who do I have to save?" I took a shaky step towards her.

"The runners." She took a step towards me, the urgency in her voice jarring me. "Three of them will die tomorrow. You must stop it."

"Runners? What runners? What are you talking about? I don't understand . . . this doesn't make any sense. You're not even real!"

"Listen to me!" she screamed, grabbing hold of the bars.

I stumbled backwards, frantic to get away from her terrifying grip. Tripping on my cubby, I fell on my side and screamed out in pain.

"What the hell happened, *Guero*?" Miguel was at my side in seconds, his eyes puffy and confused. "Are you okay?"

I strained to see around him, to the bars where she stood.

"She's here!" I gasped, pointing behind him.

Miguel spun around. Over his shoulder, I could see that she had vanished once again. Groaning, I tried to stand. Miguel threw my arm over his shoulder and hoisted me up.

"There's no one there, *Guero*," he said, setting me on top of my bunk. "This is worse than I thought."

"She was just there, I swear," I panted. "She told me they were going to die tomorrow."

Miguel ran a hand through his sleep disheveled hair. "Who is gonna die?"

"She said the runners, three of them. I don't know."

"That doesn't make any sense."

"I know," I said, swinging my legs onto my bunk.

Miguel sat at my feet, considering.

"You know what I think you ought to do? I think you need to make an appointment with psych tomorrow," he held a hand up before I could protest. "Just to talk this thing out with someone, you know? Maybe they can figure out what this woman . . . what your mind, wants."

With a sigh, I rolled onto my back and took a couple of cleansing breaths.

"You're right," I decided. "I can't do this on my own. Maybe they can give me something . . . so I don't see her anymore. I'll put in for the appointment tomorrow."

Outside the cell, footsteps sounded as the night CO approached, no doubt drawn by our commotion.

"Good," Miguel said, climbing back into his bunk. "Cuz otherwise you're gonna kill yourself for real. It will all work out, *Guero*. You'll see."

When the night guard looked into our cell, we pretended to be asleep. Even after he passed, we remained silent. I opened my eyes and stared blankly into the block, expecting to see Simone. I steeled myself for her return until my eyes closed at last and I was lost again to sleep.

Seven

"Did you see her again last night, *Guero*?" Miguel asked after he brushed his teeth and met me in the hall for morning count.

"No, but I can't stop thinking about what she said. What runners were she talking about? If she is only a figment of my imagination, then why runners?" I asked.

"Beats me." Miguel shrugged. "You gonna make that appointment for psych?"

I sighed. It seemed like a good idea before, but in the light of day I wasn't so sure. The thought of talking to a shrink made me uncomfortable. Clearly I was losing it, but there was something so final about admitting it to a trained professional.

"I don't know. What if they lock me in a psych cell?" I shuddered. "I don't think I can take that, Miguel. It'd be as bad as the SHU."

"Well, that's why you don't tell them the whole story. Don't say you've been seeing the hot woman you killed walking around the prison," he said. "Just talk out all the other stuff, like the accident and your feelings and crap. It will be good for you. It's worth a try anyway. You don't like it? Don't go back."

"I guess . . ." I started to agree when Officer Duke rounded the corner and sneered up at me.

"Well, well, well. Look who we have here. Mr. Big and Bad himself. I heard about what happened the other night. Didn't think you had it in you." Duke slugged me in the shoulder and laughed. "You and Boss have a lover's quarrel?"

I glared up at him, in no mood for his abuse.

"He got jealous when I told him I only had eyes for you," I said with a wink.

Miguel's eyes widened. He covered his mouth with his hands to stifle a laugh. Duke bristled and got within inches of my face.

"Looks like we have all the balls in the world now, don't we Foster? I bet you won't be so smug when Boss gets out of the infirmary. I hear he'll be out in a couple of days." Duke curled his lip and turned to leave with a click of his counter. "Good luck with that."

"God, I hate that man," I said to his disappearing back before going back into the cell to brush my teeth.

"What's gotten into you? You talking back to badges now?" Miguel gawked. "Did you hear what he said? Boss is getting out in a couple of days. What are you gonna do, *Guero*?"

"I'm just tired, Miguel. Of everything. There's nothing I can do about Boss right now," I said and then rinsed and spit. "I have to deal with one thing at a time. I'll make that psych appointment now, before work. Boss is a worry for later."

Miguel nodded. "You're right, one thing at a time. Talking to the doc is going to help, you'll see."

"Only one way to find out," I said as we left our cell.

Skipping breakfast, I stopped by the pill line and downed more ibuprofen and then reluctantly signed up for a psych appointment. It was the first time in my sentence that I'd ever made an appointment for anything. I wasn't expecting to be seen for a day or two, but a couple of hours after lunch Squeaky arrived at the shop to escort me to my appointment.

As Bishop and Santiago stared on, embarrassment burned my face while I stacked one last set of plates. Regret hit me like a hangover. I no longer wanted to go. It was a blissfully normal day at work and there'd been no sign of Simone since last night. Even so, I couldn't stop thinking about her warnings and what they might mean. Maybe it was best to talk to someone, to get her out of my head.

Squeaky cuffed my hands behind my back and then nervously led me to the north tunnel where he punched the code for the gate and led me through to the psych yard. The newly renovated facility sat in stark contrast against the molding fortress we called home. It's fresh, sand-colored brick and burnished windows made it look more like a hospital than part of the prison. My eyes took a few minutes to adjust to the harsh fluorescent lighting and the smell of paint and new carpet assaulted my nose as we entered the sliding glass doors.

A minimum security inmate, recognizable by his navy blue uniform, was seated behind a broad front desk. His youthful face was jubilant as he talked with the correctional officer propped up against the desk beside him. He smiled up at Squeaky as we approached.

"Can I help you?" he asked.

"Inmate Logan Foster for check in," Squeaky said.

"Just sign him in here. He can have a seat in the lobby," the inmate instructed. "He'll be ready for pick up in about an hour."

Squeaky signed me in and then removed my handcuffs. Nodding to me, he went on his way. I sat in the small waiting area where a thirty-inch flat screen television broadcasted the local news. The inmate continued his conversation with the overweight guard as if they were old buddies. I tried not to stare, but I was dumbfounded by their casual conversation. In close custody there was a clear and definitive line between prisoner and CO. I couldn't imagine discussing politics or the weather with any of them.

After a few minutes, the phone on the inmate's desk rang.

"Inmate Foster? Ms. Pritchard will see you now."

I stood, confused. "Ms.? I thought I was here to speak with a therapist?"

The inmate smiled. "Ms. Pritchard is a therapist. If you'll just follow Officer Reynolds, she's ready for you."

The plump guard motioned for me to follow and I walked to him, still wondering if I had made the right appointment. He led me into a short hallway and stopped at the last door on the left. Knocking once, he opened the door and ushered me in.

"Inmate Foster," he announced as I entered tentatively, the door shutting behind me.

The room, painted a warm shade of tan, was much more inviting than the hospital-like reception area. Light oak furnishings and a soft upholstered chairs filled the small space. A large window illuminated it with natural light.

"You can have a seat anywhere you'd like," a soft voice directed.

Standing beside her desk, a slender woman in a grey skirt-suit shuffled through folders until she found the one she needed. Then she turned to me with a smile. I tried not to stare, but I couldn't take my eyes off of her. Aside from being the only non-CO woman I'd seen in years, she was stunning. Her blonde hair was pinned back, revealing a long, delicate neck. Behind her thin-framed glasses were eyes of the deepest blue I had ever seen.

"Please, have a seat," she repeated.

Snapping out of my trance, I hastily sat in one of the soft chairs facing the window. I immediately regretted being there. *What was I thinking? How could I tell this woman what was happening with me? I should have dealt with it myself.*

"So, Mr. Foster . . ." she said, taking the seat across from me and crossing her long legs.

"Please, call me Logan," I said before she could continue.

"Logan, my name is Willow Pritchard. I'm the acting psychologist intern on staff. You're here because you requested an appointment and I am here to help you any way that I can."

"Intern? Is there a doctor I can speak with?" I asked.

Willow removed her glasses and glared at me. "I can assure you that I am more than qualified to help you. The certified staff are reserved for those inmates needing more intense treatment. I'm sure you understand . . ."

"I'm sorry, I didn't mean to offend you, Ms. Pritchard," I said, trying to dislodge my foot from my mouth. "I just mean, is it . . . safe for you to be alone with me like this?"

Willow raised an eyebrow. "Is it not safe for me to be alone with you like this?"

"No, no, that's not what I meant. I mean . . . for you to be one-on-one with prisoners. I'm used to there being a CO within sight at all times," I stammered. "And you're a very attractive woman. Is it safe for you to . . .?"

Willow seemed amused. She smiled and leaned back in her chair.

"There are certain measures at my disposal I can utilize should I feel threatened, but I've found that when I treat a prisoner like a gentleman, they tend to behave like one," she said.

I cleared my throat. "I'm sorry. This is all new to me. I was expecting a male doctor."

"I get that a lot," she said, "but I assure you that I have been well trained to help with whatever you are dealing with. So, let's get started. Shall we?"

She put her glasses back on and opened the folder on her lap. "Why don't we start with your file? It says here that you've recently been in an altercation and that before this most recent incident you were in a similar altercation several years ago with your cell mate at the time. Let's talk about that."

I shifted uncomfortably in my seat. "Why do you want to talk about that? It was a long time ago."

"It says here that you beat Mr. Williams so severely that he sustained some brain damage and is now permanently disabled. Can you tell me what lead to the fight?"

My face flushed as renewed anger and embarrassment rushed to the surface. This was NOT why I was here. The last thing I wanted to talk about was what happened when I returned to my cell after Grace's visit all those years ago.

"Look, Ms. Pritchard . . ."

"You can call me Willow."

"Willow, I didn't come here to . . ." I started.

"Sometimes it helps to start somewhere just to break the ice. I'm interested in what led you to beat that man so severely," she interrupted.

I shot out of my chair, the anger now impossible to contain. All the helplessness and desperation of that time in my life came back to me in a rush of heat and blood.

"You really want to know? Fine," I growled. "I beat him because for weeks that man attempted to sexually assault me. Every day, he waited for me so he could rough me up again and for weeks I resisted him until one day I just snapped. No one would do anything about it. I was new, scared and trapped without any options. So I took care of it myself. I spent a month in the SHU for it and I really don't want to talk to you about it. What's done is done."

"I'm sorry that happened to you," Willow said, her tone steady, calm, practiced. "I think under the circumstances, your recourse was understandable. It obviously still upsets you. Can you try to verbalize to me how you feel about the incident?"

I laughed despite myself.

"You want to know how I feel about beating a man's head in?" Sitting back down, I leaned forward and looked her square in her face. She straightened, obviously uncomfortable with my closeness, but met my eyes. "I get what you're doing. You're trying to gauge whether or not I feel remorse or if I am quick to anger to violence. Let me help you out here. I feel nothing but remorse, day in and day out. There's not a day that goes by where guilt doesn't consume every fiber of my being."

"I see," Willow nodded.

"But when I beat into Williams that day, I felt nothing. He tormented me every day for weeks. If I was quick to turn to violence, I would have killed him on that first day. He is not why I am here."

Willow studied my face, concern and curiosity on her own. "Then why are you here, Logan? Is it because of this remorse you are feeling? Talk to me about it."

The warmth in her voice and genuine interest on her face disarmed me. The anger inside dissipated. I took a deep breath and leaned back into the downy upholstery. It was finally time to talk about why I was here, but I couldn't find the words.

Refusing to talk about the accident and the remorse that was eating me alive for so long left me with no clue where to start. And I was afraid. I'd learned to live with the guilt, had accepted it as part of my life. It was mine to live with and I deserved it. Letting go of even the smallest part of that guilt would be an injustice to the woman and child I killed.

Willow sensed my struggle. "Talk to me about the accident that lead to your incarceration. Can you do that? Talk to me about Simone Kennedy. What are your feelings about her, Logan?"

Looking down at my shoes, I shook my head. "Wow, you really did your homework on me, didn't you?"

"That's my job. I have to know about you in order to help you," Willow said. When I looked back up at her she grinned warmly. She'd read my file. She knew the horrible things I'd done, yet she didn't look at me with condemnation in her eyes. There was no fear, only sympathy in their sapphire depths.

"It just doesn't seem right," I said.

"What doesn't?" she asked.

"That I get to sit here and talk to you about my guilt while they're dead and buried because of me."

Willow sighed and nodded her head, then she leaned forward and placed her hand gently on mine. I tensed with the feel of her. It had been so long since I felt the kindness of a stranger or the touch of a woman. I felt my face flush, my pulse quickened beneath my skin.

"This remorse is very natural. You made a mistake, a grave one that you can't take back. That does not mean you should spend the rest of your life suffering for it, Logan," she said. "I think what has complicated the situation for you is that there's never been an opportunity for you to do anything to assuage this guilt you are feeling."

"What could I even do? They're dead, and I have to live with the consequences." I looked away, unwilling to unload the burden I was prepared to carry forever.

"Are you really living though? Or are you just existing?" she asked, seeing right through me as though my mind and my severed heart were wrapped in cellophane.

"How is it fair to have a life when I stole theirs from them? A single mother. Her child?" I whispered through gritted teeth.

"How is it fair to them to *not* live the best possible life you can? How are you honoring them by condemning yourself to a miserable existence? Do you think that's what they would want for you?"

Everything Willow said made sense, but I didn't know if I was ready to hear it. I thought about Grace and her kind words. She too thought I should go on to live a good life, but I wouldn't hear it then. How could I now? How could I even begin to release this condemnation? What kind of life could I possibly have? How could I do anything to honor Simone and Faith's memory? I was nothing but a disappointment. There was nothing else I could ever be.

"How am I supposed to do that? There's no way to make up for what I've done," I asked.

"I think you made a big step in just making this appointment. It's a start," Willow closed my file and laid it on her lap. "Why don't you tell me what led you to make this appointment. Why now? Was it this latest altercation?"

Sighing, I warred with whether or not I should tell her about seeing Simone. I was starting to feel comfortable with Willow. She made me feel as though there was hope for me somehow, for a life beyond the hell I'd condemned myself to. Something about her made me want to cling to that hope for the first time. Would I ruin all that by telling her about Simone?"

"Not exactly . . . well maybe." I faltered. Then I thought about Simone and the desperation in her teary eyes, then decided to just tell Willow everything. It was worth the risk of being locked in a padded cell to make peace with the ghosts in my mind.

"I've been seeing her," I whispered.

Willow looked confused. "Who? Who have you been seeing?"

"Simone Kennedy. She's been visiting me," I said, looking Willow dead in her eyes. "I know it sounds crazy, and I know it's all in my mind somehow, but she wants something from me. I need your help to figure out what that is."

Willow furrowed her brow as she digested what I just revealed. I waited for her to look at me like I was insane, but she just nodded as if she were trying to work a math problem in her head. Holding my breath, I waited for her to respond.

"I see," she finally said. "I certainly understand why you made the appointment. It must be very unsettling for you to see her."

"Am I going crazy?"

She held up a finger. "Let's not use the word 'crazy'. Do you remember what I said about you not having the opportunity to assuage this guilt you are suffering from?"

"Yes, but . . ."

"Well, it seems to me that your subconscious is giving you that opportunity. I think you're seeing her because you have a desperate need for closure."

"But why all the sudden? Why am I seeing her now?" I asked.

"Your file says that you're scheduled for release next year, is that correct?"

"Yes. I only have thirteen months left on my sentence," I answered, lowering my head.

"Your subconscious is trying to tell you something, Logan. It needs you to let go of this guilt before your release," Willow said with confident authority. "It's important for you to recognize that the woman you are seeing isn't real. She's a visual projection of what's going on inside you."

"How do I make her go away?" I asked but was interrupted when the small phone on Willow's desk rang.

"I'm afraid that means our time is up," she said, standing. "But to answer your question, I think you should try to figure out what will give you some closure. What can you do to start to release some of the remorse you're feeling?"

"But how?" I asked. "How do I do that?"

I stood as Willow walked to her desk. She turned to face me with a grin on her full lips.

"Next time you see Simone, try asking her what she wants, what your subconscious wants. You have to be really honest with yourself about this, Logan. It's time to resolve these feelings of guilt."

Willow answered the phone.

"Yes, we're ready. Thank you," she said into the receiver and then hung up and turned back to me. "I would like to see you again in a couple of days to see how you're doing. Is that alright?"

"Sure . . . thank you, Willow," I said a little dumbfounded as the officer appeared at the door to escort me back to reception.

"It was a pleasure meeting you, Logan," she said, extending her hand. I took it, noting it's softness against my rugged palm. "Really consider what we discussed here today. I think we've made some good progress. I'll see you in a couple of days."

When I got back to reception, Squeaky was waiting for me. I stood beside him, deep in thought, as he signed me out and pulled out his cuffs. The plumps officer nodded to the inmate receptionist.

"Did they say anything else?" he asked.

The receptionist shook his head and sighed. "No, still no cause of death. It's a damned shame too. My little sister ran the Nevada race last year. I told her the body wasn't meant to run for two hours straight."

"I bet it's the heat that did it. This is the hottest March we've had on the east coast in a while. I'm betting heat stroke took them out. That's the only explanation for three people dropping dead in one race," the officer said. My head snapped up.

"I'm sorry. What are you talking about?" I asked the receptionist.

He nodded towards the TV in the waiting room.

"It's all over the news," he said. "That national Music Marathon series? Three people just dropped dead during the half marathon in Virginia Beach. One right in front of a high school marching band. It's a shame."

"They don't know what caused the deaths yet, but I'm telling you, it's the heat. You've got to figure it's even hotter at the beach," the officer added.

Heart galloping, I turned to the TV and remembered Simone's words. *Three will die . . .* On the screen, three pictures were displayed with names beneath each victim as the anchorman described the chaos. Two young men and an older woman died mid-race. Three people, just like Simone had warned.

"You said this is a tour? A running tour? I've never heard of that," I said, trying to keep my voice calm as Squeaky tightened the cuffs around my wrists.

"Yeah, it's a big deal too. Last year was the first tour with races in ten states. They say this year's going to be twice as big. Each race draws thousands of runners because there's a live, local band at every mile," the receptionist answered.

"It just started last year?" I mumbled. "I've never heard of it. There's no way I could have made this up . . ."

"What?" the receptionist asked as Squeaky ushered me forward.

"It isn't me," I said as I stared blankly at the TV in shock. "It's not in my head."

"Let's go, inmate," Squeaky ordered in his best authoritative voice.

I broke my stare, ignoring the confused looks that both the receptionist and officer gave me. Staggering outside, we made our way back to the tunnel. I waited for Squeaky to punch in the code. My mind was a whirlwind. There was no way I could have known about the race today. If I had no idea about the race, then what Simone said couldn't have come from my subconscious . . . *could it?* If Simone wasn't a manifestation of my guilt, that meant she was real.

By the time we were back at the shop my hands were trembling, making it hard for Squeaky to remove the cuffs.

"You alright, inmate?" he asked.

"I'm fine," I lied, joining my co-workers in time to help shut down the machines for the day.

I spoke to no one, keeping my head down until we were released from work. Metal detecting wands awaited us at the end of the east tunnel, but this time I breezed right through earning me a sideways glance from Officer Edmonds. When I got back to my cell, I threw on my running shoes and hurried out to the track. The throbbing in my side made moving laborious, but there was no time to waste standing in the pill line. I had to get to the track. I had to see Simone.

Walking as quickly as I could, I made it to the yard and was disappointed to see it teeming with inmates. The track was also heavily populated with joggers and walkers. Then I remembered with frustration that it was not a visitation day. Determined, I fell in step behind the other walkers on the track and stared out into the empty field.

The sky was grey with impending rain, casting a dull hue onto the tall grass. The steady wind made each blade sway. I stared at the movement, trying to conjure Simone's image beyond the fence. Corner after corner I rounded as the sky grew steadily darker, but there was no sign of her.

I walked until I was the last inmate on the track and the rain began to fall. Then I walked up to the fence and looked out into the mist that was forming in the field. I needed to see her, to know if she was real or if my mind was playing some kind of sick game. I had to know.

"Rec time is over, inmate. You have to leave the yard," the tower guard yelled down to me from his covered stand above the fence.

I nodded, looking once more into the field before finally giving up. Dripping and defeated, I walked back to my cell wondering if I'd ever see Simone again. She'd warned me about the runners' deaths and I'd failed to stop it. Maybe that was the end of it.

When I reached my cell, Miguel hoped off the top bunk and rushed over to me. "*Guero*! I heard on the radio in the van. Three runners died today!"

I sighed. "I know, I heard."

"Eso es un poco de materia extraña . . ."

"English, Miguel!" I yelled, reaching into my cubby for a dry shirt.

"What do you think this means? What your lady said came true," he said, sitting on my bunk.

"That's what I've been trying to figure out for the last few hours," I said. "I don't know. I guess she could still be in my head. Maybe I heard about the race and just didn't realize it. Maybe someone was talking about it. Willow thinks I need closure . . ."

"Wait, wait, wait," Miguel interrupted. "First of all, we both know that no one on this block cares about any kind of race that's not horses or NASCAR. No one around here would be talking about it, *Guero*. And second, who the hell is Willow?"

"My therapist," I answered, running a towel over my damp hair.

"You got your appointment already? And it was with a woman?"

"Yes, with a woman," I said. "And don't even think about asking if she is hot. She's my therapist. I don't want to think of her in that way, you got it?"

"Okay, okay . . . but what else did she say?" Miguel asked.

"She thinks I'm seeing things because my mind is projecting the guilt I feel or something like that," I answered with a shrug. "It all made sense when she said it, but now I don't know, Miguel. If I didn't hear about the race from someone then how the hell did my mind come up with it?"

Miguel looked deep in thought for a minute.

"Maybe she's not in your head, *Guero*," he said, a grave look in his eyes. "Have you seen her since last night?"

"No," I sighed. "I went out to the track to see if she'd show up there, but nothing. Maybe she won't come back. She wanted me to save them and I didn't. Maybe she's gone for good."

"What could you have done?" Miguel asked.

"Nothing," I said, throwing the towel back on the hook. "That's why it's so frustrating, and now I doubt I'll see her again to find out what she wanted me to do."

I thought about the possibility of not seeing Simone again and at first felt relieved. At the same time though, I felt like I'd missed something. Maybe I could have helped her in some way. As terrified as I was at the possibility of Simone somehow visiting me from beyond the grave, there might have been something I could do for her. It might have been a chance to give back to the woman I stole everything from. Now my chance at redemption had vanished with her.

"This is deep, *Guero*, and I can't think on an empty stomach. Chow's almost over, let's get something to eat." Miguel stood, and though I doubted I could eat, I followed him to the chow hall.

The smell of stale meatloaf wafted in the air as Miguel and I got our trays and took our normal seats in the corner. I picked at my mashed potatoes and found comfort in the fact that I was no longer the center of attention. Drowning out the sounds of chomping and conversation, I thought about my session with Willow. She hadn't looked at all surprised that I was seeing Simone. She was convinced that my mind was conjuring her image. I wondered what she would say if she knew Simone's warning had come true. Would she even believe me?

I was so lost in thought that I didn't notice Smiley walk into the chow hall or the eyes that turned to me with his presence.

"Look alive, *Guero*," Miguel nodded toward the double doors. "Smiley looks like he's out for blood."

When I looked up, Smiley was walking toward me, anger curling his top lip. I took another bite of my mashed potatoes and ignored him.

"Hey, Foster!" he yelled when he was a foot in front of the table. "Thought you'd like to know that Boss is getting out of the infirmary tomorrow."

When I continued to ignore him, he grabbed my tray and threw it to the floor, sending bits of overcooked meatloaf and potatoes flying. The room fell silent and every inmate in the room turned to watch the action. Miguel started to stand, but I raised a hand to him and he sat back down. I stood and faced Smiley, glaring into his golden grin.

"You hear what I'm sayin' to you?" He sneered.

"Yeah, I heard you," I said. "I just don't care. I've got better things to worry about."

Smiley laughed and stepped closer. I could see my reflection in his incisors.

"This time, Foster," he sneered, "we all coming for you. You won't get lucky again."

"So be it," I said with a shrug. "I'm not afraid of you."

"You should be, Foster. You should be." Smiley turned to leave, then stopped. "Oh, I forgot one thing. I was told to give you a message . . ."

"Watch out, *Guero*!" Miguel yelled.

Smiley whipped around, his fist jabbing out towards my injured side. Before he could make contact, Miguel braced himself in his seat and kicked Smiley so hard from behind that he went sprawling onto my food tray on the floor. Whipping around, I scanned the room, ready to engage whoever came to defend Smiley, but I was met with a sea of shocked faces.

"Did you see that?" someone whispered.

Smiley growled and struggled to get back up, slipping on gravy and bits of green beans. Officer Edmonds stormed into the chow hall and after a quick look around, marched up to me. He glared down at Smiley, now coated with mashed potatoes.

"What the hell is going on in here?" he demanded.

I shrugged at him. "He fell."

Edmonds stared at me for a second, his eyebrow raised. Then with a sigh he looked around the room.

"Everybody out! Back to your cells, now!" he yelled and then looked back at me. "You too, get back to your cell. I'll handle this."

Miguel and I backed out of the chow hall and made our way down the block to our cell.

"That's the second time I had to save your *culo* from those guys, *Guero*. We need to come up with a plan *pronto*," Miguel said when we got inside.

"You shouldn't have gotten involved again. Boss was too out of it to know that you're the one that sent his head into the bunk, but now you're going to have Smiley on your back. I wanted you to stay out of it," I snapped. "This is my fight, I don't want you to suffer for it."

Miguel jammed his finger into my chest. "You know, *Guero*? You never did thank me for saving your life the other day. If it wasn't for me, you'd be in the morgue right now. So how about a little appreciation?"

Sighing, I sat on my bunk and kicked off my shoes. "I'm sorry. I just don't want anyone else getting hurt or worse because of me. I can't go through that again, Miguel."

Miguel sat on the opposite side of the bunk and looked at me. "I get it, I do. I'm not scared of Boss and his crew. You and me? We've been looking out for one another for a long time. You'd do the same for me."

"What's going to happen when I get out next year and you're stuck in here without me?"

Miguel laughed, "Hell, they'll probably stick me with some old fart *hombre* as a cell mate, or worse, some young tortured soul like you. I'll be begging Boss to take me out."

I laughed, the tension easing some.

"Good to see you laugh, *Guero*. That therapist must have done some good," Miguel stood to grab a book from his cubby before climbing into his bunk.

"It's like she knew exactly what I was thinking, what I've been feeling for these last twelve years," I said, grabbing my own book and settling into my bunk. "I told her about seeing Simone."

Miguel's head dangled from the top bunk. "You did? Did she look at you like you was crazy?"

"No," I said to his upside down face. "She understood. She had me convinced it was all in my head, but Miguel . . . it wasn't, was it?"

Miguel sighed and his head disappeared back up into his bunk. I felt him move around and then settle into a comfortable position.

"There's no way you could have known about those runners today," he said with a sigh. "I don't think she was in your head. I think you saw something else."

"What? Like a ghost?"

"I'm not sure," he said, and then after a minute, "Do you think she'll come back?"

"No." I opened my book. "Whatever she was . . . whatever she expected me to do, it's too late. I think she's gone."

"You sound disappointed." Miguel chuckled. "Man, she must have been really hot."

"Miguel!"

"I'm just sayin'" he continued. "It is too bad you never got your closure, *Guero*."

"Maybe I did," I thought about looking into Simone's sad green eyes and remembered the things I had said to her. "I finally got to tell her that I was sorry."

By the time the bars shut for lock-down I was fully enthralled with my book. I welcomed the escape and let my mind fight alongside Jack Ryan at Buckingham Palace. Too tired to think any more about Simone or her ominous warnings or of Boss and his threats, I made it almost five chapters in before I began to doze.

When the lights went out, I set the book on my cubby and turned to Miguel who was fast asleep and snoring. I lifted his book off his chest and set it in his cubby, then I climbed beneath my covers. As I drifted to sleep, I didn't see the usual images of bloodied red hair and overturned strollers. Instead I saw the faces of three strangers as they dropped dead before reaching the finish line.

Eight

I opened my eyes to twilight. The early light of the new day seeped into the windows at the end of the block and cast finger-like shadows into the cell. It was much too early to be awake, so I rolled over to go back to sleep. Then I heard what woke me.

The sound of sobbing came from the corner of the cell. I laid there waiting for my conscious mind to chase away the sleep. When the sobbing grew louder instead of vaporizing with the remainder of my dreams, I shot up and rubbed my eyes.

Simone sat in the corner of the cell drenched in feeble shadow. Her head lay in her hands atop her bent knees as she wept. Her long red hair hung to the floor.

My breath caught in my throat and my heart sped at the unexpected sight of her. I wiped at my eyes again to be certain of what I was seeing.

"Simone?" I whispered, my voice shaking.

Her head came up slowly. Tears fell from her eyes as she looked at me, despair distorting the features of her translucent, lovely face. Steeling myself, I got up from my bunk and took a step towards where she sat against the bars.

"They're dead, Logan," she said, her voice no more than a whisper.

Taking another step towards her, I squatted down to her level. With a trembling hand, I reached out and touched her shoulder. She felt like warm static, her heat penetrating me from the inside. I gasped, looking into her swollen eyes.

"You're real aren't you? I'm not making this up . . ."

"Yes," she whispered.

"How? I don't understand what's happening."

"You have to stop it," she pleaded.

"Stop what?" I urged.

Simone sighed, the frustration on her face evident. "You're the only one who can help them, Logan. You have to stop it before it happens again."

I sat back on my heels, by mind reeling. "It's going to happen again?"

"There are others," Simone said, lifting my head to meet her eyes. "Saturday, five more will fall. You must stop it."

"But how? I don't understand what I'm supposed to do. What can I do?" I tried to keep my voice down, but I didn't understand.

Simone stood and wiped the tears from her eyes, her white dress flowing to the floor behind her. I scrambled to my feet and watched in awe as she reached up and cupped my cheek in her palm. My eyes traced the jagged scar along her face.

"I am only a messenger, Logan. It's up to you to find a way. You've been called to do this," she said.

"Called?" I repeated.

"This is your chance for redemption," she whispered. "Only you can make things right."

Simone's image blurred as my eyes filled with stinging tears.

"Redemption?" I whispered, forcing back the tears. "After what I did to you?"

"You have to believe," Simone said, her green eyes seeing right through to my soul. "Take this chance, Logan. Save them . . . save me."

There was a gasp behind me. Miguel's bunk squeaked.

"*Santo padre, es cierto!*" he whispered. I spun to see him staring, eye's wide, at Simone.

"Save them," I heard Simone plead, but when I turned back she was gone.

I stared for a moment at the place where she'd just been, then spun back around to Miguel.

"You saw her! She was just here. Tell me you saw that!" I pleaded.

Miguel stared, dumbfounded. "*Él envió a otro!*"

"English, Miguel!"

He looked at me and shook his head. "I can't believe what I just saw, *Guero*. I thought maybe you were losing it before, but this is the real deal."

"Then I'm not going crazy." I exhaled, falling back onto my bunk, my head in my hands.

"No, *Guero*. You been visited alright," Miguel said.

"She's a ghost, isn't she? I'm being haunted by the woman I killed." I whispered.

Miguel jumped down from his bunk and leaned down to meet my eyes. "You have to listen to what she says, *Guero*."

"Why?" I asked.

"Because she's no ghost, <u>*Guero*</u> . . ." The seriousness in his eyes made my heart pound faster. "She was sent here for you."

"She said I was called . . . What I'm supposed to do with that?" I asked.

"What else did she say?"

I thought about all the things that Simone said, committing her words to memory.

"She said that on Saturday five more runners would die. She said this was my chance at redemption, Miguel . . . but what can I do? What does she expect me to do?"

Miguel leaned back, his eyes wide. I ran my hands through my disheveled hair and waited for a response.

"You gotta find a way to stop it," he finally said. "You have to."

"How am I supposed to do that? Who will even listen to me? Maybe Officer Edmonds . . ."

"You want to get yourself locked up in the SHU? That's *loco*! You can't tell a badge, they'll think you have something to do with it. They'll put you under investigation if those people do die."

Miguel stood on my bunk and reached under his mattress. When he sat back down in front of me, he had Grace's Bible in his hands.

"Where the hell did you get that?" I shrieked.

Miguel held a finger to his lips to hush me. "Someone told me they saw you throw this away the other day. I know how you get when you're emotional, *Guero*. I thought you might regret it one day, and where I come from you don't just go and throw away the Good Book, *mi amigo*."

He held out the Bible. I took it from him reluctantly. There was a bulk to it that wasn't there before. As I looked down at its worn pages I noticed something wedged inside. I opened the Bible to where the bulge caused a gap in the middle of Daniel 10. As I did, the aluminum scrap that Santiago gave me fell onto my lap.

"You gonna need that too," Miguel said, meeting the shock in my eyes.

"Why would I need this, Miguel? I told you to get rid of it!"

Miguel picked up the scrap and put it into my hands. He cupped his own around mine.

"Because *Guero*, you gotta break out of here," he said, the seriousness in his voice setting my nerves on their ends.

Before I could protest, heavy footsteps sounded on the hall outside the cell. Miguel gave my hand a final squeeze, then disappeared into his bunk. I looked down at the aluminum scrap in my hand and quickly shoved it back into the Bible and then hid the Bible beneath my pillow. Then I laid down.

"Everything okay in here?" Officer Edmonds asked from the other side of the bars.

I waited to see if Miguel would respond, but when he didn't stir I knew he was pretending to be asleep.

"Just a bad dream, I guess," I said. "Sorry about the noise."

Edmonds looked around the cell, squinting in the feeble light. Satisfied, he nodded and walked off down the block. Neither Miguel nor I moved. When I felt sure that Edmonds wasn't lurking down the walkway, I sat up and knocked on the top bunk. Miguel climbed down silently and sat beside me, his face still grave.

"There is no way I am breaking out of here. Are you crazy?" I whispered. "What do you want me to do? Take a hostage with a scrap of metal? Even if I wanted to get out of here, I wouldn't make it a foot outside the block."

Miguel looked outside the bars and we both listened for movement nearby. When he was convinced that no one was listening, he turned back to me.

"That's why they can't know you gone until you are miles away. Listen," he said shifting his position at the end of the bunk. "I read about this guy, his nickname was Houdini Hines. He escaped from a max security prison back in the day by making a key out of some scrap metal."

"A key? What are you talking about?" I asked, my frustration mounting.

"With the aluminum scrap . . . you can make a key, *Guero*."

I sighed and rubbed my eyes. This was crazy. Everything was crazy.

"Even if I COULD make a key, Miguel, I don't know the codes to the tunnel gates. Besides, I'd get picked off by a block guard. Not happening, my friend."

"I'm not sayin' to make a key to the cell, *Guero*. What about your work? The shop's close to the psych wing, no? Is there a door there where you could get out without being seen?"

My mind flashed to the back door of the license tag plant, to the key wielded by Mr. Jones. "This is crazy."

"All you need is the code to the north tunnel gate. Once you in the psych wing, there's a driveway in the back of the main building that leads right out onto the main road. I seen it every time they make us pick up trash around the main gate."

I laid back on my bed and laughed as quietly as I could. "I thought I was the crazy one all this time, but this takes the cake, Miguel."

"This is no joke, *Guero*," Miguel scolded. I looked sideways at him. He was clearly getting angry, so I sat back up and took a deep breath, choosing my words carefully.

"Look, I appreciate that you are trying to help me here, but this is never going to work. It's crazy. I'll get myself killed," I said.

Miguel scooted towards to me and leaned in close.

"I thought that's what you wanted," he whispered. I met his resolute stare. "I mean, you been so wracked with guilt that you been killing yourself for over a decade. Now God himself is giving you a chance to redeem your mistake and it's suddenly not worth dying for? Better to let Boss kill you over a piece of paper in this hellhole? This is your chance, *Guero*. You have to take it. It's time."

Miguel's words hung in the air like vapor. I knew he was right. For the last twelve years I believed that there was no hope for a monster like me. Yet here it was. Hope stared me in the face, a gift from the heavens themselves, should I choose to accept it.

I thought about Simone's words. She told me to believe. She wanted me to believe that I could do this, that I was meant to do this. It was crazy. My rational mind struggled with the all of it, but I'd touched her, felt her warmth on my flesh. Simone was real. What if she really was sent from heaven? It was so hard to believe that heaven would care about me . . . that it even existed.

I'd experienced hell. I'd sunk into its fervid depths and wallowed in the wretchedness of perdition. It was as real to me as the bars that held me in their grip. How much more real could heaven be then, to find me here in my place of self-torment and offer me a life line? I thought about Grace and the hope she had once tried to offer. I asked myself what she would want me to do. With that thought, my decision was made.

"Okay," I whispered. "What do I do?"

Before Miguel could answer, the lights turned on in the cells and inmates began to stir. Chatter floated down the halls. Miguel stood and motioned to the Bible beneath my bulging pillow.

"First thing you gotta do is find a way to get the shape of the key from work back here so we can work on making a duplicate," he said, grabbing clean clothes from his cubby. "You gotta get in to see that shrink lady today too. Get a look at that north gate code. You got one shot, *Guero*. Make it count. You don't got much time."

I walked to the sink and ran water over my face, trying to convince the doubting parts of my mind of this new reality. As crazy as the decision was that I'd just made, what startled me was how I felt after having made it. It was as if I'd shed a thousand layers of dead skin and was stepping out for the first time naked and raw. It was liberating and utterly terrifying.

"Willow said she didn't need to see me for a couple of days," I said.

"Well, you gonna to have to say it's an emergency." Miguel bent to put on his shoes. "It's already Thursday. We got to figure out where the next race is going to be and hope you can get there in time."

"That won't be hard. If I can get in to see Willow, I'm sure the receptionist will know where it's being held. He seems to know a lot about the race series."

Miguel stood in front of me. He placed both hands on my shoulders and looked into my eyes, his face a mask of seriousness.

"There can be no 'if', *Guero*. Your life has just been given a purpose. You gotta do whatever it takes to fulfil it," he said. The he gave my shoulders a squeeze and smiled. "You deserve this chance, *mi amigo*. We're gonna make this happen."

"I had no idea you were such a believer." I marveled.

Miguel dropped his hands and made his way toward the bars.

"When you been stripped of everything that men can take from you, what is there left but your belief?" he said as the bars raised.

Nine

After morning count, I requested an appointment with Willow. I wrote '*Urgent, I need to see you right away*' in the comments section of the form. I hoped it was enough. Then I made my way to the east tunnel, all the while trying to think of a way to burn the shape of Mr. Jones' back door key into my brain.

The thought crossed my mind that Boss was to be released into general population at some point today, but I couldn't let him distract me from my new mission. I would deal with him if I had to. Miguel was right, I'd been given a new purpose and not even Boss could stand in my way now. There were better things to die for.

Having skipped breakfast, I was the first one in the east tunnel. I nodded to Squeaky, then made my way to the plant's back door. For a long time I stared at the lock, trying to memorize the shape and angles of its narrow opening. There was no way to remember enough of it to be able to fashion a key. I knocked on the door instead.

After a few seconds, I heard keys jingle on the other end. The door opened enough for Mr. Jones to poke his shiny head out.

"Logan, you alright? You in more trouble?" he asked, concerned.

"No, sir, nothing like that. I know I am way out of line here . . ." I fumbled for the right words to form my lie. "I was hoping you might let me have another cup of that amazing coffee this morning. It's been a hell of a week and I could really use it."

The last part was true enough. He looked to the ground and seemed at war with himself over my request.

"You can have my whole paycheck . . . and next week's too," I added.

Jones smiled and let out a chuckle. Then he stepped back from the door and motioned me inside. I watched him extract a large silver key from the door, then cradle the set in his hands as we walked through the slumbering plant to his office.

"Keep your paycheck, just promise to start training a newbie next week to be as competent as you are and we'll call it even," he said, leading me to his office.

"You got it." I felt a pang of guilt knowing I would be gone by next week. One way or another.

When we entered his office, we were again met by the divine aroma of the expensive brew. Jones threw his keys down on his desk and grabbed two empty mugs. He filled them both, then handed me one and motioned for me to have a seat. I stared at the keys on his desk, but the back door key was covered by the oversized key ring. *Damn.*

"So, how is the whole Boss situation? That is his name . . . am I getting that right?" he asked, propping his legs up beside his keys.

I tore my eyes away. "Yes, sir. He's coming back from the infirmary today. I'm not sure what will happen. I can tell you one thing, though"

"What is that?" he asked.

I leaned forward in my chair, taking a long sip of the earthy brew. "This old dog is not giving up without a fight."

"That's what I'm talking about." Mr. Jones laughed. He leaned over the desk to smack me on the shoulder. "You do what you have to do, Logan. You're so close to being out of here and moving on with your life. Don't let anyone take that away from you. Keep your nose clean though. You don't need more time added to your sentence. You report him if you have to, you understand?"

"Yes, sir."

I took my time with my coffee, trying to think up a plan to get a good look at that back door key. Before long, inmates began to file onto the production floor and Mr. Jones let out a deep sigh.

"Thank God tomorrow is Friday, huh? The weekend cannot get here fast enough," he said, throwing back the remainder of his coffee.

I started to get up, but when Jones saw that my mug was still full, he waved me off.

"No, you enjoy that coffee. I'll get Bishop to help me get the machines started. Come on out in a minute or two."

"Thank you, sir," I said as he left his office, shutting the door behind him.

I took a long drag from my mug as I watched him walk past the window. When he was out of sight, I hurriedly set it down and grabbed his keys from off the desk. Holding the back door key between my forefinger and thumb, I tried to commit its every curve and dip to memory. No matter how many times I counted each angle though, I doubted I could conjure its exact image later. This was too important to leave to chance. I needed an imprint.

I thought about tracing the key onto the message pad that Mr. Jones kept by his phone, but all I could find were pencils. If I traced the key in pencil, it might smudge on the paper when I hid it in my shoe. I needed to burn the shape of the key into my mind somehow. Then an idea hit me. . . *Burn.*

Looking back through the window to make sure I wasn't being watched, I hurriedly removed the key from the ring. Then I tucked it beneath the coffee pot and atop the scalding burner. I watched the window while the key heated up. When enough time had elapsed, I grabbed a few coffee filters and used them to snatch up the key from beneath the pot. I felt its heat through the thin barrier. With only seconds to decide, I lifted my uniform leg and exposed my calf. Then taking a deep breath, I pressed the key into the meaty flesh there. I held it firmly against my skin, clenching my teeth as I took the pain.

The key cooled after a minute, and I carefully removed it from my where it stuck to my leg. Then I inspected the results of the branding. Sure enough, the key's likeness was burned into my skin, its exact shape captured in seared, raw pink. I exhaled, wiping the sweat from my brow and gently lowering my pant leg. Then I slipped the key back onto the chain, downed the rest of my coffee, and left the office to join my co-workers. With any luck, the burn would darken and not swell.

It wasn't long before Squeaky appeared in the shop to take me to see Willow. I'd only stamped a few dozen plates when I saw him enter the plant, handcuffs in hand.

"You trying to get yourself committed before Boss gets out?" Bishop whispered.

Santiago shook his head. "See, *Ese*? You should have shanked that *vato* while you had the chance."

"This has nothing to do with Boss," I said, giving a wave to Mr. Jones through his office window.

"Yeah, sure," I heard Bishop mumble under his breath as Squeaky cuffed me and led me out of the plant.

The officer was silent as usual as we made our way to the north tunnel, and as always Squeaky looked nervous. There had to be a way to watch him punch in the code to the gate without spooking him more than he already was. I was sure he was afraid I would beat him down like I did Boss at any provocation. I also knew that since I towered over him in both height and weight, the 9mm at his hip would be his first choice of defense if he got too nervous. It didn't help matters that he was escorting me to the psych ward for the second time in as many days. Maybe there was a way to use that to my advantage.

As we approached the north gate, Squeaky paused. He looked at me over his shoulder, my signal to hang back while he punched in the code. It had to do something fast, this was my only chance to get that code. Committing to my ploy, I doubled over and pretended to hyperventilate just as Squeaky reached for the pin pad. He spun around and rushed to my side.

"Are you okay inmate?" he asked to my bent head.

"Panic attack," I said, gasping for breath.

Wobbling back and forth, I gave the allusion that I was unsteady on my feet. I stumbled towards him and as suspected, Squeaky came to my aid. He offered his shoulder for me to lean on, but his left hand remained poised over his weapon.

"Thank . . . you. Just . . . have to get to my appointment. I'm . . . so sorry." I gulped, looking as pathetic as I could.

"Does this happen often?" he asked as we stumbled toward the gate.

"Just since I found out . . ." I said, moaning for emphasis.

Squeaky looked alarmed. I continued to prey on his compassion. When we were just feet from the gate, I leaned more heavily on him. He was forced to slip his arm around mine, which was cuffed behind me. He kept his left hand gun-ready.

"Found out what?" he asked.

"Boss." I gasped. "He gets out today. He's . . . going to kill me."

Squeaky shook his head reassuringly. His tone was that of a mother talking to a child scared of the boogie man beneath his bed.

"No, that's not going to happen," he assured. "We know all about Boss and how he threatened you. We're not going to let him do anything to you."

When we approached the pin pad Squeaky made a motion to set me down on the curb, but I leaned into him all the more and coughed as though I were choking.

"He . . . almost killed me." I began to cry into the back of his shoulder, but kept the corner of my eye on the pin pad between forced sobs. "He'll find a way!"

"No, he won't," Squeaky said, looking from the pin pad back to me.

Continuing to cry against him, I feigned obliviousness. With a helpless sigh he punched in the numbers. I watched from under my downturned eyelids. *Twenty-seven, ten, twelve*. I memorized the numbers by two's, repeating them over and over again in my mind as Squeaky led me through the gate and up to the reception door. When he was sure I was stable, he let me go. I took a few deep breaths and pretended to collect myself.

"I can't go in there like this," I said. "I'm . . . so humiliated. Thank you for your help, Officer. So . . . embarrassing. "

He patted me on the back and gave me a minute to pull it together.

"You good?" he asked when I was finally able to stand.

"Yes, sir. I'm good." I sighed, faking relief.

Squeaky held the door open for me and taking a deep breath, I walked into the reception area.

"Don't worry about Boss. We're taking care of it," he whispered as he went to the desk to sign me in.

Thankfully, the same inmate was working reception. The plump officer was nearby enjoying a Diet Coke. I followed Squeaky to the desk, hanging back until he signed me in and removed my cuffs. With a final nod, he left the building and I turned to the receptionist.

"Ms. Pritchard will be with you shortly." He smiled.

"Thank you," I said, then cleared my throat before changing the subject. "So I was thinking about those poor runners all night last night. Did they find out what killed them?"

I tried to sound casual, like I was genuinely interested in the topic and not as though my very existence was intertwined in it. The receptionist leaned back in his chair, formality melting with this chance at light conversation.

"They're saying the cause of death was heart attack. Can you imagine? Three people dying of a heart attack in the same race? They said someone died in the first race in Houston last week of a heart attack too. Two races into the series and already four people drop dead of heart attacks. This tour is cursed or something," he said, thriving on the drama.

"Heart attack?" I asked, surprised. "A couple of them looked pretty young."

"They said they all must have had pre-existing heart conditions and didn't know it," the officer said as he sauntered over to join the conversation.

"Are they going to cancel the rest of the series?" I asked.

"You know they aren't going to do that, not after all the money people paid to run the damned thing. Bunch of lunatics if you ask me," the receptionist said with a wave of his hand.

"They're telling people to get approval from their doctors before they run, but you know people aren't going to do that. They're also making them sign a medical release before they get their bib numbers," the officer said, perching himself against the desk. "But you know? Thousands of people run each one of those things. You have to keep that in perspective. Three or four people out of like four or five thousand is not so bad if you think about it."

I shook my head, trying to make sense of the cause of death. *Heart attack. If that was how they had died, then how in the world could I possibly have stopped it?*

"Still, a heart attack . . ." I began, but was interrupted when the phone on the receptionist's desk rang.

"Yes ma'am," he answered. "I'll send him right in."

The officer motioned for me to follow. I made it half way down the hall when I turned back to the receptionist.

"So where's the next race going to be?" I asked as nonchalantly as I could. "Maybe it won't be as hot."

"No such luck. The next one is in Atlanta on Saturday. It will be a scorcher for sure," he answered. "Bunch of crazy people, I'm telling you."

I hurried to catch up to the officer, my mind reeling. Atlanta was a huge city, and a good six hours away. I pushed back the doubts that I could possibly make it there in time.

Willow's door swung open and I strode in. I turned to see Willow's perplexed face as she stood from her chair to greet me.

"It's a pleasure to see you again, Logan. I was surprised to see your appointment request this morning. It said this was urgent, is everything alright?" She asked, her voice heavy with practiced concern.

I was caught off guard by the sight of her. Her blonde hair hung loose in soft waves about her shoulders and the silk blouse she wore beneath her blazer matched the royal blue of her eyes. Wavering, I tried to remember what brought me here. All thoughts of the race and Simone fell to the back of my mind.

"Why don't you have a seat and tell me what's troubling you?" she said, motioning me to the same chair I'd occupied not twenty-four hours prior.

Blinking, I mentally slapped myself for reacting like a hormonal pre-teen and had a seat. I couldn't allow Willow's beauty to distract me from the task at hand. I couldn't let anything stop me.

Willow sat across from me and flashed me a reassuring smile. "So, why don't you tell me what brings you back to my office so soon? Does this have anything to do with Blake Roberts being released this morning?"

"Who?" I asked.

"I believe you know him as Boss?"

"He's been released? Already?" I kept my voice calm and steady, inquisitive, as if we were discussing politics or the change in the economy.

"Is that why you're here today?" she asked.

Seeing the worry on her delicate face, I considered telling her everything. I tried to guess what her reaction would be, were I to tell her about Simone's warning coming true. If she believed me, even just a little bit, then maybe she would help me stop the race. She had the power to make the right phone calls and I wouldn't have to attempt Miguel's risky escape. *Could I even make it to Atlanta in time?*

She tilted her head at me when I did not respond and leaned forward. She placed her hand on mine again and again I marveled at the softness of her skin.

"I felt like we made some real progress yesterday, Logan. I want you to know that anything you say to me is strictly confidential. It doesn't leave this room."

"Boss is not why I'm here, Willow," I said, standing to cross to the window.

Outside, I saw a small parking lot flanked by a rusting green dumpster. When I looked closer I saw the small driveway that Miguel said would take me right through the main gate beyond the trees and then out to the road. There would be a guard tower at the gate, and an armed guard trained and ready to prevent me from walking out. Miguel's plan was doomed from the start. Even if I did make the key and sneak away from work undetected, even if I did make it through the north gate and onto that driveway, how was I supposed to make it past the gate guard?

I turned back to Willow, who was watching me patiently from her chair, and decided that it was less of a risk to just tell her everything about Simone's warnings. She could help me, she had to. If not, if she thought I was crazy, it wouldn't matter. I was never going to see her again.

Going back to her, I sat and ran a hand through my hair as I tried to find the words. She met my eyes with earnest interest.

"Do you remember that I told you I was seeing a woman?" I asked, keeping my voice calm, rational.

"Yes, you told me you were seeing Simone Kennedy, the woman you accidently killed. I told you that she was a projection your mind created to deal with your repressed guilt."

"See, that's the problem. I don't think I'm making her up." Saying it out loud to Willow sounded crazy even to me.

"So you think she's real?" Willow raised an eyebrow. I could feel her judging my every movement and word.

"Just hear me out . . ." I said when I saw she was about to interject with more psychological wisdom. "I didn't tell you everything yesterday. I didn't tell you about Simone's warnings."

"She spoke to you? That could be a good thing. That's your mind telling you that . . ."

"I'm not done," I interrupted, sitting forward in my chair. "She warned me that three people, three runners, were going to die yesterday. I didn't want to believe it, I thought I was going crazy. That's why I made the appointment with you, but then those runners in that Music Marathon in Virginia Beach died yesterday . . . Now I know she's real."

I watched Willow's reaction, saw the interest on her face fade to something unrecognizable. She sat back in her chair and tapped her foot while she contemplated what I said.

"Did she say anything else?" she finally asked, but did not look at me.

'Yes, she said that five more people would die in the next race on Saturday." I took a deep breath and continued. "Willow, I need you to help me stop that race."

"What?" she asked exasperated.

"I know it sounds crazy, but I think Simone is some kind of . . . well, an angel or something."

"An angel . . ." Willow repeated, lowering her head.

"Yes." I tried to quell the desperation in my voice. "She was sent here to give me this second chance. Even if I'm wrong, then there's no harm done, right? It's just a race. If I'm right though, then you will have helped me stop five deaths. Help me, Willow. Please." I stared into her face, but she would not look up at me.

Willow's foot stopped tapping and she stood slowly and paced away, a glazed look on her face. She reached for a pen and paper on her desk and began to scribble.

"I'm sorry, Mr. Foster, but I don't think I can help you anymore. I'm going to refer you to my colleague, Dr. Rightenburg."

"What?" I asked, standing to meet her at her desk.

"I'm afraid I made a mistake in my diagnosis. You appear to be suffering from an acute form of Post-Traumatic Stress Disorder. I've seen this before, but I'm not . . . qualified to help you in this area," she said, holding out the note with Dr. Rightenburg's name. Still, she would not look at me.

I stood in front of her and bent down to meet her now distressed eyes.

"You said yesterday that you were qualified to help me. You're the only one who can," I pleaded, but she shook her head and grabbed the phone from her desk.

"Yes, please send Officer Reynolds down. Mr. Foster will be leaving now. Thank you," she said, then hung up the phone. "I'm afraid I can't help you after all. Dr. Rightenburg is an excellent doctor. I am sorry. I wish you luck with your upcoming release."

She didn't offer her hand, didn't offer any further explanation for why she was so eager to be rid of me, and she didn't have to. She thought I was crazy, and who could blame her? A part of me agreed with her. *It was worth a shot*, I decided as she opened her door. Officer Reynolds appeared to escort me out. I left without saying another word. Willow's door shut firmly behind me.

"I don't know what you said in there, but I've never seen Ms. Pritchard cut an appointment short like that before. Did you threaten her in any way?" Reynolds asked, the threat in his own voice clear as we made our way back to reception.

I looked forward, resigning myself to the task ahead and shrugged. "I think so, but I have no idea how."

When Squeaky escorted me back to the plant, he was still quiet, but the fear of me was gone from his eyes. Lost in thought, I tried to think of a way past the main gate guard. My plan to have Willow help me stop the race with a few phone calls had failed miserably. Retribution would not come so easily and I was okay with that. It shouldn't be that easy. Though I was sure I would be killed in my attempt to escape, there was a chance that I could help Simone. For that chance, I was prepared for whatever the outcome.

When I returned to work, I took my position back behind Papa Smurf. Bishop grinned at me as he moved over.

"You can run, but you can't hide," he whispered. "You want me to get my guy to take care of Boss now?"

I stamped the next plate and Bishop changed out the dies.

"I told you, this has nothing to do with Boss. I'll handle him if it comes to that, now please just drop it," I urged.

Bishop shot a glance to Santiago who shook his head and sent a stack of plates down the line. The hours dragged on, even lunch seemed longer than usual as I counted the minutes until I would be back in my cell with Miguel. We had a lot to do and I was eager to get on with it.

When it was finally time to shut down the machines, I glanced at the back door. No one was near it, so I made my way back to it as quickly as I could. Keeping the cameras in mind, I grabbed a broom and swept the floor along the way.

When I reached the back, I turned to see who would have a clear view of the door from their machines. Only the Papa Smurf workers would see me leave when the time came. Mr. Jones's office window was clearly visible from here though. If he was in his office when I tried the key, it would be game over.

Setting the broom down, I caught up with my co-workers as they were filing out of the front doors. We were met with a frisk-and-search coming back into the blocks. Officer Edmonds patted me down as I held my arms out wide.

"We going to have any falls this evening?" he asked.

"I'm not looking for any trouble," I said as he patted my legs.

"Boss is back in his cell. We've got a CO tracking both him and Smiley. They come near you, you come find me. You understand?" Edmonds stood and looked down at me, his authority emanating from him like expensive cologne.

"Thank you for always being fair with me and for looking out for me all these years," I said. "You're a good man."

Edmonds was taken aback by the unexpected compliment as he stood regarding me. He slapped me on the shoulder as the corner of his lip raised into a half grin.

"Just doing my job. You stay safe, Foster," he said and I walked on towards the blocks.

If I was to be caught trying to escape, if I failed, I prayed that Officer Edmonds would not be the one to have to put me down.

I struck the thought from my head when I entered my cell. Looking around, I hiked up my pants to inspect the brand on my calf. Sure enough, the burn was darkening into a mauve color. The edges, even the grooves of the key, were clearly distinguishable. Satisfied, I lowered my pant leg and contemplated what to do next.

Miguel would not be back from road crew duty for another hour. I briefly considered jogging the track to relieve some of my nerves. My side was stiff but the pain was manageable without any medication. A few laps might do me some good, but I decided that it was too risky with Boss' men on the prowl. I knew they were out there, waiting for their opportunity to strike. Despite what Squeaky and Edmonds assured, Boss would find a way to get at me eventually. It was only a matter of time. With this escape plan though, time was something Boss was running out of. One way or another I would be gone soon, either dead or headed for Atlanta.

Digging paper out from my cubby, I did something that I hadn't done since I'd been incarcerated. I wrote a letter to my parents. When the escape went down, I wanted them to know why I'd done it, that despite the disappointment I'd become, I loved them. It was hard to find the words to describe Simone's visits and her warnings. My parents would no doubt think I had gone insane, and to an extent they would be right, but I wanted them to know that I died trying to make things right somehow. If that was how this ended, with my death, I needed them to know why.

Miguel arrived, flushed and sweaty, an hour later. He smiled when he saw the stamped and addressed letter in my hand.

"You finally writing the folks?" he asked. "It's about time. You do what I told you to do today, *Guero*?"

"Yes and yes," I answered tucking the letter into Miguel's cubby. He would know what to do with it.

Miguel went to the sink and washed his face and hands. When he turned back to me he was all business.

"Okay, so did you memorize that lock? Can you remember what it looks like enough to make that key?" he asked.

"I did you one better," I said, hiking up my pant leg enough to reveal the brand in my calf.

Miguel laughed and did a small jig in the center of the cell.

"Man, *Guero*, I haven't been giving you enough credit. You are one smart *hombre*. You can even see the keychain whole in there. I bet that hurt like a . . ."

"Not something I care to ever do again," I interrupted. "You think it will work?"

Miguel studied the brand again and nodded, "Oh yes. We have exactly what we need. You get that security code?"

"Twenty-seven, ten, twelve," I said, lowering my pant leg.

Miguel did another jig and slugged me in the shoulder. "I knew you would do it. How did you get it?"

"Don't ask," I said, shaking my head. "Miguel, there's one thing I think you missed with this whole plan."

He stopped his jig and looked up at me quizzically. "What's that?"

"How the hell am I supposed to get past the main gate? You said the driveway behind the psych building leads out to the main road, but I still have to get out of the gate."

Miguel shrugged, his face a pillar of innocence. "Oh that. Yeah, you gonna to have to kidnap an employee. Have them drive you out of the gate."

"What?" I yelled.

"Just be sure to drop them off no less than thirty miles away. Oh, and take their cell phone so they can't rat you out five minutes down the road," he continued. "You gonna want to ditch the car and steal a new one too."

"Miguel! You didn't say anything about kidnapping and stealing cars. How would I even do that, IF I was even willing to?"

"What did I tell you about that 'if' stuff?" Miguel stood in front of me and crossed his arms over his chest. "There's no time for 'if'. I saw what you been seeing. She was right there in front of both of us, a messenger from God himself. It's on you to save those people, *Guero*. If you gotta kidnap someone and steal a car, then so be it."

I sighed and sat shakily down on my bunk. "How would I even do that, Miguel?"

He gave me a sly smile. "You smart, you'll figure it all out. Now let's go get some chow. I'm so hungry my belly button's about to pop out my butt."

"Maybe I should hang out here," I said, too focused for Miguel's jokes. "Boss is back in the block. Last thing I need is trouble right now. I've got to think all this through . . ."

Miguel grabbed my arm and dragged me from my bunk.

"Forget about Boss. He's not coming for you on his first night back. Plus, this could be our last supper together, *Guero*," he said. Giving in, I followed him to the chow hall.

Once again I was the center of attention as inmates stared and pointed and shook their heads in grim ceremony. Boss was out and again, I'd been labeled as a dead man.

Ignoring the stares, I enjoyed my chili-flavored slop in comfortable silence. Miguel looked around, obviously finding amusement in the constant attention we were getting. He held his head high and smiled at me knowingly while he bit into his corn bread.

I glanced at the clock above the garbage bins by the entrance and noted that the second shift inmates would be coming in for chow soon. Both Boss and Smiley worked second shift in the maintenance shop, which would explain how Boss was able to fashion the blade he tried to kill me with. No doubt he could make another.

I stood and took my trash to the can and Miguel stood to do the same. We walked from the chow hall and turned toward our block and came face to face with both Smiley and Boss as they were being escorted to chow by a CO. Boss' face was a puffy blur of yellowing purple and red. I flinched when I saw it and felt a tinge of regret.

His eyes flashed wide at the sight of me and he surged towards me. The CO, a wide, stout fortress, stepped between us. Smiley's lips tightened over his gilded teeth as he sneered at me. We stood at a deadlock while inmates gathered around, anticipating a show.

"Go around inmates," the CO yelled to us, while he blocked Boss and Smiley from our immediate path.

Without further hesitation, I walked by them, Miguel at my side. As I passed Boss, he snorted.

"Tomorrow, you die," he whispered while the CO instructed inmates to move along.

I turned to him and smiled. "Probably."

Once the bars were lowered for lockdown, Miguel and I got to work on the key. I exposed my calf while Miguel grabbed the pen and paper I'd left on my bunk.

"Okay, how do we do this?" I asked.

"You just stand still and try not to scream," he said.

"What?" I asked, but the answer came in the form of searing pain as Miguel crouched down and began to trace the burn with my ball-point pen.

He made heavy marks, sometimes going back over the line two and three times. Biting my lip, I tried to remain still. I had to try even harder not to punch Miguel in the side of his head. It didn't help that he was giggling the whole time.

When he finished tracing, he slapped a sheet of paper firmly against the ink. I howled and jumped back, the paper sticking to my now raw wound. Miguel reached for it, but I held his head back.

"I've got to take the paper off, *Guero*," he said, reaching for it again, but I held his head back.

"You didn't tell me I was going to be a used as a human stamp," I hissed between clenched teeth.

"How did you think we were going to get the imprint off your leg?" he asked. "Now let me take the paper off."

"Just wait a sec. I'll do . . ."

Suddenly, Miguel dropped his arms and pointed to the corner of the cell, his mouth agape.

"*Dios mío!* Simone is back!"

I dropped my grip on his head and turned to look, my heart pounding with anticipation. When I did, Miguel grabbed the paper and ripped it off with one quick flick of his wrist. Searing pain shot up the right side of my body. I retaliated by kicking him in the shin with a cry. We both collapsed, two writhing heaps, into the floor.

"That was a dirty trick," I panted.

"It worked, didn't it?" he asked, clutching his shin to his body.

"Did it?" I asked, taking a deep breath as the pain subsided.

We both looked to the sheet of paper lying face up beside the bars just as the heavy boots of Officer Edmonds sounded on the floor. Miguel scrambled up and grabbed the paper. He stuffed it in the back of his pants as Edmonds rounded the corner and paused at our cell. Miguel nodded to him and smiled. Edmonds shook his head, his face a cool mask of endurance, and continued on his patrol.

Sighing, Miguel took the paper from his pants and came to where I sat on the floor. He opened it up, revealing the perfect stamp of the backdoor key.

"Get the aluminum scrap," he said "We've got sanding to do."

For hours we folded and rubbed the shard against the brick wall beside the sink. Before long its sharp, jagged edges smoothed and rounded into the shape of a key. We stopped every few minutes to lay it atop the tracing, then made adjustments. By the time the lights went out our arms were stiff and our fingers were sore and bleeding. When Miguel blew the silver dust off of our makeshift key for the last time and placed it in my palm, I saw that we'd made a perfect replica.

"It looks just like it," I marveled. "Do you think it's too thin? Is it going to bend on me?"

"It only has to work once," Miguel assured me, standing to stretch out his limbs.

I took the key to my work boots and nestled it below my insole. If it weren't for my aching fingers, I might have not believed we pulled it off. Miguel quietly washed his hands and climbed up into his bunk. Changing into a clean shirt, I got beneath my covers and went back over the plan.

"Who exactly is it that I'm supposed to kidnap tomorrow?" I whispered, ignoring how much the question sounded like the line from a cheesy mobster movie. "What if there's no one back there?"

"Third shift orderlies get off at one o'clock. You need to be back there by then. Hide until you can get one alone. You'll know what to do," Miguel whispered back.

I sat up in my bunk. "How can you be so sure that I'll know what to do?"

Miguel sighed, "*Guero*, God charged you with this mission. You have to have faith that he will send provision to help you complete it. Trust in him, *mi amigo*, and it will all be okay."

Have faith. Until last night, my faith was as dead as the little girl I'd slain by the same name.

"What if I don't believe like you do?" I asked.

Miguel chuckled. I felt him roll over to get comfortable. "Even better."

Within minutes he was snoring. Staring into the darkened cell, I remained vigilant in case Simone returned. I wanted to see her, to tell her that I was going to do everything in my power to do what she asked of me. I needed her to know that I didn't want to let her down. When my eyes finally did close I felt a peace come over me, because deep down I believed that she knew I wouldn't.

Ten

"You ready for this?" Miguel asked as he bent to tie my boot laces.

I wiggled my toes and felt the lump of the key beneath them.

"I'm ready," I nodded, forcing down the queasiness that rose in my stomach.

We went out for count just as Officer Duke walked up flashing his typical, sarcastic smile.

"So, are you happy that your boyfriend's out of the infirmary? You two play nice now, I know how you like it rough," he said with a laugh.

Sighing, I looked to Miguel who rolled his eyes. This would be my last chance to tell Duke how I felt about him and I wanted more than anything to tell him just how deep my hatred for him ran, but doing so could land me in the SHU and I couldn't risk that. So I took a deep breath and laughed with him instead.

"You would know," I said with a smile and a wink.

Duke stopped laughing. He nodded as he considered my retort. Then with a snort, he patted me on the shoulder.

"I like this newfound confidence, Foster. Now you're finally interesting," he said, walking off. "Try not to run into anything sharp."

With another laugh, Duke disappeared down the block. Miguel and I turned back to our cell.

"That was my last chance to stick it to the guy," I said, clenching my fists.

"He's not worth it, *Guero*. Karma will take care of him," Miguel shrugged. "Or maybe I'll slip some of my laxatives into his coffee one day, just for you."

With a laugh I stood in front of Miguel and looked him in his eyes. Then I grabbed hold of his shoulders.

"Come with me," I urged.

He looked sideways at me, confused. "To chow? I don't think you should be going to the chow hall this morning after what Boss said yesterday."

"You know that's not what I'm talking about. Come with me out of this place," I said.

Miguel shook his head and paced away. "I can't do that. There's no way for me."

"We can think of something, Miguel," I pleaded.

Miguel turned to face me, his expression solemn. "This is your time, *Guero*. I'm not meant to go with you. This is where I belong. You don't need me anymore, *mi amigo*. You going to find what you're looking for out there. I have to stay."

I walked to him and squeezed his shoulder. "But I want you to come. "

"Yeah, well I want some of my Aunt Maria's salsa for Taco Tuesdays, but some things are just not meant to be," he scoffed. "No, this is goodbye."

Sighing, I motioned to his cubby. "My letter. If something bad happens . . ."

"I know, I know. Mail your letter off to Mom and Dad. No worries, *Guero*."

Miguel and I stood regarding one another, neither of us knowing how to say goodbye. Finally closing the gap between us, I extended my hand.

"You've been a good friend, Miguel. I don't know what I would have done in here without you. You saved my life. I can't thank you enough," I said, my voice hoarse as Miguel took my hand and leaned in for a fraternal embrace.

"*Ha sido un honor . . .*" he started.

"English, Miguel," I chuckled, patting him on the back.

"You're a good man," he continued. "You remember that, *Guero*. Trust your faith. Hope is still alive."

With one final pat, I let go of the small man that I'd grown to love as a brother and turned to leave. When I reached the bars I looked at him again and caught him wiping at his eyes.

"You never did tell me what you did to get in here," I said.

"I tell you what, *Guero*." Miguel laughed. "When you get caught and thrown back in here, I'll tell you then."

"Fair enough." I nodded in agreement. "Goodbye, Miguel."

"Goodbye, Logan," he said, as I turned to face my new destiny.

The morning was thick and muggy as the sun hurled its unseasonable heat onto the concrete. Running the plan over and over again in my brain as I walked, I made my way to the east tunnel. I was confident that I could make it to the driveway outside of the psych wing, but everything after that was still up in the air. Taking someone hostage would be difficult and I had no idea if I could go through with it or how I even would. The only weapon I possessed was now filed and rounded down into the key beneath my insole, and the thought of terrorizing some poor stranger put me in a panic. I forced the uncertainty from my mind, deciding not to think of what would happen until I got out there. Miguel said that God would provide. We'd see about that.

"How is everything going?" Squeaky asked when I passed him at the east tunnel.

I remembered my performance the day before and smiled sheepishly at him. "So far so good. Thank you."

He still looked concerned, but let me pass without any further questions.

I reached the plant early again and considered trying out the key, but decided against it. As eager as I was to see if it would work, I didn't want to risk bending it. Miguel said it only had to work once, so I saved it for my one shot. Walking around to the back door, I gave a good knock and waited for Mr. Jones to let me in.

"Is this going to become a habit?" he asked when the door opened.

"No sir," I answered. "I'm just a little early so I thought I'd help start up the machines."

"Ah, well in that case," he said, ushering me inside, "come right in."

Inmates trickled in just as the machines were warmed up and ready. Letting Santiago stamp today, I took my place by the belt and began to stack plates. Conversation was light, mostly about basketball, visitations, and new commissary items.

Looking around the room, I soaked it all in. As much hell as the last twelve years had been, this place was my refuge, the place I could come and shut out the demons in my mind and just work. A man was nothing if he couldn't work and produce. This place gave me purpose, but I had a new purpose now. If I made it out of the prison alive, I wondered if I would miss it.

Every few minutes my eyes flashed to the clock above Mr. Jones' office window. I tried to convince myself that this was any other day, but the anxiety that rose with every movement of the minute hand made it impossible to pretend. Bishop watched me out of the corner of his eye. He suspected something was off. He probably thought it had to do with Boss, but he was respecting my wishes by not calling me out on it. I had to let both he and Santiago know what I was planning to do soon, I was going to need their help.

After what seemed like days, we were released for lunch. The chow hall was quiet and a quick look around assured me that neither Boss nor Smiley would bother me as I forced my sandwich into my nervous stomach. To my surprise, Bishop stood from his usual seat with his people and came to sit beside me, tossing his tray on the table next to mine. He didn't look at me, but stared ahead as he took a bite of his runny potato salad.

"You going to tell me what you're planning or am I going to have to wait to find out when we all get put on lockdown at count this evening?"

I turned to him, eyes wide, the pit of my stomach dropping. Bishop kept his face forward, a smile spreading across his lips. He knew.

"How did you . . ."

"There's only one reason for a desperate inmate to be staring at the clock every minute like you've been doing all morning, and it ain't because he's excited about the ham and cheese," he said coolly.

I stared ahead, trying to think of another excuse for why I was so anxious. Nothing came to me.

"And I've been thinking," he continued. "You ain't never missed work for an appointment for the last ten years I've been here, then suddenly you're at psych two days in a row. You've been casing the place. You're going make a run, aren't you?"

I took another bite of my sandwich and kept my face forward, not bothering to deny it. He didn't have to look at me to know he was right. My silence said everything.

"Well, I'll be damned," he chuckled.

"You going to say anything?" I asked.

"I ain't no snitch," he said, then took a swig of his iced tea. "You sure you want to do this, man? You get caught and the CO's will put a bigger hurting on you than Boss ever could."

I shook my head and took another bite. "Like I said, this has nothing to do with Boss. This is bigger than him, but I do need your help with something."

Bishop raised his eyebrow and nodded, still looking forward. "I'm listening."

I washed the bite of sandwich down with a swig of my tea. "When the time is right, I need you keep an eye on Jones, give me a signal when he's not looking. If he asks for me later, tell him I left for another appointment."

Bishop considered my request and then nodded his approval.

"I can do that," he said with a smile. "But it'll cost you."

"Name it."

"I want three . . . no, five boxes of them Hostess apple pies. You know, the individual ones, like they sell at the gas station. Whole boxes of them, delivered to me here. IF you make it out without getting shot that is," he said, his voice stern and serious.

Smiling, I poked at my uneaten potato salad and laughed under my breath. "Apple pies."

"Boxes of them," he repeated.

"You got it." We shook hands under the table. "We've got to tell Santiago."

"Let me take care of him." Bishop rose with his tray. "I'll wait for your signal. Good luck, Logan."

With that, Bishop strode back to his usual table and I was left alone to go over the plan in my head for the hundredth time. When I'd eaten as much of my lunch as I could stomach, I dumped my tray and walked back to the shop. Another glance at the clock told me that I had an hour to make my way behind the psych ward.

When everyone returned and the machines were going full force, I watched as Bishop leaned into Santiago and let him in on what was about to happen. Santiago's face brightened with the information. A smile spread his lips from ear to ear. He looked at me and pumped his fist in the air, then settled back into lowering the stamp onto the next plate.

For half an hour we worked in silence, the anticipation floating on the air above us like a swarm of anxious bees. I sent another stack of plates down the line and then glanced at the clock again. It was time.

Taking a deep breath, I nodded to Bishop. He nodded back and positioned himself between me and Mr. Jones' office window. Bishop had a better view of the inside of the office than I did, so I watched his raised finger and waited, my palms sweating.

When he pointed to me, I made my way to the back door, keeping my eye on Bishop as I walked. When he held up his hand just above his waist, I froze and watched, my heartbeat threatening to rupture my eardrums. I was within feet of the door, with a few more steps I would be there, but the look on Bishop's face let me know that I was in danger of being spotted. Looking around, I saw the broom propped against some boxes in the corner and decided that if Jones emerged from his office to question me, I would use the premise of sweeping my area as my guise.

I was about to reach for the broom when Bishop nodded frantically and motioned for me to hurry. Grabbing my shoe, I dug the key out from under the insole and kissed it for luck. Then propping one hand on the knob, I stuck the key into the lock. It went in half way and stopped, the fragile metal scraping against the inside of the knob. I looked back at Bishop, whose face was a cold sheet of panic as he rushed me with his hands.

I turned back to the lock and forced the key in further with my shaking hands, but it started to bend in half. Yanking the key from the hole, I steadied myself and tried again. When it scraped against the inside again, I jiggled it back and forth and applied gentle pressure. After a few jiggles, the key slipped into the lock.

Taking a deep breath, I turned the key. It twisted in my fingers and I thought for a second that the weight of the lock would be too much for the flimsy metal key. But just as I was about to give up and make a dash for the broom, the key caught in the lock and began to turn. With a metallic groan, the door opened. With one final nod to Bishop, I removed the key and squeezed out of the door, forcing it shut behind me.

Leaning against the door, I took a few deep breaths and waited for my pulse to slow. Then, slipping the key into my pocket, I made my way behind the plant. It was the long way to the north tunnel, but it made me the least visible. Moving slowly, I kept out of sight of all windows and doors and tried to be as light on my feet as possible on the gravel.

When the north tunnel was within sight, I looked behind me to make sure I would not be spotted. Then I ran as fast as I could to it. I knew from my recent excursions with Squeaky that the tunnel wasn't guarded at this time of day. So I blindly ran through until a sudden sound brought me to an abrupt stop. Someone was laughing.

"And here we were, hiding out until you left work. This is going to be so much easier," a familiar voice said.

I turned to see Boss step out from the shadows, followed by a sneering Smiley.

"How did you . . ." I started to ask.

"Maintenance work requires you to leave the shop every so often, especially when someone clogs the psych wing's air conditioning compressors," Boss interrupted. "It could take all day to fix."

Smiley chuckled, a smug grin on his face. "I guess the chow hall slop is good for something around here."

"The rest of my boys are on their way. It's a shame you'll be dead before they make it. They were so looking forward to this," Boss said, drawing a blade from behind his back.

Raising my hands, I took a step back. "I can't do this with you today, Boss. I know you're pissed, I get it. But right now there's something I've got to do that's bigger than the two of us. Can we rain check on the whole homicide thing until tomorrow?"

Boss and Smiley looked at each other and laughed, Boss' puffy face shining beneath the tunnel lights.

"No see, we have an appointment," he scoffed. "I told you that today would be the day that you die. You should have marked it on your calendar."

Boss motioned to Smiley, who stepped toward me. He cracked his knuckles in anticipation.

"I'd say this will only take a minute, but what fun would that be?" he said, his golden smile glinting.

I glanced behind me to gauge how far from the other end of the tunnel I was. When I couldn't see daylight, I knew that making a run for it was futile. With my bruised ribs, Smiley would catch me before I even stopped to punch in the code.

Turning to glare into Smiley's horrid face, I considered my options. If I screamed loud enough, I could alert someone from the plant that I was being attacked. Even if I succeeded in rousing attention before Smiley and Boss shut me up for good though, my escape plan would be ruined. I would have failed Simone and the runners would die.

Simone's tear-stained face came to mind, her green eyes pleading to me from another plane of existence. I couldn't quit now. Boss was not going to stop me from this chance to make things right. Anger flashed within me, a white heat that grew from my core and within seconds consumed me. I let it take over, this suppressed rage, untethering it at last. I clenched my fists and decided to go with option number two. I had to take both Boss and Smiley down.

Before Smiley could take another step, I flew into him, knocking him to the cool cement. Then I drove my fist into his jaw with a leaden crunch. Boss rushed in behind us with an angry howl. I turned in time to catch his arm as he attempted to drive the blade into my back. Standing, I kept both hands on Boss' arm and forced it back from my body.

Smiley attempted to grab hold of my leg, so I rammed my boot as hard as I could into his side. He let out a strangled cry and dropped his grip on me to clutch at his ribs. Boss thrust the knife forward and I lost my balance. Dipping my shoulder, I turned my body as we both fell to the ground and rolled. The knife scraped the pavement beside my head as we came to a stop.

I tried to get to my feet, but Boss was on me before I could get my legs beneath me. Grabbing onto his knife wielding arm, I kicked and twisted from under him. Boss pinned me down with the weight of his body. Before I could shove him off, Smiley, still panting, grabbed my head in a strangle hold from the ground. As his arm squeezed and pulled my head back, my temples bulged. The pressure in my head was stifling. I couldn't breathe.

Boss used both hands and his upper body to force the blade downward towards my chest. I held him back as the world began to spin and blur from exertion and lack of oxygen. Smiley tightened his forearm grip and pulled back harder, increasing the pressure around my neck. Somewhere in the distance I could hear my own strangled cries. My arms lost strength and I began to lose consciousness.

All I could do was force Boss' arms to the side away from my chest. As I felt the blade slice into my shoulder, I thought about

Simone. I hoped she would know that I tried. I prayed that she would know how sorry I was from where I would now dwell within the flames. Closing my eyes, my mind flashed to Grace. *You were right about me, Grace . . . you were right.*

"Arms in the air. Now!" The shout came from behind.
Boss let go of the knife and I felt the slicing pain of the blade as it withdrew, but I couldn't open my eyes. I thought my head would explode from the pressure of my own blood being forced into my skull.

"I said arms in the air, now! On your feet!"

Smiley's grip around my neck retreated. He shoved my head aside as he stood. I struggled to catch my breath, the pain in my head and shoulder vibrating with every ounce of air I sucked in. Coughing, I looked up to see Squeaky standing in front of us, his gun pointed at Boss and Smiley. Boss hid his blade hidden behind his back, its tip damp with my blood.

"You okay, Foster?" he asked.

Nodding, I waited for the dizziness to subside. Then I got to my feet, still trying to catch my breath. It was over. We'd been caught out of bounds and would all be thrown into the SHU. I still failed.

Squeaky was sweating, his gun arm shook as he took a step forward. "What are you all doing out of your work stations?"

Boss held up his free hand as Smiley watched him from the corner of his eye.

"We just came through here on our way to fix the air conditioning in psych. Foster jumped us. He was hiding out in here, waiting for us," he lied.

Squeaky took his eyes off of Boss and met mine. With another cough I shook my head to let him know it was a lie. Squeaky's eyes widened when he saw my shoulder, the blood soaking through my uniform. Boss and Smiley exchanged looks. Then Smiley turned back to Squeaky, his jaw clenching. Like a wolf, he sized up his prey. They could smell his fear.

Choking on my own breath, I tried to call out a warning to Squeaky who reached for the radio on his belt, but it was too late.

Before he could call for back-up, Smiley lunged at him, knocking his gun to the ground. Boss grabbed his radio and threw it against the wall. The gun slid across the pavement. I dove for it. Smiley threw Squeaky back and tried to beat me to it.

When we hit the ground, Smiley's fingers brushed the grip. He swung at me with his other hand. He connected with my wounded shoulder and I cried out, the pain excruciating, but I kept my eyes on the gun. When Smiley reached for it again, I drove my knee up into his already injured side.

"How does it feel?" I seethed as he doubled over.

Getting on all fours, I grabbed the gun and then spun to aim it at Boss. He had Squeaky by the collar, the blade pressed against his throat.

"Put the gun down, or the guard goes home in a body bag," he yelled.

I had to think fast. Lowering the gun, I pointed it to where Smiley writhed on the ground.

"Drop the blade, or they'll be selling his teeth for scrap," I countered.

Boss laughed, a high pitched cackle. "You think I care about him? I've got a dozen men just like him. Shoot him, he's obviously useless."

"Boss!" Smiley choked out as he glared up in shock.

"You kill him and I'll have a clean shot," I said, raising my aim back to Boss' head.

I had a decent shot now. I could kill him in an instant and doubted I would even feel bad about it later, but the gunshot would draw every CO and employee out to investigate. There would be no hope of escape then, and I still wasn't ready to give up on hope.

Boss laughed again.

"Go ahead and kill me. It's better than rotting away in this hellhole for another ten years." He shrugged. "I don't think you have the balls."

While I contemplated my next move, Smiley stood. I turned the gun on him. He looked from me to Boss, and then with a defeated sneer, he clutched his side and ran for the entrance of the tunnel.

"Get back here!" Boss yelled to him, but Smiley didn't stop. Within seconds he was gone.

"Looks like it's just me and you again," I smiled.

Boss dragged Squeaky by his collar closer to me. I took aim at Boss' head again, getting another clean shot. If he hurt Squeaky, I would have to take it.

"This time you die," Boss said, his lips tightening over his teeth as he dragged Squeaky closer. "Drop the gun."

Boss pressed the knife harder against Squeaky's throat, a trickle of crimson ran from the wound. I pulled back the slide and readied myself to fire, my finger closing around the trigger.

"This is your last chance to do the right thing, Boss," I warned. Squeaky glared at me, the intensity in his eyes trying to communicate something.

"Oh, but this is going to feel so right," Boss said with a snicker. He stepped closer, deepening the wound in Squeaky's neck.

Out of options, I started to squeeze. Squeaky held a hand up to me at his side and I eased off the trigger. As Boss dragged him closer, Squeaky carefully unclipped the Taser from his belt. He held up one finger as Boss lugged him toward me. When he held up two fingers, he yanked the Taser free. I closed the gap at three as Squeaky armed it and jabbed it into Boss' side. When Boss sunk to his knees, I hit him in the head with the butt of the gun. He fell, an unconscious heap, to the concrete.

Squeaky put his hands on his knees and coughed. Once he caught his breath, he stood and investigated the cut on his throat with his fingers.

"Are you okay?" I asked, stepping back from him. "You did good, didn't think you had that in you."

"Yeah, it's not that bad." He sighed with relief. "Thank you Foster, I owe you one."

"If you hadn't come along, I'd be dead. You're the hero here," I said, taking another step back.

Squeaky nodded, taking in a deep breath. "You said he'd try to kill you again and you were right. This shouldn't have happened, he shouldn't have been allowed back on work detail. Now give me my gun and we'll get that shoulder stitched up."

Squeaky held out his hand for the gun. I took another step back, glaring into his eyes.

"I'm afraid I can't do that," I said. "Toss me the Taser and your handcuffs."

For a moment Squeaky stared at me, gauging whether or not I was serious. He took a step towards me and I raised the gun.

"I won't tell anyone that you were out of bounds, Foster," he said, stepping back. "I'll tell them I came to get you for an appointment and they jumped us. You won't get into trouble."

"I'm sorry," I said, "but this isn't about me. I need you to toss me the Taser and your cuffs. Please don't make me ask you again."

With shaking hands Squeaky tossed me the Taser, then unsnapped his cuffs from his belt and tossed them as well. They both landed with a clang at my feet. Tucking the Taser into my waistband, I walked to where Squeaky stood beside the unconscious Boss.

"Now, please have a seat next to our friend here," I instructed.

Squeaky glared at me, then sat on the ground beside Boss. I slid one side of the cuffs around Squeaky's wrist.

"Think about what you're doing," he pleaded. "They'll add time to your record. You only have a year left."

Tightening the cuff around his wrist, I dragged Boss' hand to the open one and secured it.

"I know. I'm sorry you got involved in my mess. Just know that I'm doing all of this for a good reason," I said, laying the gun at Squeaky's feet. "Take this, incase Sleeping Beauty here wakes up. I don't want to hurt anyone. Please know that."

He looked up to me, his face a mask of confusion. I walked to the radio, now lying on the ground by the wall. The antennae was bent, but I was sure it still worked. Bringing it back to Squeaky, I laid it next to the gun and grabbed the blade from Boss' limp hand.

"What time is it?" I asked him.

"Five till one," he said, looking down at his watch and then back up to me. He didn't make a move for the gun or the radio, but locked eyes with me as I squatted beside him.

"Half an hour. That's all I need. After that, call in the Calvary. Tell them everything . . . just give me a half an hour. Please," I asked, knowing it was too much.

"What are you going to do?" He asked. "What's to keep me from shooting you myself?"

"I'm trying to save lives the only way I can." I sighed, wiping the sweat from my brow. "If you have to shoot me, shoot me, but I'm not the bad guy here. I have to do this. Thirty minutes is all I need. Please."

"Save lives?" he asked. "What are you talking about, Foster? What's going on?"

"It's better for you to not know anything. You can't be involved," I said shaking my head. "I'm asking you to trust me even though you have no reason to. Give me half an hour."

Squeaky ran a hand through his shaggy hair. He looked at Boss, still laid out cold on the pavement. He wiped his neck wound with the back of his sleeve and lowered his head. Then he exhaled a heavy breath and looked back up to me.

"You saved me back there when you didn't have to. You gave me back my gun when you could have shot me and gone anyway. If the situation was reversed, I don't know that I'd have the guts to do that. I don't know what you're up to Foster, and you're right. I shouldn't know. I'll give you twenty minutes and then I'm calling it in. That's the best I can do," he said, motioning to Boss. "Take his watch. Twenty minutes, that's all you've got."

"Thank you," I said, my heart racing as I bent over to snatch the watch off of Boss's wrist. "Someday you'll understand why I had to do this."

Squeaky sighed. "Go, before I change my mind. Twenty minutes and the whole prison will be looking for you."

I stood and set the timer on the watch and secured it around my wrist.

"And Foster?" Squeaky continued. "If you're caught trying to escape, they'll put you down. No questions asked."

"I know, but it's a risk I have to take," I said. Then I turned and ran as fast as my bruised side would let me through the tunnel.

It took me three minutes to reach the pin pad on the other side. Punching in the memorized code, I prayed it would work. *Twenty seven, ten, twelve.* After a series of beeps the gate unlocked. Exhaling my held breath, I pushed it open.

I looked around at the psych yard for movement. When I was convinced that it was clear, I ran to the side of the building and looked down at my watch. It was one o'clock. Tightening my fingers around the blade, I leaned forward and looked around at the back of the building. A dozen third shift orderlies were filing out of the back door, talking and laughing with one another as they made their way to their cars.

I'm too late, I thought as I waited for a break in the flow of people. The dumpster sat only feet from the back door. I needed to get to it. There was still hope that another orderly was late leaving for the day. When I was sure that I wouldn't be spotted from the parking lot, I ran for the dumpster. Then I crouched and waited, my ears filling with the sound of my own breath.

Several minutes passed and the back door remained shut. My heart pounded in my chest, the fear and panic escalating with each passing second. I looked at my watch. I had eleven minutes to be as far outside the gate as possible before the alarm sounded and the prison was put on lockdown.

Looking around at the cars left in the lot, I wondered if I would be lucky enough to find one with a key left in the ignition. It was a long shot, but without an "escort" it was the only option left. There was a slim chance that I would make it past the gate guard, but it was a chance I had to take.

"Okay, God," I prayed, a shaky whisper. "Miguel said that if I did this, you would provide a way out. If you're really up there, help me get out of here. Provide!"

Taking a deep breath, I turned to make a run for the nearest car when the back door opened with a lazy groan. I threw myself back against the dumpster and listened, my breath catching in my throat. Footsteps sounded on the gravel and the back door shut behind whoever had stepped out.

"Pick up, pick up," a soft voice mumbled.

Pressing myself against the peeling green paint, I scooted to the edge of the dumpster and peeked around. Dressed in a pants suit, a cell phone pressed to her ear as she kicked at the small rocks with her strappy heels, Willow stood just feet from the back door.

"I thought maybe you'd pick up if I called you on your lunch break, but I guess not. Thanks for returning my calls. Very grown-up of you," she said into the phone. "Look, I have your stuff in the car. If I don't hear from you in the next hour, I'll just unload it all into this dumpster." With a frustration groan, she hung up the phone and stood with her arms folded across her chest.

So this was it, I thought. My provision. The flighty therapist who dumped me when I needed her the most. As much as her reaction in our last session had disappointed me though, I understood why she reacted to me that way. She thought I was crazy. As much as I didn't want to terrorize the lovely intern, I knew that fact could help me to subdue her. She was my last chance.

"Pig," she mumbled under-breath as she dropped her phone back into her purse and turned to go back in.

"Willow," I said, stepping behind her and raising the blade. When she turned, I grabbed her around the shoulders and held the blade to her throat. "I'm very sorry about this. I don't want to hurt you, but I'm going to need your help to get out of here."

"Logan!" she cried, her hand clawing at my arm.

I pushed her towards the parking lot. "Hand me the phone."

I increased the pressure of the blade against her throat and she stopped struggling. She shuffled blindly through her purse then held up her phone. I snatched it, letting go of her shoulders long enough to slip it into my back pocket.

"Which car is yours?" I asked, forcing her forward.

"It's . . . there," she said through gritted teeth. "The Jeep."

Her hair smelled of lavender. I brushed it from my face and scanned the parking lot. The black Wrangler sat in the far corner of the lot. Forcing her forward, we made our way to the vehicle, careful to not be seen from the building's windows.

"Why are you doing this?" she asked, clumsily fumbling forward in her stilettos.

"I told you why I'm doing this, remember?" I seethed.

"This isn't the way, Logan," she pleaded when we got to her Jeep. "I can help you figure this out."

"Oh, now you want to help? You had your chance," I said against her ear. "Now we both get to do this the hard way. Open the door!"

"I . . . I don't have my keys," she stammered.

"I guess I'll just have to cut through this expensive looking leather top then, and hotwire it myself" I lied, grabbing onto her upper arm and removing the blade from her neck to press it against the black leather canvas. I had no idea how to hotwire a car.

"Okay, okay," she said, digging the car keys out of her purse.

Withdrawing the blade from the leather top, I yanked her body against mine and laid the blade back against her throat. I dragged her to the driver's side and when she unlocked the door, I took the keys from her.

"You try to run and I will catch you and make you regret it" I said as she glared at me, her jaw clenched.

Pressing the lever to fold the front seat, I climbed into the back. I had to push aside two full, black garbage bags that occupied the back seat. Once inside, I yanked her arm and she got in with a huff. Reaching around the front seat, I poked the blade into Willow's side. She squirmed against its sharpness and glared at me through the rear view mirror.

"This is what's going to happen," I said, meeting her incensed stare. "You're going to drive out of the gate as if it were any other day. Wave at the guard, flutter those baby blues . . .

whatever you usually do on your way out. I know all about the distress words you people use to alert one another of a situation, so if you must speak, keep it to: 'hi', 'I'm leaving early today', and 'see you later'. Is that clear?"

Willow set her jaw and looked away. I poked the soft spot above her hip with the blade.

"Ow! Fine!" she said, jumping. "And once we're outside the gate, then what?"

Crawling onto the floorboards, I kept the knife on her as I used the other arm to roll the garbage bags on top of me. I glanced at my watch. Six minutes.

"Then I let you go," I said, tossing her the keys. "Drive"

With a frustrated sigh, Willow started the Jeep and put it into reverse. I was thankful for the small, foggy plastic windows that would offer limited visibility into the back seat. As the Jeep moved and dipped on the gravel driveway, I sunk further into the floorboard and ignored the searing pain in my shoulder and the dampness that made my shirt to cling to it. When the Jeep slowed, I knew we were approaching the gate.

"Remember what I said," I reminded Willow and jabbed her in her side with the blade again.

"Ow! Okay!" she yelled to me as the Jeep came to a stop. She rolled down her window and held my breath, trying to hear over the pounding of my heart.

"Good afternoon, Miss Pritchard," a gruff-voiced officer said. "Not used to seeing you leave this early, and in the jeep . . ."

"Hi!" Willow interrupted. "Yeah, I'm um . . . leaving early today."

"Is everything okay?" he asked, a hint of suspicion in his voice.

"I'm just not feeling well . . ." Willow started and I jabbed her in the side again making her jump.

"Ow! I mean . . . I'll see you later, Jim," she stammered.

After a long pause, the officer's voice was closer. "You sure you're alright?"

Willow sighed.

"I'm not supposed to say this . . ." she said. I started to jab her harder, but held the blade still. The officer suspected something. I decided to wait to see what she said, holding my breath and praying she would do right by me this time.

". . . but I think it will help," she continued. I felt her lean in her seat towards the guard as my hand started to shake where I held the blade more firmly against her leg.

This was it, she was going to call my bluff. She would rat me out knowing I wouldn't hurt her for doing it.

"It's that time of month," she whispered instead with an embarrassed chuckle. "Sometimes you've just got to call it a day and drown yourself in a bottle of wine. You know?"

After another long pause, the guard laughed. I took a shaky breath of relief. She was doing it, she was getting me out of here. A surge of gratitude washed over me, but I reminded myself that she was only helping me because of the sharp blade pressed against her hip. I needed to keep up the façade, needed her to fear me, if I wanted to get to Atlanta in time.

"Can't blame you for that. The missus calls in sick at least once a month," the guard said. "It'll be our secret."

"Thanks, Jim . . . I'll see you later," Willow said and then finally, the Jeep was moving.

When we were further down the driveway, I felt the jeep make a series of turns. Then the ride smoothed out and I knew we were on the main road that would take us away from the prison and onto the nearby highway. Pushing the bags off, I sat up and turned to watch the prison fade into the distance as the first wails of the alarms sounded into the warm afternoon air.

Eleven

"Okay, I did what you asked me to do. Now you can let me go," Willow said, her voice trembling.

Removing the blade from her side, I climbed into the front seat and took a minute to take a deep breath. *It worked, I was out. I'd escaped prison without being killed.* Looking out to the street, I watched civilians emerge from shops and restaurants along the road and go about their daily lives. I had to convince myself that I wasn't dreaming. For over a decade I'd been physically separated from this society, had mentally removed myself from it. It felt alien to me now.

"About that," I said with a shrug. "I lied."

"You said once I got you out, you'd let me go. You're out!" Willow yelled, her face seething as she looked down at the glove compartment and then back to me.

"I know, I'm sorry. You weren't part of the plan, but now I need you," I said, looking down at my shoulder.

Willow gasped when she noticed the blood that now soaked through my entire sleeve, the dampness spreading across my chest.

"Oh my God, you're really bleeding. It looks bad. Let me get you to a hospital so we can get you some help, Logan."

"Nice try." I laughed. "Don't waste your psychiatrist tricks on me. I can't go to a hospital now and you know it. I'd be sent back with stitches and ten more years on my sentence."

I lifted my uniform shirt carefully over my head. When I removed my undershirt, Willow's eyes widened and she turned her attention back to the road.

"You look like hell," she said. "What happened?"

Looking down, I had forgotten about the now yellowing bruise that stretched across my side. I was quite the sight. Wiping the puncture wound gently with my shirt, I tried to see how bad it was. Fresh blood pooled from the gash so I balled up the shirt and held it there and applied pressure.

"I was attacked by an inmate," I said.

"Well, you're just making all sorts of friends today, aren't you?" she scoffed.

I turned to look at her, studying the tenseness in her shoulders as she tapped the steering wheel with her thumb.

"Do you always make jokes when you're stressed?" I asked.

Willow turned to look at me and we locked eyes for a minute. I tried to get a read on her, to see if there was any part of her that could possibly understand why I was doing this.

"Now who's the psychiatrist?" She turned away, but not before I noted a softness in her topaz glare. "I get it from my mother."

"Why did you help me back there? You could have easily whispered the distress word to that guard, but you didn't. Why?" I asked.

Willow let out a sarcastic laugh. "Because I'm partial to my internal organs? And because James has a wife and four children. I couldn't let you hurt him."

I wanted to explain to Willow that I would never have hurt that guard . . . that I could never hurt her, but I needed her. When I looked at my shoulder again, I saw that my balled-up shirt was beginning to soak through. I would never make it to Atlanta on my own. I needed Willow to be afraid of me, it was the only way she would help me.

"Get on the highway," I instructed when the entrance came up on our right.

"What?" she cried.

I held the blade up, "Now."

With a grunt, Willow pulled the jeep onto the highway. I looked into the rear view mirror to see if we were being pursued, but there were no police cars, no sirens. I knew it was a matter of time before they made the connection between my escape and Willow's early departure, but I couldn't think of that now. Getting to Atlanta as quickly as possible was all that mattered.

"Take this to I-95 south. We'll have to stay on that until I can find a different route to Atlanta," I said, lowering the blade.

"I can't believe this is happening," Willow whispered as she stared straight ahead. "They train you for this kind of thing . . . I should know what to do."

Finding a dry spot on my shirt, I pressed it against my shoulder with a wince. "Yeah, well none of this would be happening if you had just made some phone calls to stop this race."

"Is that what this is about? You're mad at me?" she asked, shooting me a look of pure exasperation.

"No. I'm not mad at you. If I were you, I'd think I was crazy too." I leaned back into the soft, leather bucket seat. Sleepiness was washing over me, a mix of blood loss and post adrenaline crash. "I would have taken anyone who walked out of that back door in the moment. I was out of options."

"Lucky me," Willow sighed, her demeanor softening slightly. "And I told you, I don't think you're crazy. I think you're very confused. That's why if you'd just stop and think about what you're . . ."

She stopped mid-sentence when I laughed. "I kidnap you at knife point so that you can help me escape prison to stop a race that a ghost tells me will result in five deaths, and you don't think I'm crazy?"

Willow stared straight ahead, the muscle in her jaw twitching. "I told you, I've seen this before."

"Right, with other crazy people no doubt," I laughed again, but Willow's face remained rigid.

"Actually, with my parents." Her gaze remained on the road, but her mind wandered elsewhere. "It's why I haven't been home in years. I can't stand to watch it anymore."

I stopped laughing, watching pain spread across her face as she replayed some memory in her mind. "Your parents? They saw things too?"

"Not just things . . . Guardians. It's complicated," she said, shaking her head. "The point is, both my parents suffered traumatic experiences in their pasts, just like you. Together they built this elaborate fantasy about Guardians and supernatural visitations. My parents actually thought my dad was my mom's Guardian while he was in a coma from an accident."

"Guardian?" I asked. "Like, a guardian angel?"

"Something like that. It doesn't matter." Willow shook her head. "The point is, I've heard the stories all my life. It's what made me want to become a psychiatrist. I wanted to help them realize it wasn't possible, that none of it was real. Now I know that what they've built together is an elaborate defense mechanism that their collective subconscious made up in order to deal with the crisis they each suffered. It's a beautiful story, but none of it is real. Thanks to my training, I know that they're not crazy. Neither are you."

I thought about what Willow said. Her reaction when I told her about Simone's warnings made sense now. Her parents had experienced things too, believed that her dad had been involved. What a pill to swallow. No wonder she didn't believe them. Hell, a week ago I wouldn't have believed them either.

Hearing this was a revelation though. Of all the people who could have walked out of that back door at the right time, it was Willow, a woman raised by people who had experienced what I was experiencing. Even if she didn't believe it, on some level she understood it. That was where my provision truly lied.

"Have you ever stopped to consider that their reason for believing in Guardians . . . or angels or whatever, is a lot simpler than your diagnosis?" I asked softly.

Finally, she looked at me. "I've already told you the reason. It's a defense mechanism brought on my severe PTSD. What other reason can there possibly be?"

"That they were chosen," I said. "Chosen to see and participate in something greater than what your science or psychology can explain. Maybe you have such a hard time accepting it because deep down you're hurt that you weren't chosen."

"What? Now that IS crazy," she huffed, turning her attention back to the road.

I smiled and leaned my head against the headrest. "I have news for you though, Ms. Pritchard. You have been chosen."

She raised an eyebrow. "What are you talking about?"

"You're here, aren't you?" I asked, then closed my eyes for just a second to rest them because the world was beginning to blur.

When I opened them again, I saw Willow studying my face. When we locked eyes, she diverted them to the glove compartment again and then turned and set her jaw.

"I'm only here because you kidnapped me," she spat.

Ignoring her, I reached for the glove compartment handle, curious as to why she kept looking at it. When she saw me reach, she threw her arm out to stop me.

"Don't touch that!" she yelled as the Jeep swerved, and I knew there was something inside that she was afraid I would find.

Forcing her arm away, I pulled the handle. The glove compartment dropped open into my lap. Willow threw her hand in and desperately dug through its contents, the Jeep jerking on the road. I grabbed her wrist and lifted the blade to her neck.

Yanking her arm free, she withdrew with a cry to her side of the car. She straightened the wheel as car horns sounded angrily beside us. I rifled through the contents with my free hand, throwing trash and papers to the floor. In the back of the box I clasped cool, solid metal and withdrew a small revolver. There was no need to check the barrel, the panic on Willow's face told me the gun was loaded.

"Well, well. What do we have here?" I asked with a laugh.

"What are you going to do?" Willow's voice rose in pitch.

"The plan is the same," I smiled. "Just means I don't need this anymore."

Rolling down the window, I chucked the bloodied blade onto the shoulder and rolled the window back up. When I looked back to Willow, her knuckles were white as she clung to the steering wheel.

"You really expect me to drive you all the way to Atlanta? That's another six hours away," she asked, "And that's if we don't hit rush hour traffic."

"That's exactly what I expect you to do," I sat back into my seat and laid my head back again.

"But look at you, you're a mess. You'll never make it." She pointed to my shoulder.

"I'll be fine," I said.

"Fine. I'll just wait for you to pass out then," she whispered under her breath.

I looked back down at my shoulder, my balled-up shirt was now completely wet, the blood flow slowing, but still oozing from the wound. My head felt heavy where it leaned against the headrest. Willow was right, at this rate I wouldn't make it another hour before passing out.

"Damn it, you're right," I said. "Pull over at the next exit."

Willow glared at me, "Where are we going?"

"There's a sign for a drug store. Go there," I ordered and she flipped on the turn signal and merged into the exit lane.

Turning to the garbage bags in the back seat, I grabbed one and tore it open. As I suspected, it contained clothes.

"What are you doing? Those aren't mine," Willow protested as she slowed the Jeep to a stop at the light.

"Ex-boyfriend's? I heard you on the phone," I said, pulling out a couple of T-shirts and a red checkered flannel. I opened one of the t-shirts. Printed on the front was a picture of a muffin, the word 'stud' in bright yellow letters above it. "You've got to be kidding me."

I tore the shirt in half lengthwise. Willow fumed from the driver's seat as she pulled the Jeep into the drugstore parking lot. Folding half the shirt, I pressed it against the gash in my shoulder and then used the other half to tie it there with the help of my teeth. Then I threw a plain black T-shirt over it and carefully slipped into the flannel. Tucking my gun hand inside, I turned to Willow.

"Give me your wallet" I said, motioning with the gun beneath my shirt.

"You're going to rob me now?" she said, reaching into her purse.

When she handed me her wallet, I removed the cash and threw the rest into the glove box. I handed her back six, twenty-dollar bills.

"Cash only," I said, knowing that they'd be able to trace her credit card purchases.

When I got out of the jeep, my head was woozy, but I felt solid enough on my feet. Walking to Willow's door, I opened it and grabbed onto her arm. She got out reluctantly and I pulled her to me as she wobble in her heels.

I pressed the gun into her side through the flannel shirt and together we walked into the store. Scanning the aisles for the first aid section, I found the bandages and motioned to the large butterfly strips.

"Grab those," I ordered. "And the gauze and tape."

Willow bent to pick up the items as I looked around the store to see if we had caused any suspicion. We were the sole customers, the only other people inside were the pharmacist and front register clerk. Neither seemed to notice we were even there. Once Willow had secured the items, I dragged her to the refrigerated section and motioned to the pre-made sandwiches.

"Grab some of those sandwiches and a couple of those big waters," I ordered and she struggled to balance it all in her arms as we made our way to the checkout counter.

"Act normal. Smile a little even. Any attempt to clue the clerk into what's going on and you know what will happen," I said into her ear.

"You're not going to shoot me in the middle of the store," she whispered back.

"You really want to test that theory, doc?" I asked, then smiled at the clerk as Willow shakily set the items on the counter.

"Did you find everything alright?" the clerk asked as he eyed Willow curiously.

I jabbed her in the side with the gun until she smiled.

"Yes thank you," she said and the clerk nodded and rung up our items.

I grabbed a road map from the display on the counter at the last minute and the clerk scanned it and placed it the bag and then grinned.

"Have a nice day," he said, handing the bag to Willow. Then turning, we walked out of the store. When we were back in the Jeep, I turned to Willow and handed her the bandages.

"I need you to fix me up," I said.

"Oh no. You know I'm not an actual doctor, right?" she huffed. "Psychiatrist intern, remember?"

"Right," I said shoving the bandages at her. "Do your best."

Willow glared at me, then snatched up the bandages with a sigh while I pulled off both shirts. She was anything but gentle as she wiped the wound with the flannel and then pressed it closed with the butterfly strips. I clenched my teeth, tears coming to my eyes as she applied pressure to the wound and set it with the gauze. Then she wrapped the dressing around my shoulder.

I distracted myself with the lavender scent of her hair as she leaned in with the medical tape. When she looked up at me, we locked eyes again. She searched mine, no doubt looking for the same thing I hoped to see in hers: compassion.

Ignoring the sudden tension, I tore my eyes away and inspected the professional dressing.

"That's really good," I said, carefully pulling the black T-shirt back over my head.

Willow threw herself back into her seat and folded her arms. "Yeah, well my dad was in the military. He showed me some stuff."

I grabbed a water from the bag and gulped down half the bottle before setting it in the cup holder.

"Wait," I said with sudden realization. "Your last name . . . Prichard. I don't know why I didn't put this together before. You said your dad was in a coma for a while. Is your dad Donovan Prichard? The soldier who stopped that shooting at Fort Bragg all those years ago? Holy crap! That was his traumatic experience, wasn't it?"

When Willow turned to stare out her window, I knew that I was right.

"Wow. I remember hearing about him when I was a kid. What he did was incredible. It's a miracle he lived," I said, then chuckled. "No wonder you're so mad. Must have been hard growing up in his shadow."

"You have no idea what you're talking about," Willow whispered.

Unfolding the road map, I searched for a way to Atlanta that wouldn't require traveling any of the major highways.

"We're going to have to take sixty-four to forty-nine," I glanced at my watch. "It will take longer to get there, but it's worth the risk. They could be looking for us by now. Better to stick to the secondary roads."

"Do you really think they're looking for us?" Willow turned, hope brightening her eyes.

"If they're not, they will be," I said, motioning with the gun for her to start the car.

"You're not going to get away with this," Willow said, putting the Jeep into drive and pulling out onto the road.

"I don't need to get away with it." I sighed. "I just have to stop that race in time. Sandwich?"

We drove for hours in silence. I watched the sun dip lower and lower in the horizon until its fading rays cast a golden hue onto the landscape. My head felt lighter and the sleepiness ebbed now that I'd eaten and was hydrated. Willow refused to eat and when I turned my head to look at her, she still sat rigidly in the driver's seat and glared at the road ahead. The intense look on her face told me that she was deep in thought, no doubt trying to devise a way out of her current situation. That was fine. Once she got me to the race officials in Atlanta I wouldn't need her any more. I wouldn't stop her from happily leaving my life forever.

Turning to the window, I watched the pine trees whiz past on the quiet country highway. I admired them, each dressed in a brilliant hue of jade unlike anything I had seen in twelve years. Taking in the way the dying evening light danced between their branches, it was hard not to soak in the freedom. Infinite possibilities stretched out like this seemingly endless road before me. Too bad it wouldn't last long.

Even if I stopped the race and saved those people, I would be a wanted man, never truly free but on the run. As I stared at those trees while the evening light faded, I decided that when it was all over, I would do the right thing and turn myself in.

My thoughts were interrupted by a muffled ringing. My leg vibrated. Willow gasped and turned to me expectantly as I pulled her phone from my pocket. The screen showed that Duke was calling.

"Officer Duke?" I asked, afraid of the answer. "Officer Duke has your phone number?"

"That's none of your business," she said, reaching defiantly for the phone.

I smacked her hand away. When the call went to voicemail, I waited for the message to appear and then hit the speaker button.

"Hey Babe," Duke's disgustingly familiar voice sounded through the small speaker. "Look, we have a situation here at the prison. One of the inmates escaped. I'm going to be working late questioning inmates and working with the local authorities. I came to see you, but they told me you left early in my Jeep. You stole my car? I know you're mad about the other night and all, but you can't just take my car. Call me as soon as you get this. They're looking for you, Babe. They think you may be connected with the escape . . . and I'm beginning to think so too. I want my car back. Call me, this is serious."

I hung up the phone and gaped at Willow who simmered behind the wheel. "You're dating Duke?"

"Was. I was dating Duke," she hissed. "Not that it's any of your damned business."

"And this is his Jeep?" I asked, rubbing my temple. "That would explain the gun I guess, but the bags . . ."

"I put his stuff in here this morning. Stealing his car was the only move I had when you put that knife to my throat. I knew he would come looking for his precious jeep," she said, hysteria rising in her voice. "They think I'm helping you!"

Willow threw her hand out and tried to grab her phone again. When I snatched it away from her, she leaned further and made another attempt to get it from me, scratching at me with her fingernails. The Jeep swerved on the bare, country road.

"Give me the phone!" she demanded, but I held up the gun.

"Back off and watch the road!" I yelled.

Willow adjusted the wheel, but then turned back to me. Determination and anger distorted the beauty of her face. I raised the gun to her head and for a minute she stared at it, wide eyed.

"You're not going to use that," she spat.

"You know I'm desperate. I'll do whatever I have to do," I lied.

"You're not the only one who's desperate . . ." she said and then lunged for me again, this time using both hands to reach for the gun.

When I wouldn't let it go, she punched me in my bandaged shoulder. I recoiled with a howl, easing my grip on the gun. Willow grabbed for it again. With a cry, I yanked it from her grasp as the Jeep bounced and skid onto the shoulder.

"Watch out!" I yelled as the jeep lost control.

Willow dropped her grip on the gun to turn back to the road. She yanked the wheel with a scream, but we were going too fast. The tires squealed as they tried to grip the road. The Jeep tipped and spun onto its side. We toppled into the ditch on the side of the road with a crunching finality. The last thing I saw were the trees, brilliant in their coats of green, spinning into blackness.

Twelve

"Wake up, Logan."

The soft voice pleaded to me from the depths of darkness where my mind wandered free. I yearned to stay there, in the nothingness, where time and space no longer mattered. Where I no longer mattered.

"Please, Logan. You have to hurry," the voice called to me again, jarring me from the bliss of unconsciousness.

I recognize that voice, I realized as I struggled to raise my heavy eyelids. A blur of flowing red and white stood before me against the bright country twilight.

"Simone," I whispered.

She offered me her hand. "Hurry."

My arm ached as I reached for her, my body pressed against the jeep door which now rested flush against the grassy incline. My hand met soothing warmth. It wrapped around me and pulled me to my feet. I tried to decipher whether or not I was dreaming as I stood on unsteady legs and looked up into Simone's worried face.

"I'm not going to make it," I said, my voice weary.

"Yes you will." Simone pressed the warmth of her hand against my face. "You have to, Logan."

I stepped back from her and looked at the Jeep, now on its side in the ditch beside the road.

"How? " I asked, tears stinging my eyes. "I'm so tired, Simone."

She took a step towards me, her emerald eyes burning into mine. She took my hand. Again the warmth of her engulfed me, filling me from the inside out.

"You can do this, Logan," she said. "Trust yourself."

Wiping at my eyes, I was speechless. I had tried to trust, had believed that Willow was the provision sent to help me through this. Instead we were stuck because of her. We were stranded on an empty, country highway in the middle of nowhere and the last rays of daylight were fading into the distance.

"She will help you," Simone said, motioning to Willow who was beginning to stir from the elevated driver's seat. "Go to her."

Willow moaned and lifted a hand to her head.

"Willow!" I went to her, realizing this was no dream.

Climbing over the passenger seat, I unbuckled her seat belt and collected her into my arms. She coughed and began to open her eyes as I lowered her out of the car and onto the soft grass beside us. I looked behind me for Simone, but she had vanished with the last of the evening light.

"Logan," Willow whispered. I turned back to her and brushed the hair from her face.

"You're okay. Everything is okay," I assured her. "Can you stand?"

Willow looked down at herself and moved her limbs. "I think so."

I helped her to her feet. When I was confident that she could stand on her own, I went back to the overturned Jeep and found the gun lying in the floorboard. Tucking it into the back of my pants, I grabbed the garbage bags from the back seat and dragged them out onto the grass.

"Are there any shoes in here?" I asked. "You're not going to want to walk in those heels."

"Walk?" Willow asked, still dazed.

I rifled through the bags, throwing shirts and a bottle of cheap cologne to the ground.

"You don't want to spend the night out here do you?" I asked. "We've got to find another car, or maybe a place to get a couple of hours sleep."

Willow's eyes widened as the seriousness of the situation finally struck.

"My phone!" she shrieked, pushing me aside. She rummaged through the floorboards.

Before I could stop her, she withdrew from the jeep with the now shattered phone in her hands. "No!" she cried throwing the phone down. "Damn it."

"It will be okay," I said, turning back to the garbage bags where I pulled out a pair of beat-up gym shoes.

"Okay?" Willow asked, anger taking the place of fear and shock. "I'm stuck on the side of some country back-road in Georgia at night with an escaped con. This is the making of a horror movie! How is this going to be okay?"

"It will all work out, you just have to believe that. Have a little faith," I said, handing her the shoes.

"Faith," she huffed as she snatched the shoes from me. "In you? Yeah right."

"Yes, in me. Is that so hard? Could you just try to believe in me and what I'm trying to do for just one second?" I asked, pulling a sweatshirt from the bag.

"Why would I believe in you? You kidnapped me!" she yelled and then drew back. "Wait a minute. You saw her again, didn't you? Just now. That's why you're so inspired even though we just trashed our only means of transportation."

"You're going to need this." I tossed her the sweatshirt, ignoring the question. "And YOU trashed our only means of transportation."

Willow let it fall to the ground beside her and crossed her arms over her chest.

"What did she say?" she asked, her voice thick with contempt.

I only shook my head. It was hard to image Willow ever helping me, but I decided to trust Simone's words as I pulled a pair of sweat pants out of the bag.

"What did she say?" Willow repeated stepping closer to me.

I met her angered stare and looked her in her cool blue eyes.

"Fine. You want to know? She said that you would help me." I walked to the other side of the Jeep to change, ignoring Willow's stunned expression. "Now swap shoes, we have to keep moving."

When I came back around the Jeep, Willow was sitting inside the door frame changing into the gym shoes.

"If you think I'm going to help you, then you are delusional," she huffed. "As soon as we find civilization, I'm calling the cops. You could have left me unconscious in the Jeep to go find a new car and a new hostage, but you didn't. You were never going to hurt me or anyone else. I'm not afraid of you anymore."

I leaned over her and found the drug store bag and pulled out a flattened sandwich.

"You're right about me. You have me all figured out. I never would have shot you or anyone else," I said with a full mouth of turkey and cheddar. "But you're forgetting about something. The authorities back in Raleigh think you're helping me. If you call the cops now, they'll arrest you too."

Willow yanked off her blazer and pulled on the sweatshirt. I tried to ignore the way her silk camisole hugged the curves of her body, like water gliding over smooth rock.

"I'll just tell them that you kidnapped me at gunpoint," Willow laughed. "I had nothing to do with this."

"You drove me out of prison in a stolen car, this being after we met together in your office two days in a row. The gun was in the car, in your possession. I actually kidnapped you with a blade, but that's long gone on the side of I-95 somewhere. Point is that unless I collaborate with your story, you'll still be under investigation. You'll probably lose your internship anyway," I said, taking another bite of the sandwich.

"So collaborate my story you son of a . . ." she yelled.

"Do you one better," I interrupted. "Help me get to Atlanta, help me stop that race, and I'll let you turn me in to the authorities."

"Yeah, sure you will," Willow scoffed.

"You have my word," I said, looking her squarely in her crystalline eyes.

"How do I know you're not lying again?" she asked.

"Because it was never my intent to be a free man. I deserve to serve my prison sentence. Hell, I deserve to rot in that cell for the rest of my life, but I have to stop this race. That's the only thing I care about, I'm not interested in freedom. If you don't turn me in, I'll turn myself in anyway and then you're on your own."

Willow glared at me as she deliberated, her eyes narrowing to slats. Then she threw her hands up with a defeated cry.

"Fine," she growled. "We'll go to Atlanta. You can stop this stupid race if anyone will even listen to you. Whether you succeed or not though, I turn you over to the police there and you own up to everything."

Finishing my sandwich, I wiped my hands on my pants and extended my hand to her.

"Deal," I said with a smile.

Willow slapped my hand away and reached into her blazer for the cash and then reached past me to grab her wallet from the glove compartment. Then she snatched the drug store bag from me, dropped her wallet in and climbed the embankment to the road.

"There'd better be a diner around here because these sandwiches smell like dog food," she yelled.

Climbing the embankment with my good arm, I ran to catch up to her. We walked along the dark road a while in silence. I could feel the heat of anger wafting from her as she trudged along a foot ahead of me.

"I see those sneakers fit you okay," I said, trying my best to lighten the mood.

"Yeah, I guess," she said, not bothering to look back at me.

"So I guess Officer Duke has small feet then." I grinned. "I'm guessing it's true what they say about men with small feet . . ."

"Just shut up and walk," she snapped and we walked on in silence.

Hours went by as we walked wearily along the vacant road. Willow, finally giving in to her hunger, polished off the remaining sandwiches. We stopped once to rest beneath a billboard that advertised a motel six miles ahead. The night was cool and the moon, high in the sky, lit the road through the canopy of rustling trees.

My mind wandered as we walked. I thought about what I would say to the race officials once I got to Atlanta. What could I say? Thousands of people would be there, people who had paid to race. They would be ready and excited to go for it. How was I going to talk the officials into sending them home without the chance to accomplish what they had trained for? How could I make them listen?

"There it is," Willow said with a sigh as she pointed up the road. "You've got to be kidding me."

The Rose Hill Motel was nestled in a clearing beside the highway, a one story monstrosity of moldy brick beneath a rusting tin roof. The only light on the building came from a bare bulb that hung above the office and swung with the night breeze.

"There are no cars," I observed walking closer. "Is it even open for business?"

"Sure, for axe murderers and highway robbers maybe," Willow said, catching up to me.

"How about escaped cons?" I winked at her.

She rolled her eyes as we made our way up the small dirt path to the front of the building. The rooms were silent as we passed, no light or movement coming from any of them. I glanced at my watch. It was almost midnight.

"We might be too late," I said, walking to the office door.

"I'm not sure that's a bad thing. I've seen *Psycho*."

"Oh yeah?" I scoffed. "Ever see *Deliverance*?"

Willow stood beside me as I tried the office door. It was locked. I bent to look in the dusty window, wiping away a layer of dirt and cobweb with my forearm. The inside of the office was dark, the front desk deserted. Sighing, I looked back up the road.

"Could be another twenty miles before we find anything else, if not more. We're better off taking our chances here. I doubt anyone will be coming by tonight." I said.

"But if it's closed . . ." Willow began as I walked to the closest room and pounded on the door.

When no one answered, I kick the door as hard as I could. It opened with a violent crash, hitting the inside wall.

Willow gasped. "What are you doing?"

I went inside and turned to her. "You want to sleep out here?"

Willow looked around at the other rooms and then back to the road, no doubt considering her options. I walked to the cheap bedside lamp and twisted the switch. To my surprise, the tiny room filled with a dim glow revealing a small bed dressed in a faded comforter, a shabby dresser with a missing drawer and a rickety armchair, its upholstery ripped at the corners. The room smelled of stale cigarettes and thrift store musk.

"You coming in?" I asked going back outside where Willow stood with her arms folded, a worried look on her face.

"I don't know about this . . ." She hesitated.

I mimicked the banjo tune from *Deliverance* and turned to go back inside. Willow stepped in behind me and shut the door with a disgusted grunt.

"Not funny," she hissed as she secured the chain lock.

Walking to the small bathroom, I flipped the switch and peeked inside. I half expected it to be filled with roaches, but what I found was a small claw-foot tub and a standard toilet. Turning the knob on the bathtub, I was surprised when warm water ran from the spout.

"We've got plumbing," I said walking back into the main room. "There's a bar of soap by the tub if you want to get cleaned up."

Willow sat tentatively on the edge of the bed and laughed. "Oh no. I'm not getting naked anywhere near you, thank you very much."

"I wasn't going to watch if that's what you mean," I said, crossing my arms across my chest.

Willow shook her head. "No, I just mean that . . . well, you've been locked up with a bunch of men for a long time."

When her meaning hit me, I tried to contain my temper. "Oh I get it. You think that because I haven't been around a naked woman in twelve years that I won't be able to stop myself from breaking down that door and taking advantage of you."

Willow shrugged and looked away sheepishly. "It's a perfectly reasonable assumption."

"Three things," I said holding up a finger for each. "One, you are a horrible psychiatrist. Two, don't flatter yourself. And three, I've gone the last twelve years without seeing a woman naked, I THINK I can handle another night."

With that, I went back into the bathroom and shut the door loudly behind me, making sure Willow heard me secure the lock. Then I ran the warm water for a bath. When the thought of Willow's long, bare legs entered mind, I switched the water to cold with an angry sigh.

When I emerged from the bathroom clean and refreshed, I was ready to go another round with the blonde firestorm, but she was gone. My heart sped as I scanned the small room again and then raced to the door. I found her sitting on the curb just outside the room, legs crossed beneath her. With a relieved sigh, I joined her to look out into the blackened street.

"You shouldn't be out here," I said. "Someone could see."

Willow nodded, her expression solemn. "I know, I just needed some fresh air. Smells like an ashtray in there."

I nodded my head, my heart suddenly struck with guilt. The anger I felt towards her dissolved into a mist of remorse and sympathy. "You deserve better than to be stuck in some dingy motel room with an escaped prisoner tonight. I'm sorry I got you into this mess."

Willow exhaled slowly and looked up into the star filled sky. "Well, this is certainly on the top of my list of life experiences. Maybe someday I'll write a book about it. You might have made me a millionaire."

Right." I grinned. "Then you should be thanking me, I guess."

Willow turned to look at me and we locked eyes. Her expression was unreadable. I caught myself getting lost in the facets of her cool stare.

"Actually, I should thank you," she said to my amazement. "You could have just left me back there at the jeep."

"No, I couldn't," I said.

"Why not?"

"Because I'm not that person." I looked away. "I know I'm a bad man, but I couldn't leave you stranded like that."

Willow thought about that for a minute and turned her gaze back up to the twinkling void. "Are you really going to turn yourself in tomorrow?"

"Yes, I am," I answered. "Whether I stop the race or not."

Willow stood and brushed the back of her legs with her hands. She walked to the door and turned to me.

"You're not a bad man, Logan," she said with a sigh. "I hope you find what you're looking for."

Willow walked inside and shut the door softly behind her. Sitting on the curb, I looked up at the clear sky speckled with dozens of glinting diamonds and took a deep breath.

"Okay up there, I'm doing what you called me to do" I said, my tone hushed. "It's still so hard to believe that you'd send her, Simone, to give me this chance. I don't deserve it. So, thank you. I can't promise that I'll be able to get the job done, but I promise to do everything that I can."

I looked down at my feet and ran my heel through the gravel. "I just ask that you protect the ones I care about when everything goes down. Please look after my parents, they're not going to understand any of this. Take care of Miguel. I don't know what he did in the past, but he's a good man. He doesn't deserve to spend the rest of his life in that cell. And protect Willow. Protect her from this mess I've made for her. Help her to move on from this when it's all over."

I stood and wiped my hands on my pants then looked back to the stars with a shrug.

"I guess that's it. Thanks for listening," I said, then went back inside and latched the door.

Willow was lying on the bed with the comforter draped around her, her eyes closed. I pushed the chair in front of the door and sat, checking to make sure the gun was secure in my waistband. Then I leaned back and rested my head on the frayed upholstery.

"You're going to sleep there all night?" Willow whispered. "So I can't get out?"

"So no one else can get in," I explained, and for a second it was silent.

"Here," Willow finally whispered and she tossed me a pillow from off the bed.

I tucked it behind my head. "Thank you."

Setting my watch for 4am, I prayed that we could find a car in time to get to Atlanta before the race. Trusting that we would, that there would be a way, I let sleep entice me into closing my eyes. As I drifted to the void between consciousness and dreams I thought I heard Willow's soft voice whisper to me before I was lost to the numbing darkness.

"Goodnight, Logan," I thought I heard her say before I slipped away.

Thirteen

When my watch alarm chirped a few hours later, I woke with a start and stared into the dark room. My neck was stiff, my body ached and it took a minute for the memories of the day before, of the escape and the Jeep wreck, of Simone's pleading eyes, to come back to me. I stood with a groan and flipped on the lamp. Willow was no longer in the bed. My heart raced as I searched the small room, but she was nowhere to be seen.

When I heard the tub water drain, I leaned against the wall and breathed in relief. I wasn't sure what had scared me more, thinking that Willow ran off to alert the authorities or being without her. Shockingly, the second rang truer.

Fighting the thought back, I removed my shirt and checked my bandages in the warped mirror above the dresser. Willow exited the bathroom, her hair dripping onto her sweatshirt. I watched her surprised eyes travel the length of my chest until they met mine. Then she cleared her throat and quickly looked away.

"You bandages look like they're holding up," she said, passing behind me.

I pulled my shirt back over my head. "I thought you were gone for a minute there."

"We had a deal, remember?" Willow moved the chair from the door. "You ready to go find a car?"

Grabbing the drugstore bag from the floor, I took out the map then tossed the bag to Willow.

"We shouldn't be far from Atlanta," I said, opening the map and locating the small highway where we were. "We're only about one hundred and twenty miles away. Let's hope we find a car soon. We're running out of time."

The early morning air had cooled. The moon was now hiding above the low hanging clouds, drenching the road in shadow. We walked along for half an hour before we finally found a gas station. Though the lights were off and no one was in sight, there were cars parked in the side lot along the building.

"One of these will have to do. See if any of them are unlocked," I instructed, checking the first one as Willow tried the next.

I pulled the handle on the rusting Impala next to me and the door opened. "Got one!"

"They're all unlocked," she yelled back. "Take your pick."

"That's the country for you," I said, inspecting the inventory.

I decided that the early model Accord would be the most indistinct. There were hundreds of those on the road at any given time. It would be harder to track us down if it was reported as stolen. I circled the car, checking the tires and making sure it had a license plate. When it checked out, I took the gun from my pants and made my way towards the station.

"What are you doing?" Willow yelled.

"I'm going to see if the keys are behind the counter," I held the gun by the barrel and readied myself to smash the window above the door.

"I thought you said you could hotwire a car?" she asked, her hands on her hips.

"I lied about that too," I said raising the gun into the air.

"Wait!" Willow yelled before I could bring it down on the glass.

I turned to see Willow lean into the car. She lowered the sun visor and the keys dropped into her hands.

She waved them in the air, an arrogant smile on her delicate lips. "Looking for these?"

Shaking my head, I walked to the passenger side of the car and got in beside her. Willow adjusted the mirrors and then shifted into reverse.

"How did you know?" I asked.

Willow pulled out onto the highway. "I'm from the country."

We drove in silence as the sun peeked above the horizon, turning the sky a dozen shades of blue and gold. With every mile that ticked by, I glanced at my watch. We were cutting it close. It was time to consider a plan that would stop the race if I didn't make it to the officials, or if they refused to cancel it. If things got desperate, I would have to take matters into my own hands. Glancing down at the loaded pistol in my hand, it became clear to me what I would have to do.

"We're almost there," Willow said, jarring me from my thoughts. I turned to my window as we drove under an overpass. "What's the plan?"

Willow pulled off onto the exit where cars filled the roads, each inching to get through the race-day traffic. I looked at my watch again. The race started in fifteen minutes.

"Park as close as you can, then I'll make a run for it." I bent to tighten my boot laces.

Willow shook her head with an emphatic snicker. "Like hell you will. I'm not letting you out of my sight."

"Then you'd better keep up," I said as we passed the golden dome of the Capitol Building.

My pulse quickened as I secured the gun at my hip and prepared to jump out as soon as we were able to park.

"Do you even know where the starting line is?" Willow asked, her voice raising in pitch as she sensed my apprehension.

"Easy," I said. "Follow the crowd."

It took ten minutes to get less than a mile down the road to where traffic was being diverted into a cement parking deck. As soon as we were parked, I ran from the car to the nearest stairway.

"Let's go!" I shouted.

Willow caught up to me and we took the stairs by twos. When we hit the street, I took a deep breath and sprinted toward where the crowd was gathered in front of a large skyscraper. I had to weave through pedestrians as they meandered toward the starting line to cheer for the runners. I paused only a second to glance behind me at Willow.

"I'm right behind you," she yelled from just feet away. "Do what you have to do so I can do what I have to do."

Turning, I willed my legs to move faster though I felt my bruised lung would burst. I made it to the gathered crowd just as the sound of a gunshot sounded into the air followed by a roar of cheers and encouraging shouts.

"No!" I yelled, pushing my way through a wall of excited bodies.

When I made it to the other side, I watched in terror as the last of the runners glided past the starting line.

"No! Stop!" I yelled after them, running as fast as I could to catch up.

It was no use. My shallow breathing and aching legs forced me to stop for a breath. Willow ran up beside me and leaned on her knees as she gulped for air.

"We're too late. There's nothing you can do now, Logan. It's over," she panted.

"No," I said, inhaling a deep breath. "It's not over yet."

Looking back at the starting line, I spotted a small stage where the announcer and other race officials were gathering their things. I jogged to the announcer. The small, portly man looked sideways at me as I waved him down.

"You have to stop the race," I blurted out. "It's not safe. Those deaths that happened in the other races, it's going to happen again."

When the announcer smiled at me, I knew he wasn't taking me seriously.

"We've already thought of that. That's why we started the race an hour earlier to beat the heat," he said matter-of-fact. "Didn't you get the email?"

"What? An hour early . . . but I just saw them take off," I said, my breath still coming in heavy pants.

"No, no," he assured with a wave of his hand. "That was just the last wave. I assure you we got started right at six o'clock."

My heart sank in my chest. "Wave?"

"We have so many runners at these things that we stagger them so that no one gets hurt," he explained. "Each wave has about one hundred and fifty people."

"How many waves were there?" I choked out.

"Well this is a big race," he said. "We had forty total."

"Forty?" I whispered and stumbled backwards, my head reeling. "And they've been running for an hour?"

"Yes, the first few waves have been at it about that long." The man turned to collect his bullhorn.

"Has anyone . . . collapsed yet?" I asked following him.

He turned, puzzled by the concern on my face.

"No, no one's had any trouble." He sighed and looked at his watch. "Look, if you're worried about one of the runners, the first few waves should be reaching the quarter mark just a few blocks over soon. You could cut through and watch for yourself, but I'm quite sure there's no reason to be concerned. All of our runners have been medically cleared to run."

Taking another breath, I turned to sprint to the quarter mark but came face to face Willow, who held a hand up to my chest. Her expression sympathetic, as she met my eyes.

"It's over, Logan. The race already started, there's nothing you can do," she said and the calm tone of her voice reminded how she had spoken to me when I first sat facing her in her office.

"Don't treat me like I'm one of your patients. There's still time," I said through clenched teeth. "You do what you have to do, but I'm not giving up yet."

Pushing her hand off of me, I ran as fast as my weary body would carry me to the quarter mark. When I reached it, I stopped beside the water station and leaned against the table covered with small, white cups. My side felt like it was on fire and I wheezed more than I was able to inhale. There was a small crowd gathered to cheer the oncoming runners. Somewhere in the distance a live band pumped out eighties rock.

"We're supposed to save the water for the runners, but you look like you could really use one. Go ahead." The voice came from beside me.

When I looked over, a smiling teenage boy nodded to the plastic cups. The race logo imprinted on his red T-shirt identified him as a race volunteer. Nodding, I gulped down a cup of water, gasping for breath as I tried to keep it down.

"Dude, if you're going to run that hard, you might as well join the race and get a medal," he laughed.

"Did they come by yet?" I asked between breaths.

"Just a couple of crazy fast dudes looking to win the whole thing. The rest should be coming through any second."

"Thank you," I said, finally catching my breath.

Surveying the street, I tried to gauge who would get in my way if I walked out into the street, raised my gun, and forced the runners to stop if they refused to heed my warnings. When I spotted the armed police officer blocking the adjacent intersection, I knew I wouldn't last long. He would force me to lower my weapon and he would shoot me when I did not comply.

And I couldn't comply. If I did, he would just drag me back to jail and the race would go on. I considered jogging further up the course, but decided that this was dauntingly perfect. I realized the only hope I had at stopping the race now was to let him shoot me. There'd be no continuing a race where a police officer was forced to gun down an armed assailant in the middle of the course.

Looking up at the cloudless sky, I thought of Simone. How fitting it was that our story would end this way. I would die saving five nameless runners as penance for the one I killed, for the child that I killed with her. I thought about Faith, the little girl whose life I'd cut short and I said a bitter sweet thank-you. Faith had died on the side of that road all those years ago, but thanks to this chance to make things right, a renewed faith lived again within me.

"What are you going to do?" Willow ran up to me, spinning me around to face her as the gathered crowd began to cheer.

"Whatever I have to," I said, stepping into the street as the first of the runners approached looking tired but determined.

"Logan, no . . ." Willow tried to grab my arm, but I shook her off.

"I'm sorry," I called to her. "For everything."

"Logan, come back here . . ." she yelled, but I was already in the middle of the street with my arms raised.

"Stop running! You have to stop. People are going to die!" I pleaded as they ran past me, only pausing to hear what I was saying and then laughing and running off to get water from the water station.

"Please, stop! It's not worth it! Five of you will die if you don't stop this race!" I screamed and waved my arms, but my warnings fell on deaf ears as they parted to let the 'crazy man' through.

I tried to grab at arms as they went by, to force them to listen, but I was dismissed with angry curses and confused stares. No one stopped. There were too many of them. Lost in the crowd of huffing athletes, I screamed out my warning as the band's drums beat on like a death march in the distance. It was no use.

With a cry, I reached into my waistband for the gun as Willow screamed for me to stop, but she too was lost to me in the sea of breathless faces. I hated that she would have to see this, hated that she was even a part of it, but I hoped one day she would understand why I had to do this. Taking firm hold of the gun, I took a deep breath and began to raise it to the crowd just as a familiar face ran past me. I froze, the blood draining from my face and limbs. Spinning on my heels, I watched as her red hair swayed beneath her visor. Then she was lost in the crowd.

"Simone?" I gaped, lowering the gun as Willow grabbed my wrist.

"What the hell are you doing? You'll get yourself killed!" She screamed at me, but I struggled to look around her, spotting the red hair and visor just ahead of the water station.

"It's her," I cried, ripping my wrist free to run after her. "It's Simone!"

"Logan!" Willow yelled behind me. "I'm getting the cops. It's over, this has gone too far!"

Ignoring Willow, I ran on, struggling to keep Simone in my sights. Shouldering past runners, I sprinted forward, fueled by the shock of seeing her in person, solid and in the flesh, just as she'd looked every evening before I killed her.

It isn't possible, I thought as I got closer. The band's beat grew louder as we approached where they played from an overpass above us. I chased her for more than a mile. My lungs burned, but I couldn't stop.

When the course took a turn to the left, I cut through the sidewalk, pushing past cheering pedestrians with posters and signs to get closer to her. She turned her head as if she sensed me approaching. Time stood still. My heartbeat resonated in my eardrums. I saw the jagged scar along her face as her glassy green eyes locked on mine. No longer a misty vision, Simone turned and ran into the crowd.

With a gasp, I pursued her, pushing runners out of my way as I forced myself forward. When she was within reach, I extended my arm and felt the silk of her hair as it slipped through my fingers.

Before I could reach out again, the young woman running beside her stopped suddenly, her legs wobbling beneath her. She spun around and clutched at her chest, her face draining of color. Giving up my pursuit, I stopped in time to catch the woman as she fell. She collapsed, a lifeless heap, into my arms as Simone ran off out of sight.

"No!" I cried as other runners dodged us or stopped to help.

I laid the woman gently on the ground and tilted her head back. Leaning over her, I listened for breath but could hear nothing.

"Here's another one!" Someone yelled as they ran up to us.

"Another one?" I asked, looking up from the woman.

Race volunteers quickly diverted the flow of traffic into a bottleneck on the road's shoulder. When the road cleared, I looked down the course to where Willow knelt beside an older gentleman. He was blue and unconscious on the pavement beside her.

"Logan," she cried, tears streaming down her shocked face as she gaped at me.

Paramedics raced in, splitting up to rush to the aid of each victim. When they reached me, I was feeling for a pulse, but couldn't find one.

"It's a heart attack, just like in the other races. Treat her for a heart attack . . . do something," I demanded shakily as they began to work on the woman.

I watched in horror as they started chest compressions and placed a breathing mask over her mouth. She couldn't have been more than twenty-years old, her young face turning bluer with each passing minute.

When the paramedics lifted her onto a stretcher and ran her to the ambulance I stood slowly and watched in a daze as runners slowed as they ran by, concerned but continuing on. Some gasped and put their hands over their mouths, but when they began to stop, race volunteers ordered them to keep moving. They turned to finish the race, persisting despite the tragedy around us.

In a rage, I lifted the gun to fire into the air. I had to get them to stop the race. Did they not see what was happening? Before I could fire a shot, Willow tackled me, forcing me to lower the gun. With her arms around me, she dragged me to the side of the road as the ambulance sped by.

"No, Logan!" she cried and I felt her body tremble against mine. "Don't do this, I need you right now. There's another one back there."

"Another . . . ?" I stammered backward, my hand shook as I raised it to my brow. "Why aren't they stopping the race? Why are they letting them run on as if nothing is happening?"

"They can't start a panic, there's over seven thousand people here," Willow said, stepping back from me to look me in the eyes.

I stared at her, unseeing, as my mind fought to accept the truth. I'd failed. Somehow Simone had been just inches away while those three people were dying. None of it made sense. Where was my provision? Where was my penance? Where was the justice?

People were dead and there was nothing I could do to stop it. *It wasn't supposed to happen like this*, I reeled.

"Five people will fall," I said in a daze. "That was only three . . . there's going to be two more!"

"Two more?" Willow asked, her voice trembling. "Are you sure?"

"You know that I am." I put my hands on her shoulders. "I have to stop it. I have to!"

I raised the gun and turned but Willow grabbed my arm again and forced it down. "Listen to me, Logan. Getting yourself killed is not the answer!"

"It's the only way," I shoved past her, but she grabbed me again and spun me around.

"No it's not. Just listen to me, Logan. Those were no random heart attacks. The way that man in front of me went down . . . and that girl was so young.... There's no way those were fluke accidents," Willow said, staring me in the eye.

"What are you saying?" I asked.

"I'm saying that those people were murdered." Willow's voice shook. "Someone did this on purpose."

I lowered the gun as I considered the possibility. "But how?"

"I don't know," Willow turned her head and sobbed, her shoulders heaving. I put my arm around her.

"We have to get the police, tell them what's going on," I whispered.

Willow shook her head. "No, we can't do that. They won't believe either of us. I don't know if I even believe it yet."

I turned her to face me. "Believe it or not, this is happening. Two more people are going to die unless we do something to stop it."

"Okay," Willow took a deep, shaky breath. "What can we do?"

I looked around at the runners, the ones passing now were smiling and oblivious to the horror around them. They went by in droves, hundreds of people spread out across the course in either direction.

"Here's what we have to do," I said. "I'm going to run ahead. You go back the other way and keep your eyes peeled for anything suspicious. If you see anyone do something the least bit suspect, you tell someone right away. Maybe between the two of us, we can catch this guy before he can strike again."

Willow nodded. "I can do that."

"When I hit the finish line, I'll double back until I find you," I said as we each went separate directions. "Be careful."

"Logan," Willow called after me and I turned. "You said you saw her...Simone. Did she say anything else?"

"No," I said with a sigh. "I can't explain it, but I think she wanted me to follow her."

"Then you should go, Logan. If two more people are going to die, then we need her help," she said and then jogged off the way we'd come.

I watched her go, momentarily stunned by her words, that she believed me. Then I turned in the direction of traffic and ran as fast as I could with the runners.

For half a mile I ran as hard as my battered body would allow, searching for Simone's red hair and visor among the crowd. When I didn't see her, I slowed my pace and scanned the runners that passed me, unsure of what I was looking for. If someone was causing these deaths, how were they doing it, and why? Why kill innocent people and make it look like an act of nature?

Just past the eleven mile marker, there was a commotion. Volunteers were yelling for runners to stay to the side. The road curved and sloped downward ahead and I couldn't see what was going on, but I knew.

"No," I whispered as I sprinted around the corner, pushing my way through the bottlenecked crowd.

On the shoulder of the course, volunteers and runners leaned over an unconscious man on the street. They yelled for someone to get the paramedics. One of the volunteers directing the traffic flow tried to stop me, but I brushed past him and knelt beside the fallen man. He couldn't have been much younger than me, his face pale and ashen. A woman beside me held his left hand and I saw that a wedding ring adorned the runner's finger.

"How long has he been down?" I asked.

"Less than a minute," someone answered. "He just collapsed right in front of me."

"He's having a heart attack, a severe one. I'm going to start chest compressions. Does anyone know how to give mouth to mouth?" I asked those gathered around.

"I do," a young woman raised her hand.

I motioned for the others to move as she took position by the man's head and I started the compressions. Counting to thirty, I sat back while the woman tilted his head and blew into his mouth.

"Are you a doctor?" she asked when it was my turn.

"No," I said between counts. "But I took a CPR in college."

"Then how do you know it's a heart attack?" she asked.

"Because," I said when it was her turn. "Three more people have collapsed of the same thing. We have to keep his heart pumping until help arrives. Did anyone see someone approach this man before he fell? Did you see anything unusual?"

Those around me shook their heads.

"I was behind him for ten miles. He was going strong and then he just collapsed. We were keeping pace with the same crowd. No one touched him." A teary-eyed woman spoke up.

The paramedics arrived as I finished the next cycle of compressions, rushing onto the scene with a defibrillator. We stepped back to let them work and I looked up at the crowd. Runners looked on and gasped or clasped hands with those around them as they jogged by, forced forward by the flow of traffic. I looked back at the young man, at the husband whose wife would be waiting for him at the finish line.

"Please God," I whispered. "Don't take this man. Not this one. Not one more. You sent me here to save these people. I know I failed you. I know it's too late for the others . . . but he lives. Do you hear me? He lives!"

When I heard the shout of "clear," I opened my eyes as they sent the first shock through the man.

"Please," I cried. "Come on!"

When the paramedics shouted again for everyone to clear, I watched as they sent a second jolt through his body and then checked his neck.

"I have a pulse!" a paramedic shouted and the gathered crowd breathed a collective sigh of relief.

As they lifted him onto the gurney, the man opened his eyes with a moan.

"You're going to be alright," the paramedic said as he wheeled him towards the awaiting ambulance. "What's your name?"

"Jason," he answered as they closed the doors.

I watched the ambulance drive away and I raised my head to the heavens.

"Thank you," I whispered

"You saved his life, you know," the young lady beside me said.

"You think he'll make it?" I asked.

"He's not out of the woods yet, but at least now he has a fighting chance," She said, and I turned back to the course.

Willow stood feet away beside the flow of runners. Her face was streaked with tears, her eyes filled with devastation.

"Willow?" I said jogging to her.

When she looked up at me, her lips curved into an anguished sob and I knew. I folded my arms around her and she wept into my chest.

"She fell right in front of me," Willow cried. "A couple of us tried CPR. The paramedics got there within minutes, but they couldn't revive her. She was gone before she hit the ground. Oh God…"

I held her tighter against me. "I'm so sorry I couldn't stop it. I was supposed to stop it."

Willow looked at me, her bright blue eyes dulled by her tears. "This is my fault. I didn't believe you. I could have made those phone calls, we could have gotten here sooner if I hadn't wrecked the jeep . . ."

"Sshhh," I said, pulling her close again. "You have no idea how much that means to me, but this is on me. I was charged with the task of setting things right, and I fell short. It's time to make good on my promise to you."

I let go of Willow and looked around at the ocean of runners, huffing as they went by. Just down the course, police cars blocked traffic from a side street. Grabbing Willow's hand, I walked towards it.

"What are you doing?" she asked.

"It's over," I said, defeated. "I couldn't save them all, but I did what I came here to do. It's time to do the right thing. You have to turn me in."

"What?" Willow cried, closing the gap between us. "I can't turn you in now. After everything that's happened?"

"It's what we agreed on, remember?"

"I know it's what we agreed," she said, then lowered her head. "But that was before . . ."

"Before what?" I asked. She raised her head to look me in the eyes.

"Before I . . ." she started to explain when a loud shout made us both turn.

"There he is, that's him!" A woman pointed at me as she yelled to the officers down the street. "That's the man who was waving the gun around! He said that he was going to kill five people!"

One of them said something into his radio as the other reached for his sidearm.

"Don't move!" he ordered and they made their way slowly over to us.

"They think you're the one behind this." Willow gasped. "They'll never believe the truth. We have to go . . . now!"

"I can't do that to you," I said, shrugging out of her grasp. "I've put you through enough."

I turned to face the officers, ready to surrender. Willow stood in front of me, blocking me from them.

"You did what you had to do . . . I see that now. This isn't the right thing, Logan. If it ends this way it will all be for nothing. You didn't fail today, you saved that man's life," she said, fresh tears coming to her eyes.

"This is what I was given a second chance to do. My shot at redemption is over," I whispered.

"What if it's not? What if this is only the beginning?" She pleaded. "What if this person strikes again at the next race? Or somewhere else? If you turn yourself in now, they'll think it was you. They won't even investigate anyone else! Five people fell today, just like you said they would, Logan. I believe you now. Do you hear me? I believe that you saw something, that you've been given a gift. Use it to stop this person!"

"If I was meant to go further, there would be a way. There would be provision . . ." I stammered.

Willow grabbed my hand. I looked into her eyes as they brightened and she beamed.

"There is," she said closing her fingers around mine. "It's me. You said it yourself. I was chosen. Maybe I was chosen to stop you from doing this, Logan. I believe you're seeing Simone. I believe you, and because of my parents . . . I'm the only one who will."

Turning, I watched the officers' approach as they instructed the last wave of runners to stay to their left. Then I turned back to Willow as she squeezed my hand. I remembered what Simone said after the jeep overturned. She told me that Willow would help me and that was what she was trying to do now. Maybe this wasn't over yet.

"Let's go," I finally agreed and she sighed with relief. "On the count of three, we have to run with the crowd. They won't fire their weapons with this many people. Once we lose them we can make our way back to the car."

"Let's do it." Willow nodded.

We tuned to the runners crowding beside us, trying to get by.

"One . . . Two . . . Three!" I shouted and we darted into the crowd of runners, our hands locked together.

Behind us, the officers yelled for us to stop. I didn't look back, only tugged Willow forward as we sprinted through the crowd. For a quarter of a mile we kept pace amidst the runners. We blended with them and kept our heads low as the course turned a corner and the road slopped downward for over half a mile. From this angle, we could see officers gathering at the bottom of the hill, waiting for us to run by.

"Logan?" Willow yelled.

"I see them."

Willow tugged on my hand. "Look! On the left. It's the skyscraper we parked next to."

She was right. The tall glass building loomed from just a few blocks away.

"Make for that alleyway!" I said, spotting a small opening between the brick buildings beside us.

Pushing past runners, I edged closer to the shoulder. I dragged Willow with me against the traffic to where a gathering of pedestrians hollered and cheered. We squeezed past them unseen and sprinted through the alley and onto the sidewalk on the other side. We didn't stop running until we made it to the steps of the parking garage where we paused to catch our breath.

"You okay?" I panted as Willow doubled over to catch her breath.

"Why would people do this voluntarily?" She said between coughs.

"We have to keep moving."

Climbing the steps, we jogged to the car. Willow got behind the wheel and I threw myself in beside her. She brought the car to life as I grabbed the drug store bag and dug out the last bottle of water. I handed it to her.

"I have no plan," I confessed. "I've got no idea what to do now or where to go."

"I do." Willow took a long drag from the bottle and handing it back to me. "I know exactly where we have to go."

I chugged from the bottle, then wiped my mouth with the back of my hand as Willow put the car into reverse. "Where?"

"We're going to Saluda," she said, pulling the car onto the road. "Buckle up."

Fourteen

"Looks like you take I-85 all the way to I-25," I said, looking at the map. "What's in Saluda anyway? I've lived in North Carolina all my life and I've never heard of it."

"Most people haven't. There's not much of anything there." Willow checked her mirrors before merging onto the highway.

"Then why are we going?" I asked, folding the map to put it back in the bag.

"Because," Willow sighed. "My parents live there."

I glared at her as she stared pensively out the windshield.

"Your parents. You sure that's a good idea?" I asked. "I mean, I doubt they'll be happy about you bringing home an escaped fugitive. What makes you think they won't just turn me in?"

"It's a possibility," Willow said with a shrug. "But they're also the only ones who can help. They'll know what to do."

Watching Willow's grip tighten on the steering wheel made me wonder if she was trying to convince me or herself.

"When was the last time you saw them?" I asked.

"They came to visit before I started graduate school 2 years ago," She said. "I haven't been back home since I left for college. Our relationship has been a little . . . strained."

"Because you don't believe them." I said, putting it together. "About the Guardians . . . or whatever."

"I don't know what I believe anymore," she said staring out to the highway, seeing something more than the traffic ahead. "When I was a kid, I would ask to hear my mother's special stories over and over. My great grandmother, Gram, told me that my mother had 'the sight.' It allowed her to see things that others couldn't. My mother thought I had it too. She would point Guardians out whenever she saw them. I remember thinking that they were the most glorious things I had ever seen."

"You saw them?" I asked.

"I thought I did," Willow said with a sigh. "But now I know that children see things with their imaginations. We grow out of it."

"Maybe we just stop believing," I said.

Willow nodded, her face turning sad. "Maybe."

"What kind of special story did your mom tell you back then?"

"She used to tell me that while my dad was in the hospital in a coma after taking down that shooter in Fort Bragg, his spirit was sent back to be my mother's Guardian. When she was ten years old she witnessed her parent's murder. She said my dad was there. He saved her from being killed too. When she was my age the killer came back for her, but my dad was there to stop him," Willow explained.

"So that was her traumatic event . . ." I whispered and she nodded.

"When she found my dad in that hospital, it was happily ever after from then on," Willow said with a smile.

"I don't understand," I said, trying to make sense of it. "How could your dad have saved her back when she was a kid if he was only in a coma for a few days?"

"I used to ask the same thing," Willow said with a sigh. "She said that in heaven there is no such thing as time, no limit to what love can do. God, I wanted to believe her."

"When did you stop?" I asked quietly. "Believing, I mean?"

"When Gram died, I think. I was only eight years old when she passed. I didn't take it very well. She and I were extremely close. I told myself that she would come back to me one day as the most glorious angel of all. That she would find me, just like my dad found my mom. She never did though. She never came back to me." A tear fell onto Willow's cheek and she quickly wiped it away and cleared her throat. "After she was gone, my mother would point out Guardians to me, but I didn't see them. I realized they weren't really there at all, that they were just a defense mechanism. Up until now, I dismissed it all as just a beautiful story."

Willow stared ahead, the tears standing in her eyes. I could see the turmoil behind them, could feel the shattering of a reality she had been so sure of just yesterday.

"You know, up until a few days ago I was sure that I wanted to die, that I deserved to for what I've done," I said, lowing my head. "Everyone kept talking about how I was getting out of prison next year and I couldn't stand it. The thought of getting the chance to move on with my life knowing that the girls that I killed will never have that chance, made me want to end it all."

"Logan . . ." Willow whispered.

"Let me finish," I said, holding up my hand. "What I've come to realize over the last few days is that even though I didn't value myself or my future, the big man upstairs had a different plan for me. He gave me a purpose when I thought there was none for me. He believed in me even when I stopped believing in anything. Maybe He's doing that for you too. Maybe you stopped seeing the Guardians when you stopped believing in them."

"Maybe I didn't want to believe anymore," she said, glancing at me and then turning her attention back to the road, "When you came to my office that second time, when you told me about Simone's warning, you had that look on your face. It was the same look my mother used to get when she saw a Guardian. A look of peace and affirmation. I knew you saw what you said you saw. I knew you'd seen something. A part of me knew what was happening with you, Logan. Maybe I was just mad . . . because you were seeing something I could no longer see, something I dismissed as impossible for so long."

I took Willow's hand in mine and when I did, she looked me in the eyes and smiled.

"Sometimes believing is more than seeing," I said. "Thank you for helping me."

"I think you were right," she said, squeezing my hand. "I think I was meant to walk out of that back door when I did. We're going to figure this out, Logan. No matter what happens."

We drove on as the sun made its way high into the afternoon sky, stopping only once to fill the car up with gas and our bellies with service station snacks. When mountains began to fill the landscape, I stared out the window at their rolling peaks, mesmerized. Having been privy to only the flat scenery of the prison for the last twelve years, I couldn't get my eyes' fill their lush, green enormity. I thought we might touch the clouds as we weaved our way upward into their hills and valleys.

"You grew up here?" I asked, exasperated. "Why would you ever want to leave?"

"Well, when it's all you've ever known . . ."Willow started and then stopped herself with a sigh. "I can't believe it's been so long. I forgot how beautiful it is up here."

When the road began to twist and climb, I clung to my seat as Willow maneuvered the turns with ease. We exited the highway and the road straightened out. The small mountain town of Saluda unfolded before us.

The main street, lined with cars, was bustling with townsfolk who walked the sidewalks across from the railroad. With eyes wide, I took it all in. I marveled at the old diner and grocery shop, adorned with red and white pinstriped awnings like something out of a movie. Kids swung from the swing set beside the abandoned tracks as neighbors greeted one another with smiles in front of the tiny library.

"This is where you're from? It's so small and . . ."

"Boring?" Willow asked.

I shook my head, "No. It's just so . . . perfect."

Willow smiled as she looked around at the townspeople as they gathered together for lunch. I could tell she was seeing her home with a fresh eyes. "Do me a favor and duck down in your seat. I don't want anyone making a fuss about the man they saw me with."

I ducked down in my chair, but continued to watch the small town pass through my window. "It looks like everyone's too busy chatting over lunch to give us much notice."

"You'd be surprised," Willow said as I watched the small, green-trimmed police station go by.

I marveled at the display in the town hall's large bay windows. Spring flowers and Easter eggs of every color sat atop a table filled with hundreds of twinkling lights.

"I haven't celebrated Easter for so long I almost forgot about it," I said.

"Yeah, well if you lived here they'd never let you forget a holiday again," Willow chuckled, then turned down a side street and over the tracks.

We climbed a hill and weaved in and out of neighborhoods as I watched the A-framed houses peek above the winding streets. When we turned onto Baker Street, the hills leveled out a bit, revealing a typical-looking neighborhood lined with small houses, their yards and flower beds neatly kept.

Willow slowed the car and took a deep breath. We pulled up to a small, white house and turned to climb its sloped driveway.

"Cute mailbox," I said as we passed the white box. It was covered in painted pink flowers and purple handprints.

Willow parked the car at the top of the driveway and we got out. I looked up at the quaint house with its long porch and wooden swing. I could imagine a happy childhood spent here, could see many calm nights passed watching the fireflies float by from the porch on a hot summer evening. For the first time in my adult life, I longed for that. I let myself imagine a normal life. *What would that look like for me? Was it even possible?*

"Stay in the here for a minute. I have to try and explain this . . ." Willow said, but was interrupted when the front door opened. A middle-aged woman, short in stature but commanding in presence, stepped onto the porch.

The woman ran a hand through her grey-kissed, brown hair and stared at Willow, in shock. Willow stared back. Then with a sudden laugh, the woman ran down the steps to embrace her.

"Mom." Willow sighed, wrapping her arms around the woman. "I'm sorry I've been away for so long.

"It's okay, my sweet girl," the woman said as she put her hands on Willow's shoulders and held her at arm's length to look into her face. "I had faith that one day you would find your way back."

Willow wiped a tear from her eye as the woman looked around her to where I stood beside the car. Her eyes widened with alarm. Clearing my throat, I stepped closer.

"Willow, is this who I think it is? It's been all over the news. We've been trying to call you, but your phone just goes to voicemail. Your father is at the station ready to head out to find you," she said, taking a step towards me. "They're saying you helped this man escape from prison?"

"My name is Logan Foster." I extended my hand. "You must be Willow's mother."

The woman looked at Willow, unease and questions in her brown eyes.

"It's okay, Mom. I'll explain everything. You have to trust me," Willow held her mother's hand. "Mom, Logan's like you. He . . . he sees them too. We're in trouble. I knew you and dad would know what to do."

Willow's mom turned to me and studied my face. When she turned back to her daughter, her eyes softened, tears coming to their surface. "What?"

"Willow told me about the Guardians, that you see them. I've been seeing something too," I tried to explain. "That's why we came here. I was hoping you could help me figure out what it all means."

"You told him this?" she asked Willow. "You believe it?"

Willow nodded, a tear escaping onto her cheek as she smiled. "Yes, Mom. I think I do."

Her mom turned back to me. She looked at my outstretched hand and dismissing it, wrapped her arms around me and pulled me close. Looking at Willow in shock, I timidly held the small woman in my arms as she patted my back.

"Thank you, Logan" she whispered against my shoulder and then pulled away.

She wiped her tear-streaked face and then laughed.

"My goodness, where are my manners?" She held out her hand and I took in in mine. "You can call me Alex. Of course I'll help. Come on inside and you two can tell me all about it."

Alex turned to go back inside the house. Willow came to me and took me by the arm and together we followed her inside.

We sat at the kitchen table while Willow did her best to explain it all. I filled in the blanks where I could. Alex poured more coffee and sat, enthralled by Willow's description of the last few days.

"And you think the woman you're seeing is the same woman from your accident all those years ago? Are you sure?" she asked me.

I took a sip of coffee, savoring each nuance of its richness. "Yes. It's Simone, I'm sure of it."

"Is that possible, Mom? To see someone come back like that?" Willow asked.

She wanted to know as much for me as for herself. Deep down I knew she was still hoping to see her grandmother again. Alex sat back in her chair and nodded, a world of knowledge in her dark eyes.

"Anything is possible," she said. "The how is not as important as the why. She was sent to you for a reason. Donovan, my husband, was sent to protect me, to make sure I lived out my purpose in life. What you have to figure out is why Simone was sent to you."

"I thought it was because she wanted me to stop the race today, to save those people's lives. That's what she told me," I said.

"Now you're not so sure?" Alex asked.

"No." I looked out of the small kitchen window at the branches swaying with the breeze. "There has to be more to it. If those runners were murdered, then more people could be in danger. I think I'm meant to find the killer and stop them."

"You said you saw Simon at the race. Did she speak to you then?" Alex asked.

I shook my head. "No, she didn't say anything, but she was different this time. She was flesh and bone. I mean, usually when I see her, she's not quite clear, she's . . ."

"Fuzzy, almost like . . . warm static," Alex finished.

"Exactly like that," I said. "But this morning she looked real . . . alive. She was dressed just like she was the evening I . . . the evening she died. It just doesn't make any sense."

Alex thought for a minute. She looked at Willow to see how she was reacting to all of this. When she saw that Willow was listening resolutely she turned her attention back to me.

"When I first saw Donovan," Alex explained, "it was only through glimpses and reflections. I didn't fully believe in him, in the possibility that he was real, so I couldn't see him clearly. It's only when I believed in him with all my being that I saw him as clearly as I see him now. He was a real person to me in the moment he saved my life for the second time. Maybe Simone was more real to you this morning because you believe in her the same way now."

"That could be it," I said, but I was interrupted by the sound of a large vehicle climbing the driveway outside.

I stood to look out the window and my pulse began to race when I saw the blue and black SUV park at the top of the drive, the words 'Saluda Police Department' printed on the side in big, white letters.

"Someone called the cops. Is there a back door?" I said, frantically searching. "Willow, you should stay here. Tell them I kidnapped you, that you escaped . . . ."

"Logan," Willow stood and reached for me.

Turning to run for the back door, I heard heavy footsteps charge the porch. The front door flew opened before I could make it to the back door. The click of a 9mm slide being pulled back stopped me in my tracks.

"Don't move!" A deep voice commanded. "Turn around, now!"

Raising my hands above my head, I closed my eyes and blew out a defeated breath. *So this was how it's going to end. We were so close...*

When I turned around, I came face to face with an armed officer. The glinting badge on his belt labeled him as the chief. His jet black hair was a stark contrast to the cool blue eyes that glared at me from the other side the gun he aimed at my head.

"Daddy!" Willow shouted.

"Daddy?" I repeated, confused.

Alex walked calmly to the officer and laid a gentle hand on his arm. "Donovan, it's okay. Put the gun down."

"Evelyn almost broke her other hip running to the station," he said, refusing to lower the weapon. "She said she saw Willow with a strange man heading this way. Is this the guy? The escaped con?"

"Your dad is the chief of police?" I asked Willow, keeping my eyes on the man with the gun in front of me. "You didn't think to mention that?"

"Daddy, please," she pleaded.

"Donovan," Alex said, getting in front of the officer in order to look him in the face. "This is Logan. Willow brought him here because he sees Guardians too. She brought him here because he's been called to stop something horrible from happening. She knew we could help."

Donovan lowered the gun slowly. He took his eyes off of me to look into his wife's face.

"Willow brought him here?" he asked, almost a whisper as he looked over at his daughter.

"Just like we've been praying for," Alex said.

Willow nodded, stepping closer to her father. "I'm so sorry I didn't believe you, Daddy."

When he holstered his weapon, she ran into his welcoming arms.

"I knew this day would come," he whispered against her ear as he ran a hand over her hair.

He looked at me over her shoulder, skepticism still in his eyes, but he nodded.

"Thank you for bringing my daughter back."

"Don't thank me," I said, letting out my held breath. "Willow's the one helping me by bringing me here. She saved my life."

Donovan held Willow out to look into her face and they smiled warmly at one another.

"I knew you could help. We need you," Willow said.

Donovan looked back up to me, looked me over and then nodded. "Okay. What can I do?"

Once we went back over the course of events with Donovan, he contemplated them from where he leaned against the kitchen counter. He ran a hand through his raven hair and for the first time, I was able to get a good look at him. The wrinkles forming around his intense eyes made him look more imperial than aged. Tall and muscular, it was clear where Willow got her physique. His eyes, like hers, were the color of the deepest ocean. Otherworldly knowledge emanated from them when he looked at me.

"Here is what we have to do," he said. "I have to get back down to the station and tell everyone that Evelyn was mistaken. If everyone knows you're here, they'll start asking questions and by now word has already spread. I have to squash it."

"How is Evelyn?" Willow asked. "I'm sorry I freaked her out."

"She's over seventy and as outrageous as ever," he smirked. "I told her she was too old for those heels. Thought that fall last year proved it. Anyway, I need you two to stay here, out of sight. When I come back we'll see if anyone has posted any photos of the race. Maybe someone captured something that can give us a lead."

"We need to know where the next race is," I said.

Donovan looked at Alex who stood, suddenly worried.

"They talked about it on the news last night," she said. "The next race is tomorrow. It's in downtown Raleigh."

"What?" I said, throwing back my chair as I got up from the table. "Raleigh? Tomorrow? Maybe they canceled it. After this morning, after what happened to those people, maybe they canceled it."

Donovan held up a hand. "I'll find out. I have an old Army friend who works in the force down there. I'll find out what he knows. In the meantime, it might not be a bad idea to watch the news, see what they're saying."

Donovan walked to the door and turned back to me and Willow.

"I'm glad you came here, it was the right things to do. We'll get to the bottom of this," he said and then left the house.

Alex followed behind him to see him out.

"Like father, like daughter." I said, looking at Willow who beamed as she watched after her parents.

"You think?" she asked.

"You could have told me he was the chief of police up here," I said, running my hands over my face with a sigh.

Willow shrugged. "He took over the job when he was discharged from the Army. The position was open for over a year and since he was an MP, he was a shoo-in."

"I'm sure it had nothing to do with the fact he is a national hero. He saved a lot of people when he pounced on that shooter and took a few bullets," I said.

"My dad has never made a big deal of that." She stood and looked out the window to where her mother and father embraced and kissed tenderly. "He said he did what anyone would have done that day."

When Alex came back in we all went into the living room. I marveled at the coziness of the house and the way the afternoon sun shone on the baby grand piano in the corner. As we sat on the couch, Alex turned on the television.

It didn't take long to find my face splashed across the screen of a local news station. Willow gasped as the headline flashed across the bottom of the screen. *Escaped convict may be responsible for four deaths at the Atlanta Music Marathon*

"They think you did it, that you're responsible," Willow cried. "I told you."

I watched in horror as the newscaster explained the events of the day. Witnesses were interviewed about the man who waved a gun and threatened runners.

"Investigators are trying to determine the cause of death and how Foster may be involved. The prevailing theory however, is that the runners were poisoned. We'll know more if lab results turn up any foreign substances," the reporter announced.

"Poisoned?" I mumbled as I stared, transfixed at the screen.

"That's not what happened at all!" Willow said, outraged, turning to her mother. "He was trying to stop the race. There would be five dead if it weren't for Logan. He saved a man out there. Where was that report?"

"Foster may be traveling with this woman, Willow Pritchard," the newscast continued.

Willow's face flashed onto the screen. I looked to her as she turned ashen, bringing her hands to her mouth.

"Pritchard is the prison psychologist at Central prison who is believed to have helped Foster escape. Authorities are looking into the tragic deaths of the three runners from the race at Virginia Beach for evidence that these two were involved. If you see either Pritchard or Foster, please alert your local authorities immediately, but do not approach them as they are thought to be armed and dangerous."

"You have a gun?" Alex asked me coolly while Willow cried beside me.

"It's in the car." I sighed. "I was going to use it to stop the race, either by scaring the runners into stopping or . . ."

"Getting yourself killed," Alex said, taking a deep breath. "I understand now."

Alex turned to Willow and grabbed her trembling hand. "You did the right thing. This is all going to work out, have to have faith in that. All of this is happening for a reason."

"How do you know?" Willow asked.

"Because a long time ago, it was my time to find out that there was more at work in my life than I could fathom at the time. Before your father came into my life, I was lost. He showed me a life beyond what I thought was possible. This is your time Willow, your time to rise and fight for a greater purpose," Alex said, looking to us both.

I shook my head and chuckled, despite myself.

"What's so funny?" Willow asked.

"That's exactly what Miguel said before I left. He told me that this was my time to make amends for all those years ago," I said.

"Who's Miguel" Alex asked.

"He's my cell mate back at the prison. Up until now, he was the only one I ever really talked to. I don't know what I would have done all these years without him," I said.

"Cellmate?" Willow asked, confused.

"Yeah. He saw Simone too. He woke up when she was in our cell. That's when he gave me the idea to escape, to try to stop the race. He said this was my time for redemption," I said with a sigh. "I hope they're not giving him too hard a time about my escape."

When I looked up, Willow was staring at me, an awkward look on her face that I couldn't read.

"No, that's not right," she said.

"I know, it's not like they would know he helped me," I agreed. "All he really did was help make the key . . ."

"No, Logan," Willow interrupted. "I mean, you're talking about someone in a neighboring cell, right?"

"No, he was my cell mate," I chuckled. "As in, he was in the same cell."

"That can't be right," Willow said, confused. "You didn't have a cell mate."

"Of course I did," I scoffed. "Did you not just hear me? Miguel . . ."

"No . . . Logan." Willow leaned forward and looked me in the eye. "You didn't have a cell mate. I read your chart. It was right there on your information sheet. The warden ruled that you were to have your own cell because you were a risk to other inmates in close quarters."

"What? That makes no sense . . ."

"Why do you think I asked you about your old cell mate the first time we talked? I was trying to get your side of the story about what happened to him, Logan," she said, reaching for me. I shot up and paced away, my head reeling. "I needed to know if you were going to be dangerous in that room with me. You never had another cell mate, not after the incident with the first."

"There must have been a mistake in my records . . ."

"They don't make those kinds of mistakes," Willow assured me.

"This is ridiculous. I lived with the man for over a decade!" I brought my trembling hands to my forehead as I tried to make sense of what she was saying. "Are you saying I made him up? For twelve years? That's not possible. He's real, I'm telling you."

Alex stood and came to where I paced the living room floor. She looked me in the face until I stopped. Then she placed her hand gently on my arm.

"Logan," she said, her voice calm. "Think back to the times you were with Miguel. Did he ever interact with anyone else besides you? Did you two ever engage in conversation with other people together?"

I thought about all the times we were together outside of the cell. We rarely talked to each other outside, let alone anyone else. We didn't bother anyone and no one bothered us. That's how we stayed away from trouble.

"We never talked to anyone," I said, frustrated. "We kept to ourselves."

"What about the guards?" Alex asked. "Did they ever interact with Miguel?"

I thought back to the countless times Officer Duke greeted us with his snide comments in the morning, and the way Officer Edmonds nodded to us each night.

Then I thought again.

Duke always had a snide comment for me. He never bothered Miguel. Edmonds always nodded in my direction before he clicked the counter and moved on.

Then it hit me. With a gasp, I staggered backwards.

"The counter," I mumbled, my head spinning.

"What is it, Logan?" Willow asked.

I looked at her, my body beginning to shake.

"They only ever clicked it once," I said. "At count. They only ever clicked the counter once. I thought it was strange at first, but got so used to it I never thought about it again. I just figured they had their reasons. They didn't see him, did they? I was the only one that ever could. . . Oh my God!"

I backed away until my back hit the wall and then holding my head in my hands, I sank to the floor.

"If I made him up, if I was seeing things all these years then that means Simone . . . she's not real either is she?" I cried.

Alex squatted down beside me.

"Shhhh, listen to me Logan," she said, trying to calm me as I looked up into her understanding face. "I know exactly what you're going through right now. I had the advantage of being a child when I first met mine, so I can imagine that it's even harder for you to realize you have one."

"Have what?" I whispered. "What are you talking about?"

Alex sighed and patted my hand, then she smiled at me. "A Guardian."

"A Guardian? Miguel?"

"Donovan was there when I needed him the most, and it sounds like Miguel did the same for you. You didn't make him up, Logan, but you are seeing things, things that other people don't see. It doesn't mean they aren't there."

"It can't be," I said. "He would have told me. He went to work, ate, slept . . ."

". . . and did all the other things he had to do so he could be near you in there, so you would trust him enough to let him in. So that he could protect you, and he did, didn't he?" Alex interrupted. "Think about it. Would you have believed him if he told you?"

I couldn't grasp it, the thought of Miguel as my Guardian. My mind went back to all those countless days and nights when he was there for me. He never had a harsh word for me, never did anything but listen when I needed to talk or force me to talk when he knew I needed to. *But friends did that for each other, didn't they?* Then I thought about how he had saved my life when Boss attacked me in the cell, and how he sent Smiley sprawling into the mashed potatoes on the floor when he'd tried to punch me in my injured side, and I knew it was true.

With the revelation came sudden, fierce anger.

"If it's true . . . if Miguel is my Guardian? Then where is he now? Where was he this morning when those people were dying in my arms? Where was he that evening all those years ago? Why didn't he stop me from killing them?" I asked, jumping up and turning to go outside.

"Logan," Alex called and I hesitated. "When my parents were murdered in front of me, I asked myself questions like that. I asked why them and not me? Why didn't someone stop it? Where were their Guardians while they were being killed?"

I turned to face Alex. Her eyes were so gentle, so knowing.

"What I learned was that whether or not I can fathom it, whether or not I agree with it, everyone and everything in this life has a purpose," she said. "I may never know what purpose their deaths served, but I can tell you that you wouldn't be here talking to me today. Willow wouldn't exist, and I would not have experienced the kind of supernatural joy and love that is waiting for us on the other side of this life if they hadn't. There's a purpose that is bigger than you, bigger than all of us, that brought you here today. No one is asking you to accept what happened to you and to those girls that evening, but you have to make a decision. Are you going to get angry and walk away from all of this? Or will you fight to find your purpose in it?"

Standing there, I thought about everything Alex said as she and Willow watched me, waiting to see what I would do. I felt stifled, as though I were choking on a reality I hadn't seen coming.

"I need air," I said, turning for the front door.

"Logan!" Willow shouted after me, but I heard Alex tell her to let me go.

Walking out onto the porch, I let the warm mountain air fill me. I breathed it in and tried to steady myself and the storm of confusion and bitterness that raged within. My thoughts were jumbled and I tried to make sense of them. The implications of what I'd just learned were vast and my understanding could barely breech the surface. One question prevailed through it all: *If Miguel was my Guardian, would I ever see him again?*

Sitting on the porch swing, I remembered the last things he'd said to me. He told me that I didn't need him anymore, that he wasn't meant to go with me. As I rocked, I understood what he meant. This was my journey, my path to take. Alex was right, I had to choose which way to go for myself. As I stared off into the afternoon sky, the storm within dissipated and I knew what I had to do. I'd known it all along, I just didn't know how to go on, how to keep fighting.

Before long Donovan's truck pulled up the driveway. He got out and looked at me as he climbed the steps. I watched as he paused at the door, then turned to sit beside me. For a while we just sat looking out into the lush mountain landscape until I finally broke the silence.

"I'm sorry I got your daughter involved in this," I said.

Donovan nodded and turned over his wedding ring with his fingers as he looked down to his lap.

"You didn't get her involved in anything," he said. "This was her purpose, part of a greater plan, and I'll be forever thankful that she is involved. As scared as I am for her, being involved with you helped her to see what she couldn't before."

"What's that?" I asked.

"The truth," he said. "She made a choice to bring you here today. She is choosing to fight with you in this. You need to make a choice too."

"Your wife said something very similar to me," I said. "You two are very in tune with one another. It's a beautiful thing."

"Well, we share a very special bond. We've been through a lot together," he said. "I almost lost her a couple of times. It was my responsibility to keep her safe and I almost failed a long time ago.

So I never take one moment for granted. Each day we have in this world together is a gift."

I looked at him, studying the way his intense, blue eyes warmed when he spoke about Alex.

"So you remember then? You remember being her Guardian?" I asked.

Donovan nodded. "I remember it like you'd remember a vivid dream, or a distant memory from your childhood. What's crystal clear in my mind is waking up in that hospital bed and seeing here there and knowing that I never wanted to be without her."

"How did you do it?" I asked, bowing my head. "How did you save her from someone that wanted her dead?"

Donovan looked up at me and unleashed the fierceness of his gaze.

"What you're really asking is how you're going to save those runners tomorrow from this person who wants them dead. The answer is the same, Logan. You fight and you never stop fighting because it's the responsibility you've been charged with. You may not be a Guardian, Logan, but I believe you're meant to protect those people, just like I'm meant to help you do it. Is that something you think you can do?"

Looking back out at the mountains which seemed to roll on forever into the distance, I thought about Simone and Faith, of Miguel and Grace. All mentors with a part in shaping me into what I was becoming. I was thankful for them all, for bringing me to this magnificent place and to this crossroads where I would decide my fate. Again I was given the chance to choose, much like that evening all those years ago when I chose to send a text that would end two lives. This time I would choose life.

"Let's stop this monster," I said reaching out my hand.

Donovan took it and we shook hands. Then Donovan stood to go inside, but I remained on the bench, one final question on my mind for him.

"Donovan," I said and he paused. "Did you see it? Did you see heaven? What was it like?"

Donovan opened the door and when he looked at me, I saw the peace of eternity on his face. "I came close enough to it to know that it's beyond anything I can possibly describe. You'll see it for yourself someday."

With a nod, went into the house. I lingered a minute longer as a nameless joy came over me, filling me with peace and renewed strength. Breathing in one more breath of the mountain air, I stood and followed him inside.

Willow ran to me and grabbed my hand. I looked at her and squeezed it tight as we went into the kitchen where Donovan and Alex sat at the kitchen table. We joined them and Donovan gave us the news.

"I called my buddy in the Raleigh PD. The marathon deaths have been ruled a homicide. They found high aconitum alkaloid levels in their liver and kidneys."

"What does that mean?" I asked "Poison?"

"Yes. Aconite poisoning, the oldest trick in the murder-by-poison book, but also the least traceable. In bigger doses it causes heart complications that mimic heart attack symptoms," he answered.

"Buy why would someone want to kill runners and make it look like they died of a heart attack?" Willow asked.

"That's what we have to find out." I ran my hand through my hair. "You said that they found the poison in their liver and kidneys. That means the poison was ingested, right?"

"That's right," Donovan said. "Somehow those runners consumed it without knowing."

"Logan, Willow said earlier that you saved a man's life. Do you think he could give us any answers?" Alex asked.

"Maybe." I shrugged. "If he's awake and alert, he may be able to tell us something."

"I'm on it." Donovan retrieved his phone from his pocket. "I'm going to make a phone call, see if I can't get through to that victim."

"His name is Jason," I said and Donovan gave me a thumbs up as he walked out the door to make the call.

"I'm going to make up the spare bed and bring down some linens for the couch. You two look exhausted. Willow, you can borrow whatever you'd like from my closet and Logan, I think Donovan has some clothes that would fit you too," Alex said standing. "After a good meal and some rest, things will look better."

"Thank you," I said as she left the room.

Willow turned me to look at her. There was fear in her eyes. "While you were outside the news announced that tomorrow's race in Raleigh will go on as scheduled, but they're restricting the race area to volunteers and runners only. No one is allowed on or near the raceway unless they have a volunteer pass or a race number. They posted our pictures again, Logan. There's no way we're getting in there without being noticed."

"I've got that covered," Donovan said as he stepped back in and pocketed his phone. "My buddy is calling the Atlanta hospital now. I told him everything earlier. It took a whole lot of convincing and in the end I had to remind him that I saved his life, but he agreed to let you two into the race."

Willow brightened. "That's great, Dad."

"But he made me promise him something, Logan," Donovan continued. "I had to assure him that you would turn yourself over to him when all is said and done."

Willow looked at me and shook her head. "No."

I gave her hand a squeeze. "I told you I would turn myself in and I meant it. One way or another, tomorrow's race is the end. I have to go back. It's the right thing to do."

"His name is Derrick. He'll be waiting for you just outside the gate with your race numbers. He couldn't guarantee anything but a way in. If you're caught on the inside he'll plead ignorance," Donovan continued.

"Fair enough," I said just as Donovan's phone rang and he stepped back outside.

"If you go back now, they'll add more time to your sentence. They could move you to max security," Willow said.

I looked down at our joined hands and grinned. "No matter what happens, it's worth it."

Willow wrapped her arms around me and I let her warmth surround me as I breathed her in. I committed every second of this moment with her into my memory: the smell of her, the feel of her arms around me, and the way her body trembled against mine. We stayed that way until Donovan cleared his throat behind us. We let go of one another and turned to where he was standing in the doorway, his laptop in hand.

"So your victim, Jason, is alert and talking. He's being treated for Aconite poisoning but should make a full recovery," Donovan said, coming into the room.

"Oh, thank God." I blew out a relieved breath. "I just wish I'd have been able to do the same for the others. Does he have any idea when he ingested the Aconite?"

Donovan set his laptop on the table beside us and opened it. "He didn't know much, but he did say that he took a water from the mid-point water station. He said it tasted funny to him, so he only took one sip and threw out the rest."

"Wait," I said. "I drank a water from that station and it was fine."

"Maybe not all the water was poisoned," Willow said.

Donovan pulled up the race series website and clicked on the photo gallery.

"These are pics from today's race. Photographers typically set themselves up near the water stations to catch the runners as they slow down. Look closely at these photos and see if you can find anything strange," he said.

"I don't believe they put these pictures up of all these runners smiling and running on as if nothing happened," Willow said.

"This race series brings a lot of revenue to the hosting states. Thousands of people train for each of these races," Donovan explained. "Wouldn't be right to deny them their memories of it, good or bad."

Donovan flipped through the pictures. Countless faces flashed across the screen with each click. Nothing looked out of place. Looking in the background to the crowds of onlookers with their posters, I saw nothing but smiling faces as they cheered. Donovan clicked through for almost ten minutes until something in one of the photographs caught my eye.

"Wait, go back," I said. He went back a slide.

"There," I said, staring in awe at the screen when the back of Simone's visor-covered head filled the upper left corner. "Right next to the water table. It's her."

"Who?" Willow asked, squinting in front of the screen. "What are you seeing?"

I pointed to her blurry image and both she and Donovan leaned in as Alex entered the room.

"Simone," I answered, "How is it possible that she was caught on film?"

"Simone?" Alex asked and she too leaned into the screen to stare at where I pointed. "Are you sure that's her? The picture is blurry."

"I'm sure." I nodded. "She was wearing that visor. This is at the mid-point, exactly where I saw her run by."

Donovan zoomed in, focusing the screen on Simone's image.

"She's wearing race number 3135," he said. "Let's go to the runner's registry and see if that number is registered with a name."

Donovan started to click out of the picture when Willow held up a hand.

"Wait," she snapped. "Look at her hand. Zoom in on her hand."

Simone's hand which was partially hidden by a passing runner. When Donovan enlarged the screen there was a collective gasp. Simone's hand was poised over a water cup, a powdered substance falling from her fingers.

I looked again, unable to fathom what I was seeing. It didn't make any sense.

"It was her?" I mumbled, backing away. "She put the poison in those cups? But . . . that doesn't make any sense . . ."

"There has to be an explanation," Alex said as Donovan clicked off the picture and pulled up the runner registry.

I watched them scan the list over Donovan's finger when their eyes finally landed on number 3135. Willow was the first to turn to me, her face grave.

"Her number is registered as Simone Kennedy," she said. "She's not dead, Logan."

The last thing I saw before everything went dark was Willow's arms as she tried to catch me before I hit the floor.

Fifteen

"He'll be fine, he's just exhausted and in shock," I heard Alex say as I drifted towards consciousness.

When I opened my eyes I was on the couch. Alex and Willow stood beside me. I sat up and rubbed by eyes and they turned to me, sympathy and worry on their faces.

"How are you feeling?" Willow asked.

Disoriented and exhausted, it took a minute for my mind to clear. When it came back to me I felt woozy all over again.

"I don't understand," I whispered and they came to sit beside me. "How could she not be dead? And if she's alive, then how is she visiting me as a Guardian? What's happening?"

Alex patted my back. "Those are questions that I can't answer for you. All I can tell you is that the answers will come."

"We have to focus on what we do know, and what we have to do," Donovan said from where he leaned against the wall. "What we do know is that Simone, if it is her, is responsible for poisoning runners and that the next race is tomorrow, in your home town. We have to stop her from doing it again."

I got to my feet. "Did you look to see if she was registered for the race?"

Donovan shook his head. "She's not registered under that name, but it doesn't mean she won't be there. There's a possibility she registered under a different name to keep from drawing suspicion."

"Are you up for this?" Willow asked, coming to stand by my side.

"I have to get to the bottom of this, more now than ever," I said. "We need to leave soon, get there early in case they start the race early again."

"Please, won't you stay long enough for a meal and a couple of hours of rest?" Alex pleaded. "You won't be good to anyone of you pass out again. Please, stay a few more hours."

I looked at Willow who shrugged at me. "I guess it couldn't hurt to stay for a while longer, Logan. We both need some rest and we haven't eaten since this morning."

I considered it a minute, knowing that they were right. As much as I wanted to get to Raleigh, I knew I'd be no good once I got here if I didn't take time to rest.

I smiled at Alex. "Do you have any string coffee? We're going to need it in a few hours."

"Oh, you definitely came to the right place," Alex winked. "I'll get some dinner started."

By the time I pushed away from the dinner table I had eaten three bowls of homemade beef stroganoff. My belly was full and my head heavy as I started to collect plates from the table to take to the sink.

"That was the best meal I've eaten in over a decade," I said to Alex who took the plates from me and bade me to sit back down.

"I can't imagine what they must feed you in that place," she said.

I chuckled. "Whatever you imagine would be much better than reality."

Donovan stood to help clear the table. "Willow, why don't you two go through my closet and find some clean clothes for Logan. If the prison showers are anything like basic training, I imagine our humble tub will feel like paradise."

"You have no idea. Thank you so much for your hospitality," I said, following Willow upstairs.

She started the shower, then disappeared into the furthest room in the hall. Peeking into the room beside me, I smiled at the purple paint and bright flowers that covered the walls and furniture in what must have been the room where Willow grew up. Glow-in-the-dark stars covered the ceiling and the bed was adorned with stuffed animals.

I imagined what her life had been like growing up in such a loving home. It made me miss my own parents. With a sinking heart, I resolved to call them when this was all over. For the first time, I looked forward to a visit from them.

"Here you go, these should fit," Willow said as she handed me a pile of sweats topped with socks and a pair of black running shoes. "The shoes are for tomorrow, so we actually look the part this time."

"I'll have to thank your dad again," I said. "Your parents are amazing."

"Yeah . . . they are." Our eyes locked as her hand brushed against mine when I took the clothes from her. "I'm going to use the shower in their room. Do you need anything else?"

"No, you guys have done more than enough," I assured her.

"I'll see you in the morning then," she said with a smile, going back down the hall.

"Willow?" I said, and she turned back to me. "Thank you for bringing me here, for taking me to your home."

"No Logan, thank you for bringing ME home," she said with a grin, then disappeared into her parent's room.

An hour later I was clean, full, and laying on the couch while the last of the evening sunlight fought its way through the slats in the blinds. Setting my watch alarm for 2 am, I closed my eyes and tried to clear my mind enough to sleep, but there was so much to think about. I thought of Miguel, and was saddened. There was so much I wished I could say to him, but I knew I'd never see him again in this life. And I thought of Simone. Could she really be alive somewhere, somehow? That would mean I hadn't killed her after all, that I'd been wrongly convicted. Everything inside me screamed that was wrong. I'd seen what I did. There was no coming back from that.

Above all though, my thought circled around one question. Why? Why did she poison those runners? Why did she come to me to stop her?

As desperate as my mind was for answers, my body was just as desperate for sleep. I found my mind drifting in and out of consciousness. My last conscious thoughts were of rolling mountains, of a couple's love that had endured through space and time, and of Willow's warm arms around me. Soon my mind eased and I drifted off to sleep.

"Logan."

From the brink of consciousness, I heard someone whisper my name.

"Logan." The whispered came again.

I opened my eyes and groggily looked down at my watch. It was a quarter to 2am.

"Logan."

I recognized that voice. My heart sped as I sat up and searched the dark room. A cool breeze ruffled my hair and when I looked over I saw that the front door stood open. Rising, I went to it and looked out into the starless night.

Simone sat on the front stairs, her white dress and fiery hair floating on the breeze behind her. Her head lay in her hands as she wept. She turned to me when I approached and my breath caught in my throat.

"Logan," she whispered.

"It was you. All this time, it was you . . ." I stammered, not daring to get any closer to her. "Why?"

"I'm so sorry," she said, anguish twisting her angelic face. "You have to stop it, Logan. You have to save them."

"Save them from you!" I tried to keep my voice down, but it came out as an angry shout, every inch of me vibrating.

Simone lowered her head and took in a ragged breath. "You can't understand, Logan. Not yet."

"You're right, I can't understand. Why would you kill those people? How did you do it?" I asked, outraged. "I don't understand any of this."

"You have to stop it," she repeated.

"Stop you," I clarified. "How many more will you kill, Simone? How many will die tomorrow?"

Simone raised her blurry head. Tears streamed from her green eyes.

"Thousands," she whispered.

The air rushed from my lungs, I stumbled back into the railing. "Thousands?"

Simone stood. She climbed the steps and reached her hand out to me, but I backed away.

"You have to stop it, you must," she pleaded. "Before it's too late."

"How?" I asked. "How can I stop it? Tell me!"

Suddenly Simone's eyes shifted. I heard a startled gasp. I turned to where Willow stood in the doorway, her blue eyes transfixed on Simone.

"Logan . . ." she whispered shakily.

I looked from Simone to Willow. A single tear escaped onto Willow's cheek as she took a step closer to Simone. I went to her, wrapping my arm around her to hold her back.

"You see her, don't you?" I asked.

Willow nodded a yes and smiled, not letting Simone leave her sight. Simone took a breath, like the breeze through the blackened trees, and stepped closer to her. When she did I stepped between them.

"You stay away from her," I spat at Simone, but Willow stopped me.

"It's okay," she said laying her hand on mine. "She's the most glorious thing I've ever seen."

I stepped aside and watched Simone's face soften as she looked at Willow.

"I have a message for you too," Simone said to her, stepping even closer. "Your Gram wants you to know that she is proud of you, of the woman you've become. She says to keep dreaming. She looks forward to seeing you again one day."

Willow's bit her lip as she bowed her head and wept. Then wiping the tears away, she looked back up at Simone.

"Thank you," Willow whispered.

Simone turned back to me, her brow furrowed. "You must hurry Logan, you have to end this. You're the only one who can."

"How?" I asked as Simone's image faded into the night. "What do you want me to do?"

"Find me," she said as she vanished into the breeze. "And stop me."

When she was gone, Willow turned me to her. "I saw her . . . She's a Guardian, Logan."

"How can you be sure?" I asked. "I'm not even sure she's from heaven anymore."

Willow wiped her face with her fingers. "She is, Logan. She's from heaven. Gram always called me a dreamer. We used to bake together all the time. I would daydream with her about one day opening a bakery and selling her famous oatmeal cookies. She always told me to never stop dreaming."

"You went from baker to criminal psychologist?" I asked, brushing the hair from her face. "That's quite a leap."

"I guess I forgot how to dream." Willow took a deep breath and then straightened. "But none of that is important right now. What did Simone say before I came outside? Did she tell you about the race tomorrow?"

"She said that thousands will fall tomorrow." I stepped away from Willow, the panic rising again from my gut.

"Thousands?" she shrieked? "What do we do?"

I looked down at my watch and then back up at Willow. "We have to leave now. We have to get to the bottom of this before it's too late."

Willow ran back into the house. "I'll get my parents up."

I stared up into the black sky, terror and desperation clawing at me chest.

"I need you right now, more than ever," I said to the heavens. "Show me the way to stop this."

Taking a deep breath, I went back into the house as Donovan and Alex came down the stairs with Willow behind them. Donovan was in full uniform, his car keys in hand.

"Let's go," he ordered going to the door.

"No, no I can't let you do this . . ." I protested, but Donovan wouldn't let me finish.

"We'll get there faster if I take you, and you can use all the help you can get," he interrupted.

"It's aiding and abetting . . . harboring a fugitive," I protested, but Donovan just walked to Alex and gave her a kiss. Then he was out the front door.

"Only if we get caught," he yelled back.

Willow shrugged. Then she gave her mom a hug and followed him out the door. I turned to Alex. She smiled and ran the back of her hand down my cheek.

"Take care of my family," she said. "They'll take care of you."

I knelt down and kissed her on the cheek. Then I turned on my heels with a sigh and walked out the front door. Donovan's brought his SUV roaring to life as I climbed into the back seat. Willow grabbed my hand.

"We're going to stop it," she assured me as Donovan traversed the winding roads that took us away from Saluda.

Looking out the window, I watched the mountains' blackened peaks reach into the night sky. I burned the scenery into my mind to keep me company those long nights that awaited me in my cell. If I ever got out of prison, I knew I would come back here, to this secluded haven in the sky. Even if I didn't, this would be the place I'd think of, the place I'd travel back to in my mind when I closed my eyes amidst the coughing and the snores around me.

When the mountains were behind us, Donovan sped up. We soared down I-40. The sparse traffic on the roads in the wee hours of the morning moved aside to let us pass. Donovan was right, traveling in his police vehicle was much faster. I looked at him through the rear view mirror.

"I don't know how to thank you for helping me, for trusting me when you have no reason to," I said.

Donovan looked up into the mirror, the sharp edges of his face stern.

"Don't thank me yet. It's not you I am putting my trust in here, it's what you're seeing that I believe in," he said. "I believe you've been charged with this responsibility, Logan, and that is reason enough for me to do whatever I can to help."

"Whatever the reason," I said, "thank you both. I've felt like myself again these twenty-four hours, not just a criminal."

Willow turned to me and smiled tenderly. "You were never a criminal, Logan. What happened all those years ago was a mistake. Having to spend even one more night in jail after what you're doing to save these people will be the real crime."

"I escaped prison, kidnapped you, stole two vehicles, and waved a loaded gun around in a crowd of a thousand of people," I said, chuckling. "I'm pretty sure that last one's considered aggravated assault."

Donovan raised an eyebrow at me in the mirror as Willow shrugged.

"Well, when you put it that way . . ." She huffed and I turned back to my window with a smile.

We made it to Raleigh just before 5:30 am. The tall buildings of the downtown, sparkling and lighting up the pre-dawn sky, towered above us as we followed the signs to the race-day designated parking. When we were parked, Donovan turned to me and Willow.

"Okay, so here's the plan," he said. "Once we get your bib numbers from Derrick, you both scan the corrals for Simone. Any sign of her, you take her down any way possible. Can you do that?"

"Absolutely," I answered.

"What if we can't find her?" Willow asked.

"We have to," I said. "The race is broken up into waves, remember? We're going to have about five minutes to look through each wave before they're released onto the course. We take it a section at a time."

"Good," Donovan agreed. "In the meantime, Derrick and I will find a way to cover the water cups before the runners come through in case she gets by you. She won't be able to drop anything in them without us seeing. It's not much, but it's all we have."

"Can't you do something to stop the race?" I asked, "Can't your cop friend order them to call it off?"

"If it were up to him, it would have been called off yesterday. Unfortunately, it's up to the town government and they won't listen to a couple of hysterical cops. This race is a money maker for them. No way they're going to call it off and refund all those runners without proof," he said. "It's up to us to find her and stop her."

With a nod, we made our way to the starting line. As we turned the corner, a familiar structure loomed in the distance. The starting line sat adjacent to Central Prison, its exterior lighting illuminating the course.

"Looks like we've come full circle," I said to Willow who shot me a grave look as we walked on.

Donovan spotted his friend's patrol car parked just outside the race entrance. He waved as the man got out to greet us. A slender man, Derrick's tanned face sported laugh lines at his mouth and forehead, but right now he looked anything but happy to see us. He glared at me before shaking Donovan's hand.

"I have a bad feeling about this, Pritchard. They're saying these two had something to do with the deaths at the Atlanta race, and you want me to let them into this one? Not to mention this man," he said, pointing to me, "is an escaped convict."

Donovan patted his friend on the shoulder.

"I know it's a lot to ask, but you're going to have to trust me on this," Donovan assured him. "Logan is instrumental in helping to stop this. Willow's my daughter, Derrick."

Derrick looked at all of us, then ran a hand down his face with a sigh.

"Tell me what your plan is," he said.

"We have a good lead on the woman who's responsible for these deaths," Donovan continued.

"Woman?" Derrick asked, surprised.

"We think her name is Simone Kennedy. We went through the pictures that were posted to the race series web site from the race yesterday. If you look closely, one of the pictures shows her putting the aconite powder into a water cup as she ran by. We have reason to believe that she's going to strike a larger number of runners today."

"How much larger?" he asked, looking sideways at Donovan.

"Could be in the thousands," Donovan said.

"Thousands?" he cried. "Then we have to stop this race right now."

Donovan shook his head and looked his friend in the eye.

"It's just our word we're going on here, and we don't have time to argue the big-wigs about this. There's no way they're going to send thousands of runners from all parts of the country packing. They won't believe the truth."

Derrick motioned to me and Willow. "What are these two going to be able to do about it then?"

"I've seen her," I said, stepping forward. "So has she. If we can get to that starting line, we can find her before she even starts the race. We'll turn her over to the authorities."

Derrick thought about it for a minute. "The authorities are at the starting line looking for you two. You'll have find this Simone person before they find you. If you do, you turn her in and yourself too. That was the deal. It's back to Central for you."

Willow grabbed my hand and I looked at her and nodded.

"As soon as Simone's in custody, I'll go with them willingly," I agreed.

Willow squeezed my hand and I grinned at her reassuringly as Derrick reached into his car and pulled out two race bibs. He handed them to us.

"Where's the first water station?" I asked, pinning the bib to the front of my shirt.

"It's at the 4 mile mark," Derrick answered.

"Derrick and I will position ourselves there," Donovan said. "We'll find a way to cover the waters in case she gets past you."

"She won't," I assured.

"What does this woman even look like?" Derrick asked.

"Red hair, green eyes. She has a scar along the left side of her face," Willow said.

"She'll be wearing a white visor," I added. "But she's not going to get past us."

"We'll see about that." Derrick chided and then looked at his watch. "You two get going. Runners will be lining up by wave into the corrals shortly. If you get caught out there, this conversation never took place."

"Understood," I said.

Willow and I jogged off towards the corals as the first of the runners began to arrive.

"We should split up. They'll be looking for the two of us. If one of us gets caught then at least the other will have a chance to stop Simone," Willow said.

"Okay," I agreed. "I'll take the right side, you take the left. Try to stick close to people, make yourself look like part of a group. Keep your head down."

"Got it," she said, turning to leave.

On an impulse, I grabbed her hand and spun her back around. I took her in my arms.

"This may be my last chance," I said, bending down to press my lips to hers.

At first Willow bristled with the shock of the sudden kiss, but then she sank into it, her arms going around me. She kissed me back passionately, and a warmth grew between us, melding our very souls together. I never wanted to let go of her, wanting instead to get lost in the renewed life set alight within me by her touch.

When I pulled away there were tears in both of our eyes. I ran my hand through her hair and tried to smile at her though my heart was breaking. We both knew that this was our first and last moment together like this. Soon it would all be over and I would spend an unknown amount of years in jail. *It was still worth it, if for nothing more than this moment*, I though as I took Willow's hand. She squeezed mine back.

"Let's do this," I said.

She nodded and she wiped the tears from her eyes. "Good luck, Logan."

When she jogged off to the other side of the coral, I took a deep breath and steeled myself for the task at hand. I scanned the crowd of runners that began to form around us for Simone. When a group of four men laughed and joked in the corner, I stood close to them and tried to blend in as I watched new runners enter the coral.

The sun peeked above the horizon, shooting rays of gold and lavender across the sky above. As the crowd multiplied, I moved down the coral, looking at each person as they passed. An uneasy feeling came over me as I searched their oblivious faces. There were so many of them, too many. Older women, young boys barely out of grade school, friends, family, were all gathered at the starting line. I remembered the people who fell at the last race, the unlucky winners of a random cup of tainted water. Then I remembered what Simone said the night before. *Thousands will fall* . . . White hot panic seized my chest me with a sudden realization. Simone wasn't coming.

My heart pounding, I searched the growing numbers for Willow. I fought through the crowd to the other side of the corral where I found her lingering among a group of women by the sidewalk. Grabbing her arm, I brought her with me to the center of the crowd.

"What's the matter?" she asked. "Did you find her?"

I shook my head. "She's not coming."

"What?" Willow asked, startled. "What are you talking about?"

"Think about it." I ran a hand through my hair and looked around at the crowd, then I turned back to Willow. "How was she going to poison all of these people on her own? She wouldn't be able to get to a thousand cups before someone caught her."

Willow's eyes widened. "You think she has help?"

"No, she said to find 'her' and stop it. She didn't say find 'them'."

"Then what?" Willow asked. "How do you know she's not coming?"

"Because," I said as the announcer shouted into his bull horn for the first wave to line up. "I think she was already here."

"What? Why would she . . ." Willow started to ask. Then the confusion on her face was replaced by cold dread. "You think she already poisoned the water. All of it?"

"I don't know why I didn't think of it before," I said. "The very first race, only one person died just minutes from the finish line. Why not more? And why did he make it so far. The next race only three fell. I'm willing to bet that they didn't make it as far. Yesterday most of the runners who fell didn't make it a mile after they swallowed the poison."

"What does this all mean?" Willow asked, her voice rising as she looked at me.

"Simone was perfecting the dose," I said, looking her in her startled eyes. "She was waiting for this race. This race was her main target all along. Her hometown race. Those others were just practice for her. That's why she said to find her and stop 'it' . . . because she's the only one that knows that 'it' has already been done. She poisoned the water jugs."

"Oh my God!" Willow's face turned frantic as she looked around at the innocent women, children and men surrounding us. "What do we do?"

I turned in terror to the front of the line where the elite runners stretched and tightened their laces to prepare for the start of the race. The first wave was about to be released onto the course.

"We have to beat these runners to the first water station," I said, grabbing her hand and making my way through the crowd. "We can't let them drink that water!"

"It's four miles away!" Willow shouted through the crowd. "Is there a cut-through?"

"I don't know, and there's no way to find out," I yelled back as we squeezed through to the font of the coral. "If we start asking questions or veer off course, they'll nail us before we ever get there. This is our only shot."

"I don't know if I can do this," Willow yelled, her voice a shrill cry.

"Just run as fast as you can," I assured her. "These guys are going to pace themselves at the beginning. If we can get ahead of them and hold the pace, we can beat them to the water station. We can make it there before them, we can do it. Just run, run as if . . ."

"My life depended on it?" Willow asked with a nervous grin.

"No," I said, turning her to face the crowd where thousands of excited and smiling faces flooded the corrals behind us. "As if theirs did."

Willow turned back to the starting line and took in a deep, shaky breath. I squeezed her hand as we waited for the gunshot that would release the first wave. As the huge LED clock above the starting line counted backwards from ten, the crowd collectively shouted each number. At five, Willow and I dropped one another's hand and I gave her a final encouraging nod. At two, I took in a deep breath and focused on the road ahead. One!

The gun fired in the air and I took off with the elite runners down the strait-away, Willow close on my heels. Fueled by adrenaline and panic, I rounded the first turn ahead of everyone else. I dared not look back, afraid to take even one second to see how far behind the others were. Footsteps pounded the pavement behind me. I prayed it was Willow.

My side ached and my legs burned with each labored step. When I'd passed a few blocks, I could hear the first band in the distance. I picked up my pace, knowing I was near the end of the first mile. One down, three to go.

Rounding the corner, I could see a marching band lined up on the sidewalk beside the course. Beyond them was the first mile marker. I jetted past, my footfalls doubling the beat of the *Iron Man* theme song they played. Band members stopped playing to gawk at me as I sprinted past, but I didn't dare slow even as my breath began to come in short gasps.

By the time I heard the next band in the distance, my lungs burned and my body screamed for me to slow down, but I ignored it all. I busied my mind with thoughts of Simone and Faith, and of the eight runners who had lost their lives too soon. This was my penance, my redemption, and if I hyperventilated on the side of the road, that was fine. I could die on the pavement, a shriveled husk, as long as I stopped the thousands of people behind me from drinking the water.

The next band was perched on an overpass above the course. I could barely see them as they played. My eyes were blurred with sweat. Bluesy jazz filled the air as I sprinted past the 2 mile marker. My side throbbed and my shallow breaths started to become labored.

My body and mind screamed at me to stop, to slow down, but like an insatiable taskmaster, my spirit drove my legs forward. I pushed faster past the band at the three mile marker whose music was lost to me, drowned out by the pounding of my heart and wheezing in my head. When I rounded the next corner, I could see in my peripheral that Willow was no longer on my heels, but further down the course. Her face was red, but her stride was strong. Ahead of her, two men were closing in on me. Flanking me on both sides, they upped their pace to catch me.

By the time I heard the fourth band in the distance, the men were beside me and threatening to pass. I closed my eyes, focusing all of my being into my legs. When I opened them again I saw the band on a street corner, opposite the water station on my right. Hard rock filled the air as I pulled forward, my knees threatening to buckle beneath me. Through my blurred vision, I saw Donovan and Derrick placing a sheet over the filled cups of water. They instructed volunteers to reach beneath it to grab the cups to hand to the crowd.

"No . . . water!" I tried to yell, but my voice was a horse croak as I charged forward towards the table, locking eyes with Donovan.

"No water!" I yelled again as I waved, but again my voice refused to work.

The volunteers stretched out their cup-filled hands as we approached, three wide. When the runner to my right reached out, I dove into the volunteer and knocked the water from her hands. Then went after the next volunteer, ignoring the curses being shouted to me by the runners.

"No water!" I croaked again to Donovan. "It's in the water!"

He finally understood my hoarse words and sprang into action, running to the closest volunteer and knocking the water from their hands.

"No one gets water from this station!" he yelled to the crowd of elite runners who passed by agitated and confused, but compliant.

I ran to the water table and threw it on its side, sending hundreds of small white cups rolling across the sidewalk. Then I spun around to make sure there were no more being handed out. When I was assured that no one was drinking the water, I leaned over and put my hands on my knees to catch my breath.

"Are you crazy?" the volunteer manning the water cooler screamed at me. "What the hell are you doing?"

"There's . . . poison . . . in the water," I panted.

"No there's not," The guy scoffed at me, anger making the veins in his bony temples bulge. "My partner and I filled every cooler on this course ourselves last night. There's nothing in the damned water!"

Donovan placed his hand on my shoulder and squatted down to look in my eyes.

"Are you sure about this, Logan?" he asked. "Because if not, she could be running to the next station right now."

I nodded my head violently as I stood upright.

"I'm sure of it. It's in the water, all of it." I said with a gulp of air. "We have to shut down all the stations."

"Like hell we will," The volunteer screamed. "Those people will dehydrate without water stops. You could kill someone!"

"If they drink the water, they're all dead!" I shouted back.

"You'd better be damned sure of this, Foster," Derrick growled.

"It's in the coolers," I panted. "I know it . . ."

"If you're wrong, Donovan and your girlfriend will be tried for malicious mischief with you. You'll all be in jail."

"I'll prove it. Pour me a cup," I said to the volunteer.

He hesitated, made uneasy by my conviction. With a sigh, he grudgingly filled a fresh paper cup from the water cooler beside him and handed it to me.

"Logan, I should be the one to do this," Donovan said, trying to take the cup from me. "If anything happens, I've lived a full and incredible life."

I ripped the cup away from his grasp.

"This is my responsibility, not yours. Not this time," I said, quickly tilting the cup to my lips.

"No!" Willow screamed from behind me. I turned to see her running up as the liquid hit my tongue.

The water tasted rancid. My tongue numbed as soon as the bitter liquid touched it. I spit it out onto the ground, coughing violently. I glared up at Donovan through glazed eyes.

"Stop those runners, now! This race is over!" Donovan screamed to Derrick who nodded, wide eyed. He grabbed his radio and began ordering his officers to detain the runners and quarantine the water supply.

Willow took my face in her hands and used her shirt to wipe out the inside of my mouth.

"This guy is faking it," the volunteer said. "I'm not going down for this. My partner can vouch for me. The water was clean!"

"Simone got to the water supply," Willow said to Donovan.

"Yeah, that's her. Simone, my partner," the volunteer snapped. "She'll tell you, the water was fine last night."

I pushed away from Willow and cleared my throat, my tongue now burning. "Your partner's name is Simone? What did she look like?"

Donovan and Willow came to stand behind me. The volunteer looked from me to Willow and his eyes widened as he stepped back.

"Wait a minute, I know you two," he said. "You're the ones from the news."

Leaning over the downed table, I grabbed the man by his collar and yanked him to me.

"What did she look like?" I asked again through gritted teeth.

"Red hair, green eyes. Kind of hot if it weren't for that scar on her face," he blurted out and I dropped him.

"Do you know where she lives?" Donovan asked.

"Yeah, she lives at 1100 King William Street, right off of Oberlin Drive. I dropped her off last night," he said. "Good luck finding her, though. When I went by there to pick her up this morning she was nowhere to be found. She left me to haul all those water coolers by myself."

Donovan looked at me as I wiped the sweat from my brow. "Do you know where that is?"

"I know exactly where it is," I nodded solemnly. "It's my old neighborhood. The street where I hit her. That's where she lived before . . ."

The volunteer nudged Derrick's arm. "Officer, he's the guy from the news, right? Shouldn't you be arresting him?"

Derrick glared at me, waiting for my next move. I turned to Donovan.

"I have to go to her," I pleaded. "I have to know."

Willow put her arm around me and looked at her father. Donovan sighed, nodding his head.

"I'll drive you," he said. "We can cut across this next street and follow Western Boulevard back the car. It will be faster."

"No one is going anywhere," Derick said, resolute. "That wasn't the deal. I just pissed off thousands of runners, hundreds of volunteers, and a handful of state officials. You're staying right here to help me explain this mess. Then it's back to where you belong. I'm already in enough trouble here."

"He's coming with me, Derrick. You do what you have to do, but we have to find Simone. It's the only way to clear Logan's name," Donovan said. We followed him down the sidewalk to the next street.

"I have to call this in, Prichard," he called after us. "I can't just let him walk away! Damn it!"

Donovan walked on unaffected. We followed him down the side street to Western Boulevard where the prison loomed, monstrous, beside us. The burning spread to my throat. I coughed as I stared at the prison's high brick walls and razor-wired fences.

"We have to pick up the pace or we'll never make it out of here. Can you jog it back to the car?" Donovan asked.

We nodded and jogged with him. I made it a few blocks when the burning in my throat spread to my chest. It was hard to catch my breath. Stopping, I bent over to suck in air, the sidewalk tilting and whirling beneath me.

"I'm okay," I said to Willow when she doubled back for me. I knew it was a lie.

"I'm just tired," I assured" "I have to do this."

"We're almost to the car," Donovan said. "Stay here. I'll grab it and pull up."

Donovan ran off and Willow bent down beside me.

"Why did you do that?" She demanded. "Why did you drink that water? Are you still trying to get yourself killed?"

Having caught my breath, I stood and faced her.

"It was the only way to know for sure. I couldn't let you and your dad face the consequences if I was wrong."

"It wasn't the only way," she said, her voice rising. "We could have found another way. Someone else could have tried it."

"Someone like your dad? Because he was about to try it himself," I said. "Look behind you, Willow."

Willow turned and faced the prison as the sun, still low in the sky, cast a shadow over the ominous facility.

"That is my future over there," I said, motioning to it. "That is what I have to look forward to in life. It was better me than *anyone* else."

Willow lowered her head, defeated. She looked at me, anguish in her ocean eyes.

"You have to go to the hospital then, let them check you out at least," she begged.

"You know I can't do that. Not until I find out the truth," I sighed. "I'm fine. I spit it out before I swallowed it. I just sprinted four miles in less than twenty minutes. I'm exhausted, that's all."

Before Willow could argue, Donovan pulled up and we climbed into the SUV as sirens wailed in the distance.

"We're about to have company," Donovan said. "Where am I going?"

"Follow this to Martin Luther King, then take a left onto Raleigh Boulevard," I said, my stomach lurching with the car's movement. "Then a right onto New Bern and another right at King William. Her house was half-way down on the left."

"Sounds like it still is," Willow said as Donovan flipped the switch for his own siren.

We weaved in and out of the morning traffic, running red lights and blazing through stop signs. I gripped the door handle and kept my eyes shut as the inside of the car started to spin. I felt drunk. The burning pain in my chest intensified and my limbs felt rubbery, like they were floating apart from my body. I knew I was in trouble, that enough of the poison had made it into my system to do damage, but I said nothing. I had to know the truth.

Opening my eyes, I tried to focus on Willow as she glanced back at me every few seconds. I silently prayed that she would one day move on from the trauma of the last few days, from the trauma she would sustain when I finally fell. I prayed that she would live a long and happy life, one without the worry and sorrow I had to offer.

Turning to the window, I watched as we turned into my old college neighborhood. I prayed for forgiveness for what I'd done the last time I drove this street. I prayed to make it long enough to see my redemption.

Donovan parked in front of 1100, but it felt as if the car was still moving. I held onto my seat to keep from falling into the floorboards. Willow hopped out and opened my door and I rushed through it, stumbling out onto the sidewalk. My stomach heaved and I threw up into the gutter.

"Dad!" Willow yelled and both she and Donovan were at my side.

"I'm okay," I said, holding up my hand to them. "I feel better now. Let's find Simone."

My stomach clenched and tightened. I felt unsteady on my feet, but I forced myself upright. Willow stared me down and reached out a hand to help me.

"We have to get you to a hospital, Logan. Please," she pleaded. "This isn't worth it."

I brushed her hand away and walked towards the house, while Donovan followed me closely.

"Yes it is," I said.

We passed the front gate lined with a row of evergreen bushes, and the house came into view. Its yellow paint and white trim seemed oddly cheerful for the circumstances. As I haved myself up the porch steps, I saw that the window shades were drawn. I leaned closer to get a peek through the cracks between them. The house was dark.

Willow pounded on the door, waited a few seconds, and then pounded again. When no one answered, she tried the knob.

"Locked," she said, looking at me. "Maybe no one's here."

"Let's try the back door," Donovan said, already headed for the side yard.

As we followed behind him, I looked into the windows on the side of the house, but again the shades were drawn and nothing but darkness emanated from the cracks between them. I kept one hand on the siding to steady myself as we rounded the house. My heart raced like a speeding locomotive in my chest.

In the back yard, an in-ground swimming pool sat nestled between blooming dogwood trees. A flowerbed filled with thousands of delicate purple flowers ran the length of the pool against the back fence. Whicker patio furniture adorned the small deck. We carefully stepped around each piece as we came to the sliding glass door.

I looked through the glass at the darkened living room and could see only a tan leather sofa drowned in shadow. Donovan reached into his back pocket and withdrew his phone. He clicked on the flashlight and held the light to the glass as we looked again.

"There!" Willow gasped as she pointed into the house. "Beside the fireplace!"

On the floor beside the brick, a splay of red hair caught the light. Frantic, I searched the deck and yard for something solid. I spotted a garden shovel leaning against the house beside the deck and darted to the stairs, but I lost my balance and pitched forward, stumbling down them. Willow ran to my side. I steadied myself against her and grabbed hold of the shovel.

"Step away from the door," I said to Donovan and with Willow's help, I climbed back up to the back door.

Donovan stepped aside as I took a deep breath and swung the shovel as hard as I could into the glass. The glass cracked as the shovel bounced off, and the exertion sent waves of pain throughout my chest. I doubled over and gasped for breath. Willow cried out, coming to my side.

"Dad, call 911. He needs emergency care now," Willow pleaded.

"No!" I croaked, pushing her out of the way to try and stand. "Please, no."

I was too close, Simone was right there in front of me. Fighting against the stabbing pain in my chest, I tried to lift the shovel again, but Donovan took it from my unsteady hands. As I panted, I looked into his face. I saw in his eyes that he understood my urgency, my need to get to the truth before it was too late.

Taking a step back, he lifted the shovel above his shoulder like a major league player at a home run derby. Then with one fluid stride, he swung the shovel into the door, shattering it into a million scattering shards that flickered with the sunlight as they fell to the ground.

When the glass settled, I staggered inside and flipped on the first light switch I could find. Soft light filled the room, illuminating the woman who lay motionless on the floor beside the fireplace. She was dressed in a white dress which flowed behind her on the floor. In her hand, she clasped a small purple flower.

Kneeling beside her, I lifted her head into my arms and brushed her red hair away from her face. For the first time, I looked clearly into the lovely young face, marred only by a thin, red scar that ran down the left side of her cheek. It was the same woman who had haunted me, who had warned me of the devastation to come, and who had guided me here to this house.

But it was not Simone.

"It's not her," I cried out. "This can't be Simone, not the same one I killed, at least. I don't understand . . ."

Donovan bent down to examine her. He put his fingers to the side of her neck.

"Logan?" Willow said, her voice no more than a whisper, behind me.

"She's too young," I said, the devastation hitting me as if I had killed her all over again. "Simone would be older by now, in her forties. This girl can't be more than twenty. I don't understand what's happening. Who is this?"

"Logan," Willow said again, louder, but I couldn't respond, couldn't speak. My mind was reeling, going a thousand different directions at once. Nothing made sense.

"Is this the woman you've been seeing?" Donovan asked as he checked for a pulse.

"Yes." I breathed, a ragged breath. "That's her . . . I never saw her face this clearly, this close. This is the woman I've been seeing, but it's not the woman that I killed. This is not Simone!"

"You're right, Logan," Willow said and I finally looked up to see her staring, stunned, at the mantle in front of her. "That's not Simone. I think you need to see this."

I stood, transfixed on Willow's eyes as she glared in awe at a row of frames on the mantle. The world around me spun as I stumbled to stand beside her. When I looked up at the mantle I stared into the real Simone's face from where she smiled back to me from half a dozen framed photographs. In many of them, Simone smiled goofily beside a younger Grace, the love of a mother and daughter forever captured in film.

My eyes skimmed past those to a larger photograph in the center of the mantle, and my breath left me in a sudden rush. I doubled over, my stomach clenching, but I glared at the eight by ten glossy image in utter shock.

In the picture, Simone was dressed in her running gear and visor as she posed proudly beside her jogging stroller, the same stroller I struck with my car that evening all those years ago. The stroller held not one, but two red-headed little girls of the same age. Their identical freckled faces smiled at the camera. Simone's baby girls.

"Twins?" I gasped, staggering backwards, as the room lost focus. "That can't be . . ."

"She has a pulse!" Donovan yelled and he tilted the woman's head back and checked for blockage.

I collapsed on the ground beside the woman, my head flooding with disjointed memories of that evening twelve years ago, of the overturned stroller, bent and broken in the ditch. A stroller which had held not one child, but two.

Willow knelt beside me and gasped as she looked into the girl's face.

"It's her," she said. "That's the Guardian I saw last night."

"How is it possible?" I asked, stunned. "She couldn't have been lying here for more than a few hours, right? I've been seeing her for days. How is that possible?"

"Where she's been, time doesn't exist" Willow said as a tear streamed down her face. "Just like with my dad, maybe she was given a second chance. You both were . . ."

Donovan looked at his daughter and she grabbed his hand and met his eyes. "That's how this works, doesn't it?" she asked him.

"Anything is possible," Donovan said, pride emanating from his gentle face. "Time is no obstacle for the one who sent her to you, Logan."

I sank onto my heels, my mind losing focus as I tried to understand it all. Willow looked back to the woman and reached for the purple flower clutched in her white hand.

"Don't touch it," Donovan warned. "Monkshood flower . . . Aconite."

"There were thousands outside . . ." Willow gasped and drew her hand back. "That's how she did it, that's how she poisoned those people."

"Wait," Donovan said, frantically pressing his fingers to the woman's neck again. "I lost the pulse. We're losing her."

He started chest compressions. "She must have eaten part of the flower."

"She can't die," I wheezed. "She can't."

"Willow, grab my phone and call 911." Donovan ordered. "Quickly."

"They're already here," she said as sirens screamed in the distance, gaining in volume as they approached.

When Donovan was finished with the first round, Willow leaned over the woman to breathe into her mouth.

"No!" I cried. "The poison . . . let me do it."

Bending over, I delivered two rescue breaths. Then I gulped for air, a spasm rocking my body. I fought to catch my breath before Donovan finished the next round of compressions, then I leaned in again. Flashing lights strobed into the house from the front windows, turning the room into a horrid blue and red disco.

When Donovan started a third round of compressions, there was a commotion on the back porch as Derrick, followed by two more officers, charged into the house, their guns held out in front of them.

"Derrick, call for the paramedics!" Donovan shouted. "Tell them to bring in the defibrillator!"

Derrick hesitated, the other officers waiting for his lead. He glared at me as I struggled to focus on him, then his eyes shifted to the woman on the ground. Lowering his gun, he grabbed his radio and called for an ambulance as the other two cops holstered their weapons and went to Donovan to help. Derrick kneeled beside me and looked the woman over.

"Is this her? Simone?" he asked.

"No," I said with a violent cough. "But she is the woman who killed those runners . . . who tried to kill them all today."

Donovan looked up from where he pressed into the woman's chest.

"She's got an aconite blossom in her hand, Derrick," he said, "There are thousands more growing outside."

Derrick stood and went to the back door to look out.

"My God," he whispered as the sound of another siren wailed in the distance.

"The ambulance is coming," Willow said, relived.

She looked at me and grabbed my hand. The warmth of her touch was lost to me, my hands and legs completely numb. I fought to keep her in my sight.

"Hang in there," she said. "You have to hold on for me."

Time and space sped around me and my head struggled to stay in the present, to stay conscious. The paramedics rushed into the room as Donovan was finishing another round of chest compressions. Donovan, Willow, and the officers made way. I crawled to the woman's head, running my fingers through her hair as they opened the bodice of her dress and inserted the paddles.

I looked down at her face and tears came to my eyes as I imagined her as a child, broken and torn in that ditch. Running my finger across the scar on her face, I tried to imagine her grief, her agony as she was forced to grow up without her mother and twin sister, all because of me.

When the paramedic called for all to clear, someone behind me dragged me away, but I held the woman in my eyes. When the first charge went off, her torso lifted briefly off of the floor and I closed my eyes. Remembering the anguish and despair that was so heavy in her eyes when she visited me from someplace beyond, I prayed that she would be given a second chance at life, a chance for redemption like I had been given. I prayed that despite the fact that she had taken lives, she would be given hers back to start again.

"Take me instead," I whispered. "Please, take me instead."

When the second charge went off, I forced my eyes open. Through blurred vision, I saw a paramedic raise his hand and then bend over to the woman's head.

"She's breathing," he announced and I dragged myself to her just as she opened her glossy emerald eyes.

"Logan?" she whispered, barely audible.

"I'm here," I said, fighting to see her clearly.

She reached up weakly with her empty hand and laid it atop mine. I expected to feel her static warmth against my skin, but her touch was cold.

"Did you stop it?" she asked. "Did you stop me?"

I nodded, fighting to take a shaky breath.

"Yes, we stopped it," I said, looking down to her. "It's over."

Tears formed in her eyes as she stared up at me, her lips quivering as she spoke.

"I was so angry," she said. "So angry that they could run, that they could go on running with smiles and music. That's all she ever wanted to do, Logan. My mom only ever wanted to keep running. She never got that chance. I didn't think they should either. So I used my mom's name to stop them. I couldn't see past my anger . . ."

A tear fell from my eyes. It landed on our joined hands.

"I am so sorry that I did this to you," I cried. "This is all my fault, everything."

The woman shook her head and smiled up at me, tears spilling from her own eyes.

"No, Logan, you saved me," she said. "You saved me from killing thousands more. I can see everything now, how our lives were always meant to entwine. You're a good man, you deserve this redemption. Take it and live your life without any more guilt. What I did is not your fault. You're not the villain of our story, Logan. I am."

The paramedics wheeled in a gurney and lifted the woman onto it, forcing her hand from mine. Laboring to stand, my legs barely held my weight as I forced them under me. I clasped onto the gurney before they could wheel her away.

"What is your name?" I asked. "I need to know."

"Hope." The woman grinned, a joyless smile. "My real name is Hope."

They wheeled her away. Wobbling, I started to collapse, but Willow caught me and held me up as my mind careened. Her name was Hope. Thinking back to the trial, my memories were fuzzy and disjointed. *How could I have not known?*

I remembered how Grace had pleaded to the judge for mercy. I thought, in my dismayed stupor, that she was trying to save me because she couldn't save Simone or Faith. Now I knew it had everything to do with Hope. She wanted us to move past the accident, to live on to honor what she'd lost. If only I had known.

I thought about all the things Grace said to me in that visitation room all those years ago: *Hope is still alive, still with me. Hope is not dead.* She was talking about Simone's living child all along, the one that had survived my greatest sin.

My legs buckled again and I sank to the floor, but this time Derrick caught me and supported me beneath my arm.

"I know you've been through a lot, Foster, but I'm afraid I have to take you into custody," he said as he escorted me out the back door.

Willow and Donovan followed after us.

"Leave him alone, he's sick! He needs help!" I heard Willow yell, but her voice sounded distant from where my mind wandered.

"The poison got into his system, Derrick," Donovan protested as Derrick helped me down the stairs and onto the lawn.

"You have to let him them take him to the hospital," Willow pleaded. "He's dying!"

Startled, Derek turned to look at Donovan and Willow. When he did, another white-hot spasm erupted in my body and I pitched forward, clutching at my chest. Derrick lost his grip on me and I staggered blindly forward.

As Willow screamed, I toppled over the side of the pool. The cold water enveloped me, a watery tomb, and swallowed my crippled body whole. I watched drowsily as bubbles floated up around me to the surface where Willow's beautiful face looked down on me. Then I closed my eyes and let myself be carried away into the cool darkness.

Sixteen

Into the abyss I sank, deeper and deeper. I became one with the darkness, with its insipid lifelessness, and resigned myself to reside in its obscurity forever. As I awaited the fires of hell to devour me, I thought only of Simone, Faith and Hope, of how different their lives would have been had I never existed. My only comfort in the murky depths came from the knowledge that I couldn't hurt them anymore.

As I sank deeper into my liquid grave, a flicker of light caught my eye. I watched it, dazed, as it sent shimmery rays throughout the blackened waters like a thousand glinting diamonds. Transfixed, I watched as a hand emerged from the light and grabbed hold of me. It pulled me towards the surface. The light intensified as I floated towards it. I had to close my eyes against its brilliance. My body eased and the pain dissipated and dissolved into the wake behind me. Then I was floating. A warmth unlike anything I had ever known enveloped me like a soft blanket as I was pulled to my feet.

"Logan," a gentle voice said.

Opening my eyes, I squinted as they adjusted to the silky luminance around me. There was no sky above or ground below my feet, only the warm glow that surrounded me. My mind was clear of all despair, anger, and worry as I gazed around at this light. For the first time in twelve years, I felt completely at peace.

"Logan," the voice said again and I turned towards it.

She stood behind me, dressed in a cloud of shimmering gold. Her red hair flowed in waves behind her and her serene face held the wisdom of a thousand years. When she smiled, her jade eyes came alight with joy.

"Simone?" I whispered and she nodded.

I took in her mature, lovely features and a tear came to my eye. The real Simone stood before me, the one I'd killed a lifetime ago.

"I'm so sorry," I said to her. "I would give anything to take it all back. I'm sorry."

Simone stepped closer and grabbed my hand. I gasped at its solidity and warmth as her fingers wrapped around mine and she looked me in my eyes.

"There is no need to be sorry, Logan" she said. "Not anymore . . . not ever again."

"Am I dead?" I asked, not afraid of the answer if it meant I could stay here in this brilliant warmth forever.

Simone shook her head, her smile deepening. "No, Logan. You're not dead, only asleep. You still have so much life to live and so much purpose yet to fulfil."

I reached my hand to her face and ran my fingers down the side of her cheek.

"Am I dreaming?" I asked as I stared into her flawlessness.

"No," she assured me. "This place is more real than anything you've ever known. That is why you have to let go of your guilt, Logan. You have to know that I am okay, that we are all okay."

Simone motioned behind me, but I hesitated to turn from her beauty.

"Logan," another voice called to me, a familiar one.

I turned at last as two figures approached in the distance. A young child with long red hair and a freckled cheeks smiled as she held the hand of an older woman whose silver hair and gentle face I knew well. It was a face I'd thought of every day since her visit a lifetime ago. Grace grinned at me and raised her free hand to wave.

"Thank you, Logan," Grace said as she came to stand before me. "Thank you for finding Hope."

"If you hadn't," Simone said, going to stand beside her mother and daughter, "she would have been lost to us forever. If she can just see past the guilt of her sins, we can be together again."

Beside me, the little girl let go of her grandmother's hand and wrapped her arms around my waist, hugging me to her.

"Thank you for saving my sister." She beamed and I let the tears fall freely as I hugged the girl to me.

I bent down to her and took her shoulders in my hands as I looked into her cherub face.

"Faith," I whispered. "I am so sorry I took your life from you before you had a chance to live it."

Faith laughed, a blissful laugh, and cupped my face in her little hand. "You're silly. Don't you know I'm home where I belong? We're going to have so much fun together once you come home to stay too."

Faith stepped back and took her mother's hand with a giggle.

"You'll see," she giggled again. "Here at home, there is no 'sorry'."

As I stood, I reached up to wipe the tears from my face. Grace stepped closer to me and took my hand in hers. I looked into her grey eyes, soft and filled with compassion.

"There are no tears here either, Logan," she said with a grin. "You'll see when you come back home. We will meet again. I always knew you were a good man."

"But how could you know that?" I asked.

"Because there is so much love inside of you, Logan," she said and her smile grew wider. "And there is so much love here for you. That's why He sent Hope to you . . . because you are both so loved. You needed one another to realize that."

I tried to grasp what she was saying, but I couldn't comprehend the kind of love that could forgive me or Hope, people who had taken lives either by intent or careless accident. Yet I could see the peace and warmth in their eyes and could feel the tranquility that danced in the light around us.

"Why?" It was all I could think to ask.

"Close your eyes," Grace instructed and I obeyed. "Can you feel it? His love is everywhere, it always has been."

I felt it. The warmth of it embraced me, wrapped around my heart and filled every empty, guilt-filled darkness of my being. Falling to my knees, I let tears of joy flow from my face, a crystalline release from all the pain, the guilt and the sorrow that had ruled my life for so long.

"I feel it." I laughed.

When I opened my eyes again, Grace stood in front of me and extended her hand. "It's not your mistakes that make up who you are, Logan. It's what you do about them, what you learn from them, and how you use that knowledge to better the world. You are going to make the world a much better place."

"I think about you all the time," I told her. "I want you to know that I understand what you were trying to say to me that day when you came to visit. It stuck with me all these years. You gave me hope when I thought it was lost forever."

Grace squeezed my hand and then pulled me close into an embrace. Her arms were solid and strong around me.

"And now you've done the same for me," she said.

When Grace pulled away, I stared deep into her slate eyes, memorizing each facet. Then I looked at little Faith and took in the way she swayed when she giggled against her mother's arm. Lastly, I looked at Simone who smiled to me warmly. I committed to memory the way her full lips turned up at the corners as she looked at me, approval and esteem emanating from her warm eyes.

"I don't know what to do now," I said. "You all have been such a big part of my life for so long. How do I let you go? What will I do without you?"

"You will never be without us," Simone said. "We are a part of your story, of your journey, and you are a part of ours. You carry an important message inside of you now, a message that the world needs desperately to hear. Tell them. That is your purpose, Logan."

"Go," Grace said, with a smile. "Live a long and happy life."

Faith giggled and tugged at her mother's arm. "We'll see you when you come home."

As I watched, the three of them turned to walk back into the light. The luminance engulfed them and they started to fade away, Simone turned to me once more and smiled.

"Thank you," she whispered.

As fresh tears came to my eyes, her image blurred and she disappeared into the warm glow.

"No, thank you," I said with a shaky breath.

Then the light around me faded and melted into liquid shadow. My heart raced as the warm glow was replaced by damp, cool darkness. I couldn't breathe. The pain in my chest returned with a vengeance. When I opened my eyes, the world around me was a blur of refracted daylight and water. My back scraped against the bottom of the pool as a dark figure dove in beside me.

I struggled to stay conscious as I looked up into Donovan's strained face through the water. He grabbed me around the neck and shoulder, and heaved me to the surface. I closed my eyes again, succumbing to the pain and weariness. When we broke the surface, I gasped for air as helping hands pulled me from the water. I rolled onto my side and coughed, clutching at my chest.

"He's conscious!" I heard Willow scream. "Hurry! We have to get him to the hospital."

I felt Willow's hand grab hold of mine as I was rolled onto a gurney and wheeled into a waiting ambulance. With her at my side, the ambulance doors shut and within minutes we were flying through traffic.

With my eyes closed, I held Willow's hand as I tried to force my mind back to the warm glow, to the place where pain did not exist. I yearned to be there surrounded by that overwhelming love and comfort, but as I opened my eyes and looked up into Willow's tear streaked face, I realized that I already was.

"Stay with me," Willow whispered as the paramedics placed a heated blanket over me and started an IV.

I slipped in and out of consciousness, trying to comprehend the slur of lights, strange faces and hospital equipment. I was not afraid, I knew I would make it. It wasn't my time. I had a purpose to fulfill. Instead, I clung to the warm glow and to Willow who refused to leave my side as all went black again.

Seventeen

I awoke to whispers. Excited voices did their best to keep their voices down. My eyelids felt as if they had been shut for years and when I finally opened them, the room was a blur. Harsh florescent lighting burned into my corneas and my throat felt scorched. When I coughed, the whispers stopped and three familiar faces looked down at me, blocking out the fluorescent rays.

"Looks who's finally awake," Alex said as she smiled at me.

Willow came to stand at my side, relief washing over her beautiful face.

"You had us worried for a while there." Donovan patted my shoulder. "How do you feel?"

"Like hell," I said, my voice barely above a whisper.

Alex rushed to the door of the small room. "I'll get the nurse."

"How long have I been out?" I asked. "Alex is here?"

"You've been unconscious a few days," Willow said. "Mom came as soon as she heard what happened. They didn't expect you to make it past the first twenty-four hours, but they don't know how tenacious you are. I knew you'd pull through."

Donovan laughed as Alex rushed back into the room, followed by a nurse.

"Don't be fooled, Logan," Donovan said with a chuckle. "We've all been praying for you. Willow was a wreck."

The nurse checked my vitals and shone a light into my groggy eyes. When she was done, Alex handed me a glass of water and helped me sit up. My body ached, but the pain in my chest was gone, the numbness in my hands and legs replaced with tingling cold.

I looked around the small, sterile room in shock. Balloons and flower vases, filled with every imaginable bloom, cluttered the small table near the window and overflowed onto the floor below.

"What's all this?" I asked.

"There are a lot of thankful people who wanted to show their appreciation for saving their lives, or the lives of their loved ones," Willow said.

"News travels fast." I coughed, taking a tentative sip of water and letting the cool liquid ease my sore throat.

"You're somewhat of a celebrity," the nurse said after pressing a stethoscope to my chest. "Your vitals look good. I'll go page the doctor. He'll want to have a good look at you."

The nurse left the room and I looked up to Willow who smiled down at me, her eyes puffy and sleep-deprived.

"The press caught wind of what happened," she explained. "It's been all over the news for the last couple of days."

I took another sip of my water as the memories of what happened all rushed back. "Wait, what about Hope? Is she okay?"

"She was released into police custody yesterday," Donovan said. "She pulled through too."

"What's going to happen to her?" I asked.

Donovan looked to his feet with a sigh. "She's been charged with the deaths of those runners, and for the attempted murder of thousands more. She's going to prison for a long time, Logan."

My heart hurt for her. I wished things could be different for Hope, that I could have stopped her before she was able to take even one life, but I was thankful that she was given a second chance at life, a shot at redemption like I had. She had only to accept it. She had to know that her family waited eagerly for her to come home to them where suffering no longer exists and shimmering light takes the place of all pain.

"Logan," Alex said and I looked up. "There are some people here who would like to see you. We called them, I hope that's alright."

Alex was at the doorway when my parents entered the room looking anxious and worried. My mother had tears in her chocolate brown eyes. I took in the wrinkles that had formed around them. Grey had mixed into the blonde of her hair over these last twelve years, but seeing brought me back to a more innocent time. Suddenly I was her young son again, oblivious to the harsh world I would get to know so well.

"Mom?" I asked, reaching for her.

She ran to me and for the first time in over a decade, I embraced my mother and let her hold me tight. Her body shook as she cried against my shoulder. I breathed in her scent of vanilla and sweet flowers.

"I've missed you so much," she cried.

"I'm so sorry," I whispered. "I'm sorry it's been so long. I was . . . lost."

My mother straightened and wiped her eyes, then held my face in her hands.

"None of that matters now," she said. "We thought we'd lost you for good, but we're all together now."

My father, tears brimming in the corners of his worn eyes, came to me and I embraced the stocky man as he patted me on the back.

"I'm proud of you, son," he said. "The way you saved all those people. It's good to have you back. We've prayed for this moment every day for the last thirteen years."

As my father stepped back from me, my heart sank. I looked at all the people standing in my small hospital room; at Alex and Donovan, my mom and dad, and at Willow. My family. *How would I ever be able to say goodbye to the ones I loved most in the world to go back to my cell for what could be many, many years*?

"How long do I have until they come to take me back into custody?" I asked, bowing my head.

When no one spoke, I looked back up at them. Willow looked to her dad and my mother looked to mine, no one knowing what to say. Then they all smiled sheepishly.

"What is it?" I asked, confused.

Finally Willow turned to me and sat beside me. She looked me in the eyes and took a deep breath. "Derrick, my dad, and I made statements to the police department and state government. We told them what you did to save those people, and what you've been through. It was hard to explain everything, but Logan, after what happened at the race . . . they listened. Once they found where Hope dried and powdered the aconite in her house and tested the water at the race, it was clear what you did. You saved thousands of people."

I looked from Willow to my parents. They all looked down at me with joy in their eyes. It didn't make sense.

"I don't understand what you're telling me," I said. "They know I wasn't involved?"

Willow shook her head. "They could find no connection between you and the poisonings. They still have a lot of questions for you, but other people gave statements too, about your character."

I looked sideways at Willow, still not understanding where this was going.

"Who?" I asked.

"Jason, the runner who survived in Atlanta," she explained. "He made a statement about how you saved his life. Mr. Jones told them that you were a model employee, and Officer Brady reported to the authorities that you stopped Boss from killing him, that you told him you were trying to escape in order to save lives."

"Squeaky?" I asked stunned.

"The governor was here, Logan," my mother said with a grin. "He's going to grant you a full pardon."

"What?" I asked, staring blindly at the smiling faces around me. "A pardon?"

"You can come home," my mother said with a relieved sigh.

"Home . . ." I repeated as my mind struggled to comprehend the idea freedom, of home.

The news should have brought me relief, elation even, that I was being granted this merciful liberation. As much as I wanted to stay with my loved ones though, with Willow, it felt wrong. To skip out on what justice had deemed my punishment for taking Simone and Faith's lives felt like I was cheating them. As I thought about them, and how they had welcomed me in the warm light, I knew I had to go back to Central. It was only right. My purpose there was not yet fulfilled.

"No, I have to go back," I said and the faces around me skewed in confusion.

"Go back?" Willow asked. "You're free, Logan. You don't have to go back there."

"Yes I do. I haven't finished serving my sentence," I tried to explain, "I have to finish out my year."

My mother stepped forward, wringing her hands.

"Logan, no," she said, "Don't do this . . ."

I looked at both my parents who had no idea what I had been through these last thirteen years, and had no way to comprehend what had happened to me the last week.

"Mom, Dad, I love you very much, but this is something I have to do," I said. "I don't expect you to understand, and I know this must be hard for you, especially after what I've put you through all these years, but I made a mistake that day. A mistake that took two lives. I have to finish my sentence, I have to. For them."

My father stepped forward and placed his hand on my mother's shoulder. "I understand, Son. We're just glad to have you back in our lives, whatever you decide to do."

"We love you so much," my mother said, standing beside him. "As long as we're family, we'll get through anything."

Alex cleared her throat and looked at my parents sympathetically. She motioned to me and Willow. "Why don't we give these two some privacy to talk about it?"

My father wrapped his arm around my mother and they both gave me a final worried glance before they let Alex lead them out of the room. When they were gone, Donovan looked sideways at me, a grin spreading across his face.

"You saw it, didn't you?" he asked, knowingly. "You saw the light. Now you know why I couldn't explain it."

Willow looked from Donovan to me, her eyebrows raised.

"There are no words," I said with a smile, "but I understand why you came back."

I took Willow's hand and Donovan nodded in approval.

"Some things definitely are worth living for," he agreed, walking to the door.

"Donovan," I called after him. "Thank you for your help, and for saving my life."

"No thanks necessary. I'll see you soon," he said and with a wave, he left the room.

Willow turned to me, an inquiring look on her face. "You two were talking about heaven, weren't you? You saw it?"

"I can see it now too, just as clearly," I said staring into her ocean blue eyes.

Willow smiled and squeezed my hand with a sigh. "Then stay with me. Don't go back there."

I brushed the hair from the side of her face. "I have to do what's right. I have to finish out my sentence because Simone and Faith deserve that much. I was given this sentence because of my mistake and what it cost them. It's only right that I finish it, for them . . . and for Hope."

Willow thought about what I said as she looked out of the window to the trees budding with fresh spring growth. I watched her foot tap lightly on the side of the bed and waited for her to respond. When she turned to me, she chuckled under her breath.

"It's funny how life can change so much in just a few short days," she said.

I looked down at our joined hands and laughed with her. "A week ago you wanted nothing to do with me. You thought I was . . . confused?"

The smile left her face as she looked into my eyes. "I was the one who was confused, Logan. I understand why you don't want to take the full pardon, and even though it scares me to see you go back to that place, I know why you think it's the right thing to do."

"Thank you."

"But . . . Logan, I'm not going back with you," she said. "I'm quitting my internship."

"What?" I asked, surprised. "Why?"

"Because you were right," she said, squeezing my hand. "We were chosen to see and participate in something that science or psychology could never explain, something wonderful that can't be reasoned or diagnosed away, and I no longer want to try to. How can I go back to my practice knowing what I know now, after what I've seen with my own eyes?"

"What will you do now?"

"I'll figure something out," she said. "I have some ideas."

I lowered my head with a sigh. "I can't ask you to wait for me while I'm gone."

Willow pressed her finger under my chin and raised my face to hers. A tear escaped onto her cheek and I wiped it gently away with my thumb as I cradled her face in my hand.

"You don't have to ask," she whispered.

I drew her in close and took her lips with mine, immersing myself in the taste of her, the feel of her against me. She melted into me as sublime heat bubbled up between us and threatened to carry us both away. I was reminded of that luminous, warm glow and I longed to get lost in it, in her, forever. When I could stand it no longer, I pulled away, and taking a shaky breath I looked into her eyes.

"We're in for one hell of a ride, aren't we?" I breathed. "You sure you want to stick around? I'm a lot of trouble."

"I'm sure. We're in this race together, remember?" Willow laughed and squeezed my hand just as the door opened and the doctor walked in to examine me.

Willow stood and made her way to the door, but turned to me with a devious grin. "If you're lucky, you won't even have to kidnap me this time."

With a wink, she shut the door behind her. Just as it had in the warm light, my heart filled with unspeakable peace and joy. Although I was unsure of what the future held for me, I knew that I had a purpose and that there were people who loved me that would support me in fulfilling it. As the doctor made small talk and examined me, I breathed in and let my healed lungs fill with renewed life.

Eighteen

As the bus drove through the towering front gate, I clutched my tall paper bag and looked up at the razor wire. I took a deep breath. There were no second thoughts, no regrets as I was led from the bus into processing. When I was handed my khaki uniform I changed into it, but for the first time I didn't feel as though the uniform changed me. It was no longer a reflection of who I was and I brought that assurance with as I was escorted back to my block.

The governor had been shocked when I requested to finish my prison sentence, but he respectfully honored my decision. He asked if there was anything he could do to make my stay more comfortable. I requested four things.

The first was to return to the same cell, the cell I'd spent the last twelve years in. My second request was to be assigned the same work duty with Mr. Jones, if he would have me. The third was to be allowed this one, full, paper bag to enter with me. My fourth request had been more difficult to get approved, but in the end, that too was granted.

It was early in the morning and inmates were just beginning to stir when the guards led me through the block. By the time I reached my cell, the gossip and whispers had started and I was greeted with awestruck stares and cheers. As I dumped my linens and my paper bag onto my bunk, the guards left to ready themselves for morning count. I looked around the cell, at Miguel's cubby, and felt the bitterness of his absence. Leaning down, I riffled through his books and wondered if he had actually read any of them. *Did angels read Dan Brown?*

My letter to my parents lay atop the small stack of books and I picked it up with a sigh. Of course Miguel had never sent it. He must have known there would be no need. As the call for count sounded through the block, I wondered if he had known how things would turn out for me. Did he know I would make it?

I stepped out into the hall just as Officer Duke rounded the corner, the usual arrogant sneer spreading his thin lips across his teeth. He looked at me and nodded cockily as he ran his tongue across his bottom lip. Meeting his beady eyes, I crossed my arms and stared contently at him.

"Well, well, well," he sneered. "If it isn't the escaped con turned hero. I heard they tried to turn you loose. I guess you just couldn't stay away from all this man meat in here, could you?"

I looked down at the floor and chuckled as I shook my head. When I looked back into his smug face, I smiled. "Were they able to get your jeep out of that ditch in Georgia? I'm sure they can straighten out the front end no problem, make it look like new."

The smirk fell from Duke's face and he stepped closer, poking his finger into my chest as he seethed.

"You're lucky I was told not to touch you, or I'd shove my foot so far down your throat you'd piss shoe polish," he spat. "You stole two things from me that day, Foster. I intend to get them BOTH back."

My anger rose when he referred to Willow as a thing, but I stepped back from him and held my smile.

"The jeep is all yours," I said calmly, "but you should really learn to take better care of your 'things', or else they find new homes with someone who will."

Duke's face twisted into an angered grimace as he stepped toward me again, his fist raised. "What can you possibly offer her, inmate? You're nothing but a criminal."

"I used to think so too," I said with a sigh, "but love changes everything, and even if it's all I have to offer her, it's more than you ever gave."

Duke tightened his fist and raised it to my head and then punched the wall beside me with an enraged grunt. Then he straightened and took in a deep breath as he collected himself. He plastered on an indignant smile.

"This isn't over," he said with a click of the counter and then he spun on his heels and began to walk away.

"I've missed our talks," I called after him. "See you tomorrow . . . Stud Muffin."

Duke bristled, and then with a huff he continued down the hall. I strode back into my cell feeling satisfied, and I made up my bed. Skipping breakfast, I went on to work early. I wasn't ready to face the crowded chow hall that would undoubtedly greet me with a slew of whispers and questions, so I grabbed my paper bag and made my way to the east tunnel.

Tilting my head to the light of the fresh, spring morning, I let the sun's warmth fall onto my face. I closed my eyes and imagined the warm luminance and smiled, my heart light and my soul content. Then I continued into the tunnel and spotted Squeaky at his post near the end. He looked up as I approached and a grin widened his scrawny face.

When I reached him we stared at one another for a moment and then I reached out my hand to him. He looked at it a second and then with a chuckle, he shook it.

"I want to thank you for what you said to the governor," I said, "for giving him a statement on my behalf."

Squeaky shook his head, a serious look taking place of his smile. "For all the good it did, Foster. Here you are."

"No, being back here was my choice. It's just something I had to do. What you said meant a lot though, so thank you." I said.

"I should be thanking you for saving my life." He shrugged. "There is one thing I don't get about that day, though."

"What's that?" I asked.

"Why didn't you just tell me . . . about the runners?" he asked. "I might have been able to help more."

"Would you have believed me?" I asked and watched as Squeaky thought about it and then with regret in his eyes, he shook his head no.

"I barely believed it myself." I grinned and started to walk away.

"Hey, Foster?" he called after me and I turned to meet his questioning face. "How did you know? I mean, about the poisoning."

With a sigh I looked down and kicked at the gravel beneath my boots, thinking of an easy answer, but there was no easy answer. Only the truth.

"Do you believe in angels, Officer Brady?" I asked.

He shook his head with a chuckle and then stopped abruptly when he looked at my face and saw that I was serious.

"I guess I've never really thought about it," he said with a shrug.

I smiled at him and nodded.

"You should," I said, then turned to walk the rest of the way to the plant.

When I reached the back door, I took a deep breath and then banged on the door. Within a minute the door opened and Mr. Jones stuck his head out to look at me. He didn't seem surprised to see me, only grinned as he raised an eyebrow.

"I thought this wasn't going to become a habit," he teased.

I reached into my paper sack and pulled out a five-pound, gourmet coffee bag and raised it up for him to see.

"I thought you might reconsider," I said with a smirk.

Mr. Jones' eyes widened. He laughed as he stepped back and let me inside.

Mr. Jones' propped his feet on his desk as we sipped the heavenly brew and waited for the other workers to arrive.

"I'm not going to ask how you did it," he said, taking another sip, "but I'm glad you're back."

"It's good to be back to work," I said. "Can't say the same for my cell, but it was the right thing to do."

"Think you can make it to the end of your sentence?" he asked, looking at me over his coffee mug.

"Oh yeah," I said with a smile as I sipped the last of my coffee. "It helps to have something to look forward to on the other side."

"What's that?" he asked as workers began to file in.

I raised my mug. "A new life."

"Cheers to that," Mr. Jones said as I stood to leave. "New workers will be coming in tomorrow. You can start training your replacement."

"Looking forward to it," I said as I set my mug down and grabbed my paper bag. Then I left his office to join the other inmates.

When I walked onto the production floor I was met by applause as my co-workers, my fellow inmates, stood by their machines and stared at me in awe. I paused, taken aback by their unexpected show of support and then waving them off, I made my way to Papa Smurf where Bishop and Santiago smiled at me.

"They're just clapping because I found a way out of here and they want in on it," I chuckled as I took my place stacking plates.

"No," Bishop said solemnly. "They're clapping for what you did once you were out there."

"And for what you did to Boss on the way out," Santiago laughed as he changed out the die before Bishop stamped his next plate.

"So, Bishop," I said and the large man turned to me after stamping the next plate. "I know I said I would send you five boxes of apple turnovers once I got out, but I didn't get around to it with all the excitement."

"Hey, man. It's all good," he said with a wave. "What you did out there . . . makes me proud to have been a part of it, man."

"So . . . I brought you six boxes instead," I said, handing him the paper bag filled almost to the brim with apple turnovers.

"Six boxes . . ." Bishop repeated in a daze as he clutched the bag to him. A full-toothed smile spread across his dark face.

"You sure you don't want to keep that for yourself?" Santiago chuckled, and Bishop slapped him in the back of the head. "I'm just sayin', you might need it to barter with here soon. You might need to acquire some protection."

"What are you talking about?" I asked.

"Didn't you hear?" Santiago continued with his usual dramatic flair. "Word is they're releasing Boss from max security today and putting him back in here."

I tried not to laugh, only nodded as I placed a stack of plates on the belt behind me.

"Oh, I know all about it," I said. "I requested that he be released and brought back here to Central."

Bishop dropped the bag, and Santiago stared at me, his jaws hanging open. I looked at them and laughed, reaching over Bishop to lower the stamp for him.

"So, you are crazy," Bishop gawked and shaking his head, he handed me the plate and lowered the stamp on another.

"Why would you do that, Homes?" Santiago asked as he glared at me.

"Because," I explained as he changed out the dies. "I have a message for him."

Lunch came quickly and I was met by another onslaught of applause and stares as I entered the chow hall. I told myself that the attention would die down in a few days as I sat in my usual corner and picked at my ham and cheese. To my surprise, both Bishop and Santiago came to sit with me, their lunch crews following behind them. Before I knew it, the whole table was filled with inmates eager to hear my story.

So taking a deep breath, I told them. Every detail of the last week, of that fateful evening all those years ago, I relayed to them as they listened and ate their prison issued lunches. I spoke to them of the hell my life had been and of the mistakes I had made that left me hating myself for so long. I spoke to them of forgiveness, and of the overwhelming peace and acceptance that I found in that warm, luminous place where my past was healed and my future sealed.

When it was time to go back to work, some laughed at me, some mocked my story and brushed off my words. It didn't matter. As I looked into each of their eyes as we made our way out of the chow hall, I could see the spark of a storm brewing inside of each of them and I knew I would never eat in the corner alone again. They would come back to me with their questions and more would join them. And I would be ready for them.

The rest of the work day flew by and before I knew it, it was time to shut down the machines. A metal detector sweep was waiting for us on the other end of the east tunnel and when it was my time to be checked, Officer Edmonds smirked at me as he ran the wand down the outside of my leg.

"Funny how it's not making a sound at your boot now," he said.

"New boots?" I shrugged.

"Stay out of trouble," he said in a serious tone, but the corner of his mouth turned up into a half-grin.

"You know me," I chuckled and walked off towards the block.

"Yeah, that's what I'm afraid of," I heard him yell behind me.

When I reached my cell, I changed into my running shoes and then walked down to the track. The yard was crowded, but it didn't deter me. Running along the track, my heart beat strong in my chest as I looked out to the browning field beyond the gate. I knew I would no longer see Hope's image amongst the swaying blades of grass and flapping blackbirds. As I watched the sun lower in the sky, I wondered if she ever thought of the days she'd visited me. *Did she know that she saved my life?*

By the time I left the track, I was the last one in the yard. The sun hovered just above the prison and cast shadows down on me, cooling my now sweating skin. I didn't want to stop running, stop thinking about the week before and the life-changing events that unfolded. I felt as though I could run on forever and a part of me wondered if Simone was up there, in the glow, running with me.

The block was quiet as I walked the hall to my cell. All the inmates were at chow or holed up in their cells for the night. Welcoming the solitude, I decided not to go to chow just yet. I needed to rest. As I reached my cell though, I saw that I had company.

"I knew I'd find you here," Boss sneered from where he leaned against my bunk.

Setting my jaw, I entered my cell and prepared for the worst, but prayed for the best.

"Well, this is my cell," I said going to the sink to wash my face and hands.

I could feel Boss' eyes burning a hole in my back as I cleaned myself up, but when I dried my face off and turned around, he was still leaning, unmoved.

"What can I do for you?" I asked.

"Spare me all the fake formalities," he spat. "I know why you did it. I know why you had them spring me from max."

"I don't think you do," I said calmly.

"You had me brought here so you could kill me once and for all," he said, stepping into the middle of the cell and raising his arms. "Well, now's your chance, Foster. I've got no weapons, no one to watch my back and thanks to you, I no longer have any respect around here. So just come at me now and we'll settle this once and for all, like men."

I stared at Boss as he stood there, his ebony face still bruised and battered from our first altercation which seemed now like a lifetime ago. He glared at me from the center of the room with something more than hatred in his fierce eyes. Behind his tough façade, I saw a glimmer of fear and sadness and I knew that I'd made the right decision by having him brought back here. I stepped towards him and crossed my arms at my chest.

"I don't want to fight you, Boss." I said, my voice low and calm. "I didn't ask to have you brought back here so I could hurt you."

"Yeah, right," he snickered and I took another step towards him.

"I had you brought here so I could tell you that I'm sorry," I said, then watched as his face morphed from anger to confusion and finally settle on amusement.

"Let me get this straight," he chuckled. "I try to have you killed . . . numerous times, and you bring me back here to tell me that you are sorry? You really are a whack job if you think I'm going to believe that."

"I'm sorry for everything that happened between us, Boss." I said again, my tone steady. "I'm sorry that you are so filled with hatred and anger. I'm sorry for whatever happened to you to make you hate yourself so much."

"What the hell are you talking about?" He raised his voice and took a step towards me. "You don't know anything about me."

I held his glare and did not move as Boss brought his face in front of mine and waited for a response, his jaw clenching.

"I know you more than you think," I said. "I hated myself too. I remember feeling the anger so acutely that it seemed to burn in my veins."

"We are nothing alike, do you hear me?" He seethed. "Nothing."

"We are exactly alike, Boss." I said unflinching. "The only difference is I grew up in a supportive home and I've been surrounded by . . . people who have helped me through my anger. I suspect that you haven't been as lucky."

"Quit talking like you know me, like you know anything about me," he said inches from my face, the heat of his anger palpable against my skin.

"Am I wrong?" I asked, staring him right in the eyes.

Boss glared at me for a second and then the anger in his face turned to a grin as he backed down with a cynical chuckle.

"So what?" he asked. "You just had them bring me back here so you can lay all this psycho-babble on me?"

"No. I had them get you out of max security because everyone deserves a second chance," I said.

"A second chance," he laughed. "The parole board sure doesn't think I deserve a second chance. I'm going to rot in here until I'm an old man."

"So change their minds. Turn your life around," I pleaded, stepping towards him. "I can help you."

"Like you helped with that letter?" He laughed. "How the hell are you going to help me?"

"I can teach you how to forgive yourself." I extended my hand. "From there anything is possible."

Boss looked at me and then at my outstretched hand. He nodded his head and then turned away from me.

"That's enough of this," he said as he spun back around, his fist flying towards my face.

I caught his arm and hooked my leg around his, dropping him to the floor. He looked up at me, the anger on his face giving way to fear as I crouched over him and grabbed his shirt in my clenched fist.

"You're right," I said. "Enough of this! I'm not going to fight you. There's no reason for this."

I dropped my grip on him and let his shoulders hit the floor beneath him. Then I extended my hand again. Boss just stared up at it and didn't move, only stared me in my eyes.

"Look, I don't expect you to trust me any more than I trust you right now," I continued. "It's something we're both going to have to earn, but you said yourself that you have no one left in here. So give me a chance, hear me out. Come to chow with me."

"Chow . . . ," he repeated apprehensively.

"Imagine the stares we'll get," I said with a smirk. "It's just one meal. If you still want to throw a punch when it's through, then so be it."

Boss looked again to my extended hand and then up to me. With a defeated sigh he took it and I heaved him to his feet. He brushed himself off as I went into the hallway and then turned to wait for him to follow.

"This doesn't mean that I won't still want to kill you," he yelled to me.

"Fair enough," I said and Boss hesitated, then straightened and followed me out of the cell.

As suspected, we were greeted by stares and whispers in the chow hall. Boss followed me with his tray to the back corner and sat across from me as Miguel had so many times before. We were alone for only a minute when inmates, nameless to me, began to fill the seats at our table. On all their faces was a look of curiosity and wonder.

"People are talking," one of them said. "They say you see things and that's how come you knew that all them people was going to die."

"We want to hear about it," another said.

I looked around at the men crowding around us and then to Boss who stared at me inquisitively.

"What is it you want to hear?" I asked them.

"Tell us what you told those folks at lunch," yet another said, and they all nodded in agreement. "Tell us about the angels."

So I told my story again, leaving no detail out as more and more inmates gathered. They sat in silent awe as I talked about Miguel, and Simone, and Hope. They cheered when I told them about flipping Officer Duke's jeep. I took each of them along with me on what had been my journey of discovery. To each of them, I relayed my message of forgiveness and I tried my best to describe the acceptance and love that I'd felt in that brightest of places.

Some laughed and walked away with sarcastic curses. Others called me crazy and dismissed my claims as the rantings of a madman. But more stayed. More listened. And by the time we were forced to leave by the call to evening count, I saw the same spark of hope in their eyes, even in Boss who waited until the others left to follow me out.

"This Miguel guy," he asked, "He's the one who kicked me into the bedpost, isn't he?"

I nodded in response and watched his face as he pondered further while we walked.

"If you ever see him again, you point him out so I can return the favor," he continued and I laughed.

"I'll do that."

Boss turned in the opposite direction with a nod and walked off towards his cell.

"This place you talked about," he said, tuning back to me. "The place with the light. Was that heaven?"

"If it wasn't, I can't even imagine how much better heaven could be," I said.

Boss looked around as inmates settled into their bunks for the night. Then he looked back at me. His eyes were soft and in them I could see a flicker of hope where the fear and anger used to be.

"Do you think I could go there one day?" he asked quietly.

I looked him in the eyes and let him see in mine that I was telling him the truth.

"I don't see why not," I said, "but in the meantime, what is it you like to do that's just for yourself? Something that feels to you like heaven on earth?"

Boss thought for a minute. He seemed shy for the first time, as if admitting that something outside of the hard life of drugs and gangs was a sign of weakness.

"It can be anything," I prodded. "I won't say a word."

Boss looked around and when he was content that no one else was listening, he came closer.

"I like to paint," he whispered with a wry smile. "I used to be pretty damned good at it too . . . before I got caught up in other things."

I smiled and slapped him on the back.

"Then painting is what you should do," I said. "Let it help you find yourself again. Who knows, maybe it will lead to a life far, far away from all of this. Think about it."

Boss seemed to consider, his head nodding up and down, deep in thought. When he looked at me again, his eyes were alight.

"Maybe you can pull some more strings and get me some paints . . . maybe an art pad?"

With a laugh I shook his hand. "I'll see what I can do."

"Okay then." With that, Boss grinned and walked off. "Same time tomorrow."

With an exhausted sigh, I returned to my cell with a smile. Grabbing my book, I kicked off my shoes and slid into my bunk. Though I stared at the pages, my mind couldn't register the words. Instead I thought about the day I'd had and of all the nameless faces who'd gathered at my table not only at lunch, but at supper too. I prayed that I'd said the right things and I felt assured that I had. *How many more would be at my table tomorrow?*

Though I laid in bed alone in my cell, I felt the presence of love and acceptance around me and I knew I wasn't truly by myself. When the lights went out, I tossed my book into my cubby and I thought of Miguel.

"I wish you were here, Miguel." I whispered into the darkness. "There's so much I want to say to you. Most of all I want to thank you for watching over me all these years. I wish I had known what you really were. Then maybe I could have told you how much you meant to me. You were my best friend and I find comfort in the fact that we will see each other again one day."

I rolled over with a sigh and closed my eyes.

"I hope I made you proud," I said as my body began to relax. "I know you're up there looking down on me."

My mind started to drift into the nothingness, the tranquility of sleep, when a voice above me made me jump.

"Of course I'm up here, *Guero*. Where else would I be?"

I turned over with a gasp and met Miguel's upside-down face as he hung down from the top bunk.

"How's a heavenly portrector supposed get a *siesta* around here though, with all of your yapping?" he asked. "I think I liked you better when you was all quiet and brooding all the time. Emo Logan was easier to fall asleep to."

With a smile, I sat up as Miguel hopped down from his bunk and sat down beside me. I stared at him, my heart filled with joy, but my mind could not find the right words.

"I . . . I didn't think I'd ever see you again. Not until I . . . Well, you know," I stammered.

"Croaked?" he asked and I nodded. "Well, there's a much higher chance of that now that you're back in here, you *idiota loco*! Why would you come back here? And you asked them to bring Boss back too? Are you trying to get yourself whacked still? I thought we were over that."

I smiled even though Miguel's face was a mask of seriousness. "Coming back here was the right thing to do."

Miguel waved me off. "So is changing your underpants every day, but I've gotten by just fine."

"Do Guardians even wear underpants?" I asked with a snicker.

He shrugged. "You'd be surprised."

"I'm glad you're here." I sat back and looked at my friend, my Guardian and smiled. "Can you stay?"

Miguel rolled his eyes. "As long as you're here, I'm here. We're bunk mates, *Guero*."

"And when I leave this place for good?" I asked.

Miguel stood and hopped back into his bed. I felt the familiar shake of the bunk as he got comfortable.

"When you leave, I get to go back home and prepare for when you get there . . . many, many years from now," he said with a loud exhale.

I laid down in my bunk, overwhelmed with gratitude that Miguel was here with me for the duration of my stay . . . just as it should be.

"How do you know it will be many, many years?" I asked him.

"Because," he said with a yawn, "you and the hot lady doc get to live happily ever after first."

With a smile, I rolled over onto my side and imagined Willow and I as an old couple rocking together on the front porch. The thought filled me with contentment and I chuckled into the darkness. In a little over a year I would have the chance to start that life with her, and as I lay in the darkness, I knew I'd be forever grateful for that chance.

For a while all was silent except for the snores and coughs of the block. I took in a deep breath and let my mind wander to a place surrounded by mountains and sky. Then I remembered something . . .

"Wait, now that I'm back you have to tell me what you did to get in here," I reminded Miguel before I fell asleep.

He moaned and turned in his bunk.

"I was sent to babysit a big white boy who just needed a kick in the *culo* to realize how special he is," Miguel said drowsily. "I think he gets it now."

As I closed my eyes, I thought of all the people who had surrounded me in that hospital room. I prayed a prayer of thanks for each and every one of them, and for finding my redemption after all. Bringing my mind back to that lush, green town, and to a warm little house with glow-in-the-dark stars, I drifted closer to sleep.

"He does," I said before I faded away. "He understands everything now."

Epilogue

I sat in the flimsy, plastic chair and waited nervously for her to arrive. The visitation room was filled on this hot summer afternoon with the anxious faces of eager family members. Turning the small, wrapped gift over and over in my hands beneath the table, I wondered how she would react to it. After what seemed like hours, they were sent, one by one, into the visitation room. When I saw her, I stood with a warm smile as my heart sped.

She stared me down before having a tentative seat across from me. I could tell from the suspicious look on her face that she knew I was up to something, though I tried to hide it. It had been thirteen months since I'd seen her and I had so much I wanted to say. But as she looked up at me with those glassy green eyes, I forgot everything I'd wanted to say.

"Thank you for letting me visit, Hope." I said. "It's good to see you again."

Her young face looked older, like it had aged a decade since the last time I'd seen her. In her eyes was a sadness, a torrent of guilt that I recognized all too well. I wished more than anything that I could wipe it away, replace it with the purpose that she'd once given me when she appeared to me while she lay unconscious on her living room floor.

"What do you want, Logan?" she asked, despair thick in her voice.

"I brought you something," I said.

Hesitating for a second, I fumbled with my gift under the table and then with a sigh, I handed it to her. She took it and glared at the package in her hands. Then with shaking hands she opened the wrapping and gasped.

"You need this more than I do," I said.

Hope stared down at the small white Bible in her fingers, tears forming in her eyes. "This was my grandmothers."

"I know," I said, leaning over the table. "Open it."

Hope opened to where the golden angel wing held the page at Hebrews 12.

"Therefore, since we are surrounded by such a great cloud of witnesses, let us throw off everything that hinders and the sin that so easily entangles. And let us run with perseverance the race marked out for us," I quoted as she read along.

When she looked up at me, tears streamed along the scar on her face.

"We're still running that race, Hope," I said. "It's time for me to hand you the baton."

Hope shook her head, anger and hopelessness rising in her face. "I can't. Not after what I've done."

Reaching across the table, I took her small hand in mine. It felt and feeble against my skin.

"Your grandmother read that verse to me once," I explained. "She came to me at a time when I thought I didn't deserve the mercy and forgiveness she was offering. She read that verse to me because it speaks of forgiveness, of letting go of past sin. She forgave me for what I did to your sister and your mother . . . and to you. She wants you to forgive yourself now."

Hope began to sob across the table, defeated and lost.

"I saw them," she said as she wiped the tears from her eyes. "I was there with them, in the light. They said that they forgave me, that they knew they would see me again someday. I felt so loved and accepted, but now I don't know how to get past what I've done. I murdered those people . . ."

"You made mistakes, horrible mistakes that cost eight people their lives," I said. "But Hope, it would be the worst kind of tragedy for you to loose yours too. Especially when they're up there, all of them, and I know they've forgiven you. You have to find a way to forgive yourself. We were brought together for a reason. You have to keep running the race."

She looked up at me through her tears. "How?"

"After all you've seen, all you've witnessed. . ." I explained. "You have a message within you that the world needs to hear. A message of redemption and forgiveness that's been lost to people like you and me, and so many others who have lost hope. It's up to you to give that back to them, like you did for me. Give them hope."

Standing to leave, I pressed her hand to my lips. I watched as the helplessness in her eyes faded and a spark of belief lit them from within. She dried her tears and grinned at me as I walked out of the visitation room. When I opened the door to the warm summer air, I felt at peace knowing our story had come full circle.

A car waited for me at the curb. I opened the door and hopped in. Willow turned to me from the passenger seat.

"How did it go?" she asked, concerned.

I sighed and looked out the passenger side window at the Women's Correctional Institute.

"I think she'll be okay," I said as Willow started the engine and pulled onto the main drive that would take us out of the gate. "She is surrounded by so much love. If she could just let go of her guilt, she would feel it."

"She will," Willow said, grabbing my hand.

I looked at her and smiled, my heart warmed by her touch.

"So," she said with a smirk. "Now that you're a free man, what's the first thing you want to eat? Anywhere for lunch, you name it."

I smiled devilishly at her. "I've been dying to try some of those famous cookies of yours."

Willow laughed as she pulled onto the highway. "You'll have to wait until we're home in Saluda. There are plenty of those at my bakery waiting for you."

"Then you'd better step on it," I teased.

"Logan, it's three hours away." She huffed. "I'm hungry now."

I looked at her and laughed, the joy within impossible to contain.

"We can stop at a drug store and grab some sandwiches," I said. "Just like old times."

Willow dropped my hand and punched me in the shoulder. "No way, those things smell like cat food!"

We laughed as we traveled down the highway towards our haven in the sky. I looked over at Willow as she smiled and I was filled with a warm glow that I was sure would last forever.

The series continues with:

Muse
Book Three

When Blake Roberts is released from prison, he
follows his dream to become a successful
impressionist painter. But when an accident leaves
him completely blind, he becomes a recluse - shutting
himself away in his Wilmington, NC studio with only
his shattered dreams as company. Blake is lost to
total darkness until he is visited by Julian, a small
boy, who comes out of nowhere.

And Blake can see him.

Inspired by Julian's visits, Blake paints the boy's
likeness and within six months is heralded as an
enigma. He finds his second chance in this mysterious
relationship with Julian, until one day when a knock
sounds at Blake's door. A woman, claiming to be
Julian's mother, demands to know where her son is.
Julian has been missing for six months.

Available now!

A.L. Crouch

A.L. Crouch, author of the Guardian series, graduated with honors from North Carolina State University with a degree in English. She currently teaches high school creative writing in her hometown of Cary, North Carolina. She is a member of the NC Writers' Network and spends her summers off from teaching formulating tales of suspense and the supernatural. When she's not at work raising up young writers or keeping her readers jumping, she is spending time with her husband and two sons exploring the majestic mountains and coasts of North Carolina.

For more information and other titles by A.L. Crouch visit:
www.alcrouch.com

Made in the USA
Columbia, SC
11 August 2019